LOIS WALDEN

AFTERWORLD

ARCADIA BOOKS

Arcadia Books Ltd
39 Highlever Road
London W10 6PH
United Kingdom

www.arcadiabooks.co.uk

First published in the United Kingdom by Arcadia Books 2013
Copyright © Lois Walden 2013

A catalogue record for this book is available from the British Library

ISBN 978-1-908129-85-7

Design and typesetting in Garamond Premier Pro by 2h Design, York
Printed and bound by CPI Group (UK) Ltd, Croydon CR0 4YY

Arcadia Books supports English PEN *www.englishpen.org* and
The Book Trade Charity *http://booktradecharity.wordpress.com*

Arcadia Books distributors are as follows:
in the UK and elsewhere in Europe:

Macmillan Distribution Ltd
Brunel Road
Houndmills
Basingstoke
Hants RG21 6XS

in the USA and Canada:
Dufour Editions
PO Box 7
Chester Springs
PA 19425

in Australia/New Zealand:
NewSouth Books
University of New South Wales
Sydney NSW 2052

in South Africa:
Jacana Media (Pty) Ltd
PO Box 291784
Melville 2109
Johannesburg

AFTERWORLD

Lois Walden is an American writer, singer, songwriter, librettist, record producer, performer and teaching artist. The author of the novels *One More Stop* (Arcadia, 2010) and *Afterworld* (Arcadia, 2013), Lois Walden worked as a television writer in Hollywood with many major artists, including Dionne Warwick and Jane Fonda. As founder of the gospel group, The Sisters of Glory, she performed at Woodstock '94 and at the Vatican for the Pope. She co-produced the group's critically acclaimed album, *Good News in Hard Times*, for Warner Bros, as well as writing and co-producing her solo album, *Traveller*. She was the lyricist for *American Dreams Lost and Found*, based on the book by Studs Terkel. Her life and music have been profiled on CBS *Sunday Morning* and *Good Morning America*. Her debut novel, *One More Stop*, was a Lambda Literary Awards finalist and a Waterstones New Voices finalist. For the past 15 years, Lois has travelled America for The Acting Company, teaching teenagers in small towns and inner city schools how to tap into their emotions and understand their world through classic theatre and literature. She is currently co-writing the libretto for the opera *Mila* and working on her third novel.

For Tommy & Betty

THE DUVALIER FAMILY TREE

William Duvalier & Mrs William Duvalier
**She has no name of her own.
She lives in the shadow of his name.**

They give birth to Carter Duvalier — Carter Duvalier marries Lily.
He is and always will be — **She is the best thing that
nothing but trouble.** — **happens to him for sure.**

Lily Duvalier gives birth to Steven and Winston Duvalier.

Steven Duvalier marries Doreen. — Winston Duvalier marries Charlotte.
Doreen gives birth to — **She is his sweetness.**
Carter Jr and Daphne.

Carter Jr — Charlotte gives birth to
marries Faith. — Alice and Theodore.
**Faith gives birth
to Steven Jr the
football hero.**

Daphne hooks up — Alice marries Rob
with Chris. — **Alice gives birth
They have no** — **to the twins
children.** — **Lily and Billy.**
**Thank god for
small favours.** — Theodore,
Suitcase Boy.

That is the tree.

BOOK I

REVELATIONS

AFTERWORLD

Where are we? We are in the place before thought, before you were you, before you came into form. We created this place for you, for you and your family. I am your dreamer. You are my dream. I dreamed you into being. You are not in the image and likeness of me. You are very much you, whoever you are. I am but the beginning of you. All that has been, all that is ... includes you. All of your *'The Lord is my shepherd; I shall not want'* is what you think I need to hear. I do not need to hear any of it. I am too busy dreaming you. You want to know how it works? How can I answer unanswerable questions?

Rheta's questions: *'Why did I give away my son? Is he dead or alive?'* Doreen's question: *'Why do I drink?'* Doreen is here with us, still trying to get over her psychological stupor; years and years after her death ... a difficult transition for her. Steven's questions, which have everything to do with Doreen's drinking: *'Why boys? Why Theodore?'* Winston's question: *'Why did Charlotte have to die?'* How many times do I have to listen to that one? Melanie's heartfelt question: *'Why? Why my baby girl. Why did they take her so soon?'* Understandable. Then there is Charlotte. Charlotte. Melanie's daughter, Winston's wife, Charlotte, who has been driving me crazy with her moods and never-ending questions: *'Why can't we fly like the peregrine falcons? Why can't we be like the cypress trees? Why, why, why?'* Do not ask me. I haven't the faintest idea. Finally, there is Theodore and his questions: *'What do I want? Will I ever be content?'* Who is content in any world?

There are so many individuals, dead and alive, seeking answers. I have better things to do with my time than answer every single one of their questions, thoughts and prayers. Have I made myself clear?

Let me explain. When I created you, and I did create you, I dreamed you into form. My dream was your awakening. I chose your family, chose your fate, gave you the life that you call '*my life*'. When you call it '*my life*', it is as if you believe there is some personal purpose to your residency on earth. Your ego is my greatest frustration. If only you understood that I dreamed you up in the first place, maybe you would be less resistant during those final moments when I am finished dreaming you. So what if you no longer exist? If you did not exist in the first place, why should it matter? Why wouldn't you want to time travel on your iridescent silver thread back into '*My Kingdom*', as you put it, which sounds a bit grandiose, but you need to call it '*A Kingdom*' and I cannot stop you from calling it that, can I?

Imagine my frustration? '*Thy will be done on earth as it is in heaven.*' There is no heaven! There is no hell! And Purgatory is the most peculiar notion you have ever invented; a purification process for all who have sinned? There is simply not enough time to purify each and every soul who aspires to achieve the holiness necessary to enter the joy of some imagined heaven. Sometimes, I wish we had never started this experiment. I could stop dreaming, but that wouldn't be any fun. I like the drama, too.

The Duvaliers are but one example of my infinite manifestations. When I came to the end of my dreaming Charlotte, she was relieved. She thanked me. She travelled on her silver thread without any resistance whatsoever. She left Theodore; her beautiful infant boy. The family wept, they moaned, they asked so many questions of me, I wondered if I had misunderstood the directive. Charlotte asked nothing. She knew it was the end of my dreaming her. She understood it was an even trade. I do not understand why Charlotte has been so petulant since she arrived. After all, it was she who was so anxious to get out in the first place.

I hope Lily awakens soon. Maybe she can help with Charlotte, talk some sense into the girl. When she was alive, Lily never asked anything of me. Never. She never complained about her marriage to Carter. What a mess that was. I wonder which world has got a hold of him? I am delighted he is not here.

I seldom know when I will awaken, when I will call you home to be with me, when it will be your time to leave. There will come a mysterious moment when I have no choice but to dream you back into life, only to wonder when we will be together again.

RHETA B.

Fourteen. I was fourteen years old when Minister Cleveland had his way with me. When it comes to bein' taken down by your minister in The House of The Lord, who you gonna tell? Nobody. You don't say nothin' to no one. You let yourself swell up like a hot-air party balloon; ankles swell, fingers swell, bosoms swell, until everyone around you realizes you are swollen with child. Such shame don't come free. You pay. And the minister, he don't pay a penny for what's happened behind his altar. He don't even know that this future bastard is his child. He's too busy sleepin' with the female population in his congregation to consider whether or not this bastard is his bastard. Pardon me for saying so, but his dick has been in just about every woman's hole in the Church of Heavenly Saints. Heaven help all the bastards seeded by Minister Cleveland.

Cleveland Alexander was born on a wet spring day in May of nineteen hundred and fifty-four. Baton Rouge clinic was a haven for fallen women. They greeted me with open arms. They didn't care whether I was black, white, red or yellow. No one asked me who was the father of my child. I was one of many black, unmarried women who walked through those green wooden doors.

When my water broke, which took me by complete surprise, they drugged me. When I woke up, they put Cleveland Alexander in my arms. He was smaller than a white rabbit, cuter than a Kewpie doll. His hands were two-toned; the inside milky white, the outside chocolate brown. I remember his smell; syrup, maple; sweet sweet sweet. Nobody visited. My mother wanted to visit, but my daddy wouldn't allow it. It was when I gave birth to Cleveland Alexander that my daddy made a hard and fast decision to disown me. Nothin' quite like bein' disowned; no place to go, no one to call on the telephone, no one to help me through the most important decision of my wicked life.

'Why me?' I asked myself. 'How do I deal with this helpless infant, who the good Lord has placed under my watchful eye?' Soon after his birth, I put Cleveland Alexander up for adoption. Never went back home. Never saw my daddy again. Spoke to my mama once or twice on the telephone. But, I never saw her kind eyes again. There are some disappointments that break your heart. That was the biggest disappointment of 'em all. One misstep in an unforgivin' direction forever changed my life. But, was it not for that one misstep, I might never have known the other child I call my own: Theodore Faulkner Duvalier.

Mr Steven Duvalier is a gentleman. Did you ever see the movie *Gone with the Wind*? Mr Duvalier looks like the Mr Ashley character: slim, quiet, easy on the eyes; a good man with a sweet heart. When I look at him, I see a deep wound; an enormous ache that he can't shake. His brother has the same kind of ache. I understand his brother's ache; what with his wife, Charlotte, dyin' so young.

Mr Steven Duvalier's wife, Doreen, was a strong-willed woman with a mean-ass temper. When she screamed, the sugar-cane lost its sweetness. I mean, you could hear her bitterness resoundin' throughout the sugar-cane fields for miles and miles. I don't like a hot temper. Reminds me of my daddy. And I don't need to be reminded of him, especially by someone who is my employer.

When you clean houses, you want to feel confident. If you don't get any praise, you don't feel like you've done the right kind of a job. That's how I felt when I worked at Mr Steven and Miss Doreen's house; like I was walkin' on eggshells. One misstep and the whole damn job would crack apart and I'd be out the door, on my ass, with egg on my pretty little face. What would I do then? Now I know the answer. Clean. I can cook and I can clean. There'll always be a job for me. Have to keep remindin' myself that things are goin' to work out. 'Things are goin' to work out'. I will land on my two feet. I can clean. I don't mind gettin' my hands dirty. I can be of service to those folks who don't know the first thing about pickin' up after themselves. I pick up for them.

Every evenin' I anxiously waited for Mr Steven to come home from work. His calm presence quieted down Miss Doreen. She was a handful. But, from the moment he walked through the front door, she was a very different person; on her best behaviour, almost a human bein'. Almost.

When Miss Doreen drank her bourbon on the rocks, which was every single afternoon, she became another person altogether. At around four o'clock, she would kick off her shoes, sit in the recliner and ask me to bring her the bottle. I did what she asked. It seemed awful early to be gettin' tight. Not to her. She wanted her liquor. Now! After a couple of bourbons she'd be hurlin' insults at every corner of the room. Nobody was listenin'. Maybe there were things in that great room that never revealed themselves to me. She certainly had some deep-seeded resentments bubblin' up inside of her. I'm tellin' you. Those chintz curtains got quite an earful.

Chewin' ice. She had a talent for chewin' large cubes of ice; like a cow chewin' its cud on a hot afternoon. Never broke one tooth. Wonder what she was thinkin' about while she chewed away her afternoons. Never chewed at night. Miss Doreen is no longer with us, rest her soul. Fortunately, long before she died, I was already workin' for Mr Steven Duvalier's brother, Mr Winston Duvalier. I didn't have to watch Miss Doreen drink herself into the grave. Mercy comes in many ways; that timely change of employment is but one example of mercy's watchful eye. I'm on loan. It's permanent. Glad of it. Mr Steven knew the situation was dire at Mr Winston's house. Mr Winston's wife had passed away durin' childbirth leavin' Mr Winston with a five-year-old girl and a newborn baby boy. Charlotte Duvalier gave her young life so that Theodore Faulkner Duvalier could enter the world. That's how Mr Winston saw it. He didn't want anythin' to do with Theodore. Whenever he looked at his son, he thought about his wife. Sugar-cane fire burned out of control in his heart. Even though he married two more times, he'd never forget her. Even though the child needed his father's love, the father couldn't give it, because he wouldn't forgive his son for changin' his imagined future into an unimaginable nightmare.

Alice, Theodore's big sister, was tickled pink to have a newborn baby brother. She loved him to pieces.

The Duvalier family has been in sugar for over a hundred years. Mr Steven, who runs the business now, ran the business with his father, Carter Duvalier, who inherited the business from his father, William Duvalier, who inherited the business from his father, whose name I don't remember.

When the pressure from a hurricane blew a manhole cover sky high in New Orleans, it hit Mr Carter Duvalier in the head. Killed him in an inhale. Carter Duvalier's wife, Lily Duvalier, the mother of Mr Steven and Mr Winston, insisted that the sugar-cane business remain in the family. Without missin' a beat, Miss Lily called a meetin' with her two sons and their respective wives. She informed them that it was her intention to take over the affairs of Pine Grove Plantation. Miss Doreen was pretty pissed off. She hated Miss Lily's strong will. Miss Lily never liked Miss Doreen much either. She could not tolerate her daughter-in law's drinkin' indulgences.

The brothers knew there was no changin' their mother's mind. Mr Steven was delighted to keep the business intact, so as to have a job that made him feel useful. Mr Winston, who at the time of his father's death was married to his second wife, Miss Francine, had become a successful heart surgeon in Baton Rouge. He didn't much care who ran the damn sweet mess, as long as he kept his beautiful home, which was situated on the edge of one of the sugar-cane fields in Vermilion Parish. Miss Francine, who was from the north, didn't know the first thing 'bout sugar, except that the family's successful business made her life just a little sweeter.

Miss Lily reminded me of Scarlett O'Hara. She fought with all her strength to keep the land in the family. Unlike Miss Scarlett, Miss Lily got what she wanted. Miss Lily *always* got what she wanted. Though she's no longer with us, her iron-fisted ways play a big part in how the business is run. Even from her grave, she's still the boss of Pine Grove Plantation.

Couldn't have been nicer to me. Grateful that I took care of Theodore. She loved that boy. 'Rheta B.,' she said, adoringly. 'He is different than the rest of us. This boy's got the soul of his mother. Look at those eyes. No one can escape his charm.'

Only time I ever saw Miss Lily cry was at Miss Charlotte's funeral. She loved Miss Charlotte. Everybody loved her. Mind you, Miss Charlotte was not easy. She didn't take any bossin' around from anybody, not even from Miss Lily. Miss Charlotte came from a fine southern bankin' family. Didn't put the slightest financial demands on Mr Winston. If she needed somethin', she had her own personal fortune at her disposal. Miss Lily liked that about her daughter-in-law.

Miss Doreen, on the other hand, came from a poor family without a cent. She never stopped complainin' for one minute about not havin' enough of anythin', 'cept an overabundance of heartache. I could have given her a few lessons in heartache. I didn't. Not my place to give her a lecture on life.

Theodore was magical; even when he cried, there was somethin'

special 'bout his tears. They fell in perfect circles. Whenever I held him in my arms, I thought 'bout my son Cleveland Alexander. Where was he? Who was takin' care of him? Did I do the right thing by givin' him away? But when I looked into Theodore's eyes, I knew I was meant to be where I was; takin' care of Miss Charlotte's little boy. Were it not for me, no one 'cept Miss Lily, when she had the time, which wasn't very often, would have taken care of Theodore. That is until Miss Charlotte's mother, Miss Melanie, moved from Atlanta to Baton Rouge. She wanted to be close to her only grandson.

Every other week she visited her husband, Bud, in Atlanta. He didn't seem to care one bit about the arrangement. I thought it peculiar. But, Miss Melanie was different, just like Theodore; unusual, independent. She did *what* she wanted *when* she wanted. Nowadays, we'd say she's a free spirit.

Charlotte was her only child. I can't imagine how painful it was for her to lose her only child like that. I just can't. When Miss Melanie first arrived at Pine Grove, she refused to talk about the girl. She buried her sorrow in the curves of her heart and the marrow of her bones.

She loved Theodore like he was her own. Come to think of it, he was her own. Any child born into a family belongs to every generation of that family. Theodore belonged to everyone but his father. Miss Melanie found Mr Winston's prejudice against his own child unforgivable. Often, there were harsh words between them. I disappeared during those confrontations. Don't stick around when the dirty laundry is bein' hung out to dry; one of the tricks of my trade.

The boy had three women takin' care of him. But, I was the one changin' his diapers, burpin' him, throwin' him high up in the air every single day of his early life. I am still the woman who takes care of that boy. Every blessed Sunday he calls me from New York City.

I ask him, 'Are you takin' care of yourself up there in that mean ol' city?'

He laughs. 'I always take care of myself, Rheta B. You, Melanie and Grandma Lily taught me how to do that better than you will ever know.' The boy tickles me no end. But, I do worry 'bout him. He seems so restless. Wish he'd settle down. Now that would be a true blessin'. Amen.

✳

Durin' those every other weekends, when Miss Melanie was in Baton Rouge, Theodore begged his daddy, 'Please let me visit Grandma! Please!' He made a pest of himself. Sooner or later, after he'd pestered his father to the point of absolute annoyance, he got his way.

I packed his cardboard suitcase, made sure he had plenty of clean underwear, ironed and folded his shirts and slacks, packed his penny loafers, placed 'em on the bottom of the bag, handed him his Bible, took him to the Greyhound bus station and sent him on his way. Missed him when he was gone. Hardly knew what to do with myself. But it made him so happy to be with his grandma, so I gave up my missin' him for more productive activities.

Miss Melanie spoiled Theodore like you can't imagine; gave him coffee milk every mornin', peanut-butter sandwiches for lunch, cookies in the afternoon and pulled pork for dinner. Every evenin', before he went to bed, she pulled out photo albums filled with pictures of his mother. Often she'd tell him stories 'bout Miss Charlotte that would bring tears to her eyes. 'She's watchin' over us, son. God took the sweetest girl to heaven so we could have the sweetest boy on earth.'

Other than walkin' through the sugar-cane fields, there was nothin' that made Theodore happier than spendin' time with his grandma.

✳

Before Miss Charlotte died, Mr Steven promised her he'd be there for the boy. He promised. It was sweet how much time he spent with Theodore. When Mr Steven wasn't visitin' with Theodore, he was out on the road sellin' sugar. Seemed like he focused on the business with a vengeance. Had no time for his family. His children, Carter Jr and Daphne, practically raised themselves without a father. And then there was the problem with Miss Doreen, their mother. The more time Mr Steven spent away from home, the more time Miss Doreen hit the bottle. I'm tellin' you, poor Miss Doreen just up and disappeared into her drink. So sad; sad for everyone in the family, 'specially for poor Miss Doreen. Fortunately, I had switched households by then.

Things got worse and worse with Miss Doreen. When Mr Steven finally came off the road, some days he would walk for miles through Pine Grove's sugar fields, come over to Mr Winston's and beg me to do him a favour. 'Rheta. Go over to our house and put Miss Doreen to bed. Please, Rheta B. Please! I need your help. I don't know what to do with her any more.' He looked so unhappy. It broke my heart to see such a good man in so much pain.

Miss Doreen wouldn't let any of the other help bring her upstairs; threw glasses full of ice cubes at every single one of 'em. As soon as she saw me, she smiled, let down her guard just a little bit. 'Rheta B. Things aren't goin' right with me. I am so unhappy.'

It broke my heart, but not enough to leave Theodore. I'd never leave him. When he was grown up, ready to face the grown-up world, he'd be the one to leave me.

THEODORE

You can bet my white, male, sweet as sugar, southern ass I love to travel. Packin' is the most pleasurable part of life. Getting' where you're goin' is the saddest.

I loved my black mammy, Rheta B. I still love her. In truth, she had been my cousins' mammy. She came to help Daddy after my mother died, which was soon after I was born. Rheta B.'s parents threw her out when she was fourteen. She must have gotten herself pregnant. If that be the case, I never met her children. My father would not allow such minglings in our house. When I was but a small boy in my hometown of Napoleonville, Louisiana, Rheta B. packed my bags, got me on the Greyhound bus to wherever I was goin'. I loved the Bayou. I loved travellin'. Most of all I loved walkin' in the sugar-cane fields. I felt like they were my fields. I owned them. Actually, they owned me. As a boy, I never loved anyone or anything more than I loved that sugar.

Sometimes, when I was on school break, I would ride the bus for a very long time just so I could look out the window and gaze at the sugar-cane in the most southern part of my home state. I loved it when Rheta B. packed my bags, got me ready for the journey. She took care of every little detail down to my socks and underwear. No matter where I was goin', she took that brown cardboard suitcase down from the shelf inside my closet, made sure I had my Bible in tow, sent me on my way to whatever great adventure was in front of me.

Day in day out I begged my daddy to let me visit Melanie, my grandma on my mother's side. When he got good and sick of my persisting, he'd let me go. I took the Greyhound bus to Baton Rouge all by myself; one hour, just one hour from home; alone lookin' out the window. I could not wait to see her. She showed me pictures of my mother. She loved my mother. I could tell from lookin' at the pictures why everyone loved my mother.

I am always ready to move. Home is my suitcase. There is not a place in the world that makes me feel at home any more. Not lookin' for that in this life. Be damned if it ever happens. You know things don't happen if you don't want them to happen.

I have a couple of cousins: Carter Jr and Daphne. I like 'em a lot. When we were kids, we played games, played doctor, had oral sex, bent-out-of-shape sex. I always liked that fuck-me-upside-down crazy kind of sex. I'm not afraid to admit it. I'm not afraid to admit anything. It doesn't mean I'm proud of it. I am not proud. Shame is in this here bag I carry.

When you're at an airport, there are millions of guys waitin' for it. You see it in their eyes. Follow the suitcase boy, boys. Passengers get ready. Married commuters, I advise you to take the latest flight you can book. Let me give you a thrill before you get home to see that little missus who's keepin' your dinner warm in the microwave. Before you get on the plane, look my way. I'm there waitin' for you; ticket counter, baggage claim area, to the left of the security check, I am there. Look me in the eye. Where do you want to go to? I know a corner. Where do I live? Right here in this bag. That's enough about this here geography lesson.

Rheta B. was a rock. She rocked me on those big black bosoms of hers. She was estranged from her family, I was estranged from my father, even though I was living in his house. Rheta often asked me, 'Theodore Faulkner Duvalier, what you day-dreamin' about now, chile?'

I always gave Rheta B. the same answer: 'Travellin', Baton Rouge, Grandma Melanie, pulled pork, gettin' the hell away.'

I wanted to go to boardin' school so bad. I wanted to look at those pretty boys in their skin-tight underwear. But, Daddy wouldn't let me go. No. No. No. The son of a bitch ran our house like it was the military. Funny thing is, he was never a soldier, sailor, pilot, none of those fightin' hero types. He just had it in him to be meaner than a coiled snake in a bad mood. He had rules for this an' that and every itty-bitty thing you could imagine. He watched me like a hawk. It seemed to me he didn't like me very much. Rheta B. said he missed my mother. That's what was botherin' him. I was too young to understand his missin' or his meanness.

Daddy's mother, Grandma Lily, was a killer. She didn't let him get away with anything. When he was a boy, any time he took the Lord's name in vain, she washed his mouth out with borax and castor oil. Can you believe that lethal combination? Only a very strict person could come up with such a wretched punishment. Over time, he learned never to mess with her during her pre-, post- or menopausal years. She couldn't have been sweeter to me. I got the best part of her. He got the worst.

My daddy was a hunter. Even in his dotage, he is still a hunter. He will shoot at anything that's killable. The fact is, he believes every day is huntin' season. On Easter Sunday I have seen him shoot a rabbit with a sawed-off shotgun from at least two hundred yards. Bang. Right through the heart. Daddy is a doctor. He is a heart surgeon; a heart surgeon without feelings; one of the great ironies of life.

He and I have a mutual understanding. We do not hug, never did, never will. We shake hands. Like it's some kind of contract of obligation to say hello. We are gentlemanly about it. Civil. Even now, when I get home after this flight, I will walk into his house, the house where I lived during my formative years and we will shake hands.

Daddy will say, 'Hello T.F. How was your trip? Glad you had

it in your heart to see your poor old father.' That's what the son of a bitch will say.

I'll carry my bag up into my room, store it on that top shelf inside my closet. Won't unpack. Why bother?

My father's brother, Uncle Steve, is more like a father to me than my own father. His son, Carter Jr, is one of the cousins with whom I had oral sex. When we were children, Uncle Steve's daughter, Daphne, and I played for hours and hours in the sugar fields. We laughed and laughed and touched each other in those forbidden places. I adore Daphne. She's more like a sister to me than my own sister, Alice. My Uncle Steve molested me when I was but a child. Of course I never told my father about Uncle Steve's shenanigans. You don't squeal on family members. You live with the memory. You try to understand why things happen the way they happen. You forgive. You try to forget.

Gettin' back to the Bayou. I love fishin' and water skiin' in the Bayou. Freedom is what you feel when you are out beyond civilisation's reach. The Bayou is not about civilization. It's about playin', ridin' motorcycles on the water's edge, gettin' hard from thinkin' you don't have to worry about tomorrow or the next day. It's about jerkin' off while fishin' for red fish, almost fallin' in the murky waters when you hit orgasm and a fish pulls on the line, laughin' out loud, laughin' till your belly aches. It's about nobody tellin' you what to do or where to go. No father to make you feel like you don't belong in his family, like you don't belong in the world.

'Your mother would be saddened by your reckless behaviour, son.' My mother, they say, was the sweetest girl. She was his goodness.

Louisiana State University (LSU) is my alma mater. It's hard for me to believe I have a college diploma, but I do. In those years of later learning, though I felt trapped and confused, I felt it was my obligation to complete a business curriculum. I knew it would lead me nowhere. But, since it was the single most boring major I could find, I assumed business studies would allow me the endless opportunity to ask myself the same unanswerable questions I had been asking for years. 'T.F., what the hell do you feel? What do you want? What in the name of the good Lord are you lookin' for? What?'

Now I understand that what I wanted was to find somethin' better than what I had at home. I wanted to believe that somethin' luminous was waitin' for me, somewhere ... somethin' would assuage ... assuage ... beautiful soundin' word ... my symptoms of unrest, my shame.

Have I ever been in love? I have been close to that feelin'. It feels so good, then suddenly I feel a pressure in my intercostal muscles, right in front of my heart and I think I'm gonna suffocate from feeling. When these symptoms occur, I fall apart. Too much feelin' causes me to recognize all that I am missin'.

Because I had so much longin' inside me during my college years, I drank copious amounts of the finest twelve-year-old bourbon day in and day out. I drank to forget where I was, what I felt, what I feared, what I wanted. I became a loner. I played sports to work out my aggressions: tennis, basketball. I was good. My father was proud of my athletic accomplishments. He didn't have a clue about my other extracurricular activities. In my freshman year of college, an older man groped me after a tennis tournament. Unsolicited. Uncle Steve always showed up for the games. I love you, Uncle Steve.

I hid in the swamp after Uncle Steve jerked me off. I was confused. I knew I wanted more where that came from. For that matter, I wanted more from any male who would do me the honour of takin' my dick in his hand or his mouth and givin' me pleasure. To this day, I have not given up that hope. Every bus station with a glory hole gives me hope.

Do you want to know what I think about gay people? There are gays who don't want anyone to know they're gay. Hypocrites. I don't like them much. Then there are flamers who flaunt it. I could care less about them. Then there are the hot guys, like my best friend, James. If he weren't already taken, I'd be on his back like a monkey. Cuban guys are hot. I hardly know what to do with myself when I hook up with a Latino at the check-in line. Eyes. It's right there. Eyes are the soul's door. We all know what we're lookin' for, so why waste time. Sex is like a drug. When you know it's available, you gotta have it. One rule of thumb; never see them again, whoever they are. Don't tell them where you come from or where you're headin'. Zip and leave. No tears in these eyes.

Daddy was a doctor. Didn't I tell you that already? I didn't like either one of his other wives. Of course he got married a couple of more times after my mother passed away. He is one of those types who do not want to be alone. Ugly, cunning, whining gold-diggers those women, his wives, my stepmothers.

My mother was a looker. My grandma, Melanie, says she looked like Carole Lombard. Melanie wants me to settle down. I am her son. By no fault of my own I am hers. Her love lights my heart.

Have you ever been to Riverside Park in Manhattan? That park is a park for strangers to meet and become fuck-buddies. The front of the park is for straight guys lookin' for girls. Usually, everyone is walkin' a dog. Damn! You see more dogs tied up to trees in that park than you could imagine. And why are they tied up? Their owners are busy gettin' it on in the bushes. That's why. The back side of the park is for mysterious men; men addicted to other men, men looking for blow jobs, hand jobs, ass jobs, men at the end of a day's job, straight men going home to Connecticut, not quite ready to go home.

I ride my motorcycle to Riverside Park. I don't need a dog to sniff out the action. I have never come home empty-handed from that West Side sex haven. I am extremely interestin' to men on foot. I just sit on my bike real nonchalant like, peruse every single guy that walks by. Sooner or later, someone gets on the back of my cycle with a hard-on. I turn around, see if I want him. When our eyes meet, if my heart races and my dick hardens, off we go. Sometimes we go as far as the Palisades. I love New Jersey, especially at night when the lights from the George Washington Bridge light up the sky like it were Christmas or a Fourth of July celebration. I have heard that my mother loved Christmas. I would have liked to have celebrated just one Christmas with her. That would have been a fine memory to carry with me through life.

I believe in safe sex. What do you think? I'm some kind of animal because of my proclivity? Look at your own proclivity. When I was ten or eleven years old, I read an article about HIV that changed my life forever. After reading that article, I decided I would never have unsafe sex. Never. I did not, do not, will not end up a statistic because of my desires. Desire is holy. Desire is its own temple; the temple of temptation.

My strict upbringing has taught me to be a man of manners. I am very careful about how I say what I say to any person I meet. This suitcase boy will never be rude to any man because of his accent, the colour of his skin or his socio-economic status or lack thereof. Black is beautiful, so is brown, baby so is white trash. I believe in the rainbow coalition of sex appeal.

It is true that I am forever tryin' to get somewhere. When I get there, I am forever disappointed. When I am disappointed, I need to disappear by having sex with myself or with some other lucky so-and-so. I think sex is a great stress buster. Give me one last splendid orgasm before this world blows up, this plane goes down or this body gets sick with some incurable disease; one majestic masturbatory farewell.

Transient. I am that word. I live that life. Transient is hot and sexy. Anal sex is hot and sexy. We are primal beings. We are on a quest, one that continues long after we settle down. So why settle down?

✳

'Hey! I thought you understood the rules. All right. I'll tell you one more time. Do not tell me you love me when you're comin', just come. Do not tell me your name. I don't want to know where you come from, where you're goin', where you've been. The truth is I don't want to know a damn thing about you. And I don't think you need to know a damn thing about me. You got the rules. What's not clear? You want to know where this tattoo came from, do you? I told you no questions. But, since you are so pretty, I will answer this one question. My mother gave me this tattoo. On my twenty-first birthday, she took me to a tattoo parlour in Baton Rouge. This tattoo was her gift to her favourite son; this heart on my ass. She watched while the tattoo artist needled my skin. She cried so hard. She thought I was in pain. I stopped the tattooer, got up from the table, walked over to my mama, hugged her, swore on my life it didn't hurt. I lied. She left the room, waited outside. Mama never liked to see anyone in pain, especially her favourite boy ...

'Damn! Didn't I *just* explain the rules? Never mind. I've gotta go. Gotta make a phone call. Tell 'em the flight's delayed. I'll see you on the plane ... It's crazy we're on the same flight. Maybe we'll check out the bathroom. I said ... maybe.'

WINSTON

The boy is a faggot. He had too many women fawning over him as a child. 'Isn't he the most beautiful baby? Who's the best boy? Who's the sweetest boy? Have you ever seen such beautiful tears?' I tried making a real man of him, a straight man of him. But, you cannot straighten a bent man. You cannot change certain unassailable situations in this life. It's like open-heart surgery; either you get into those arteries, ream them out real good, so they are clean as a whistle, functioning to the best of their abilities or the patient is never quite right in his body or his mind. If things go completely haywire, the patient dies on the table. It is better to die than to be gaga for the rest of your life. That is a terrible burden on the entire family. Nowadays, it is rare that a patient dies on the table. In the old days it was a different story. In the old days you never knew who was going to make it through surgery. When I started out, I told my patients, 'You have nothing to worry about. You are going to have a fine outcome.' Bullshit.

Let me tell you a secret: back then, I didn't know what I was talking about. I was scared out of my pants. I learned medical facts from cutting open cadavers. I learned from reading textbooks until my brain was crammed with so much information I thought my head would explode. I had learned enough to understand that the human embryonic heart begins beating almost at the identical rate as its mother's heart. I learned when the human embryonic heart begins beating, around twenty-three days after conception, it was a true miracle. I knew there was a region of the heart called the sinoatrial node, the pacemaker, which is wholly and completely responsible for the rate and time of all cardiac muscle contraction. I knew the heart was the centre of emotion, that feeling deeply made a hollow man whole. My darling Charlotte taught me that significant piece of information. I knew you could have your heart broken. She taught me that, too. She taught me so many wondrous things. She was my sweetness; dear, dear Charlotte. She was the most beautiful, complicated woman who ever walked the earth.

Of course I knew where the heart was situated. Imagine if a heart surgeon didn't know that? I knew the cessation of any man or woman's heartbeat meant he or she was in a critical emergency. Critical. I remember many of those critical emergencies like they were yesterday; blood spurting every which way, nurses handing me that cold clamp, nurses wiping my forehead dry, nurses scurrying around the operating room, beeping noises, clocks ticking, heart racing, racing against time, trying to breathe, trying to think straight, trying to save a dying man; too much pressure for an anxious man ... I do not perform heart surgery any more. Where was I? I was talking about the heart, wasn't I?

The boy! I was talking about the boy, my son, Theodore. Theodore Faulkner Duvalier is my only son. I have a daughter, Alice. She's a lovely girl; nothing at all like her mother, but she is a good girl; practical, down to earth. Alice is married to Rob, who is a doctor. He makes plenty of money. They seem happy. They have two crazy kids, Lily and Billy. Those twins are inseparable, just like Alice and Theodore were when they were kids.

From the moment he was born, Alice loved Theodore. She loved having a baby brother. She wouldn't let him out of her sight. The boy was surrounded by nothing but women; my mother, mother-in-law, his sister, his black mammy. Lord! I know that was the problem. What else could it be?

What is a father to do with a son who has no real mother?

You take him to the swamp, teach him how to love nature and

her seasons, teach him how to hunt, how to be a man. When you spend time in the Atchafalaya, the seen world disappears. That seen world has a way of tearing your heart into a thousand pieces; lost pieces, pieces of how you hoped life was going be. The swamp and its unseen world have a way of giving you back *most* of what you are missing.

✳

Charlotte loved the swamp. She sat for hours upon hours on the green and grey woollen blanket her mother, Melanie, knit for her; peering through her high magnification binoculars, watching the peregrine falcons circle high above her head. She wanted to fly with them. She wanted to climb the cypress trees, stand on their uppermost boughs and dive into the swamp.

'*Winston,*' she said. '*Why can't we fly? Why can't we grow as tall as these glorious trees? Why is man so puny in comparison to the natural wonders that surround him? Why?*'

There are some questions you simply cannot answer. They are unanswerable. Charlotte asked those questions. Melanie told me that even when Charlotte was a little girl, she asked big questions. She desperately wanted to understand the ins and outs of how this world worked; what came after this world and what came before it? That was my Charlotte.

Charlotte's father, Bud Brickman, was the top tax attorney and financial wizard south of the Mason-Dixon Line. His firm Brickman & Stein had business offices in Atlanta and New Orleans. Bud ran the Atlanta office. Though he lived full-time in Atlanta, somehow he became a great friend of my mother's father, Daddy. Daddy worked for my grandfather, William Duvalier, and that is how Bud came to work for my grandfather and finally ended up working for my miserable father, Carter Duvalier. To this day, I have no idea how they met. But, it is an undeniable blessing for the Duvalier family that they met.

After my father's untimely death, it was Bud who saved my mother's ass from a thousand land-infringement litigations and at least that many business catastrophes. He was, single-handedly, responsible for my brother's and my mother's acquisition of thousands of acres of untouched farmland, so they could expand the family sugar business into a lucrative, albeit, back-breaking enterprise, which I had and continue to have absolutely no interest in, except for the financial remuneration.

Bud figured out how to manage the family funds and where to invest the family funds. He kept the books squared away. He kept the Duvaliers informed. He made sure every member of the Duvalier clan received a quarterly report on the developments involving the family business; even those of us who weren't the least bit interested. On numerous occasions Bud rescued the Duvalier's from the grip of the corrupt Louisiana government. He created loopholes out of fertile soil. Bud charged as much as he could honestly get away with; always with a smile on his face. Bud Brickman is a Jew, so is his wife, so was Charlotte.

Bud's wife, Melanie Brickman, was and still is the biggest pain in the ass I have ever known. Their daughter, Charlotte Brickman Duvalier, was and still is the love of my life; rest her soul. It was Bud's idea that Charlotte and I should meet. I am sure Melanie had something better than me in mind for her clever, cultured daughter.

I can hear Melanie reading Bud the riot act. '*I don't want my baby having anything to do with the likes of those sugar-cane people, those greedy rednecks without an ounce of culture in their perverted souls. Louisiana isn't fit for the swamp. Honestly, Bud Brickman,*' I'm sure she moaned, as she gave him that condescending look of hers, '*The one and only thing you have any sense about is numbers. My mother warned me about you.*'

Bud brought Charlotte to the plantation. For once in his hen-pecked life he refused to kowtow to his wife. When we met, Charlotte was finishing up her senior year of college: Emory University. I was finishing up medical school: LSU. When I fell in love with Charlotte, which was the moment I laid eyes on her, it was the first time in my life I believed in God or fate. It was the first time I believed I could love somebody forever.

*

As a child, my mother dragged me by the short hairs, kicking and screaming all the way to our local church; every single Sunday morning. I hated it worse than having my mouth washed out with borax and castor oil for taking the Lord's name in vain. All that changed when I met Charlotte. Charlotte was my religion. Because she was Jewish, she didn't go to church. Because she wanted our little girl to be part of a religious community, I took Alice to church. That made Charlotte happy. My children still follow the Catholic faith. When he comes home, even Theodore goes to church.

*

Before Theodore was born, Charlotte, Alice and I spent as much time as possible on Gran' Isle. Because my medical practice was thriving, I made arrangements for another doctor to be on call. September was my favourite month down there. It still is. On the way down we drove by hundreds of oil platforms and drilling rigs in Port Fourchon. I hated those rigs. I still hate them; three miles from the shoreline. If those rigs were up north, those smart ass Yankees wouldn't allow those rigs within ten miles of their shoreline. How we hard-working people are treated in this state. It is not fair; not fair at all. What good is a government that steals from its people?

When Charlotte, Alice and I drove down to the Gulf, the roads were a mess from one hurricane or another. But, when we got to Gran' Isle, we were glad to be there. Even if the roof had blown away during the latest hurricane, we were happy. We considered it free air-conditioning. I love getting something for nothing. Our camp, a wooden house on stilts, overlooked the Gulf waters.

Charlotte unpacked, got Alice situated with her toys, went food shopping and visited friends. I had my ritual: walk out the door onto the wooden deck; smell the ocean and gaze at the soft brown waves in the late September sun; like nothing or nowhere in the world. It was paradise.

Everywhere else in the Gulf of Mexico the water is blue, but in southern Louisiana the water is brown. It is rare to see anything blue here, except a roof that will most assuredly be blown away in the next storm. So what if the water's brown. It is our water. Those oil companies, they don't own our water; the rigs yes, the water no. Here in Gran' Isle the women play cards, the men fish and everybody drinks.

On those memorable weekends, I would take the fishing boat to Queen Bess Island, watch the pelicans dive for their afternoon meal, the seagulls glide and the blue heron pose for us fisherman who wished we could catch what those birds had already eaten. At night, after Alice was tucked in and the babysitter was positioned in front of the television, Charlotte and I went dancing. We danced to the music of Ray Conniff and his orchestra; cheek-to-cheek, close my eyes, smell her sweet perfume, rest my hand on the crook of her back and pray the night would go on forever.

When the weekend was over, we made a point of leaving at the most beautiful time of day. We followed the sky's incredible sunset all the way home. Winston and his women chased the magical creatures in the sky. Alice saw dragons and giants. Charlotte saw dragons, giants and some mystical world beyond my imagination. I saw the sky change from one colour to the next. That was enough for me.

Sixty-five years old! Why have a birthday party!? At my age, there is nothing to celebrate. Social Security! Social Security will be gone soon enough. So will I. The family mausoleum will be a nice resting place. I hope my father isn't there. When I am dead and gone, who the hell is going to visit *me*? Alice, maybe? She loves her old man. Maybe the kids? Certainly not Theodore.

I have quite a bit of money hidden in various places. I don't have as much money as my brother, Steven, but I have more than either one of my children might imagine. Money! That's all anyone talks about these days. Money. Poor Doreen. She came from nothing, she felt like nothing. She never got over her poverty mentality; ashamed of her parents, hated her father, hated all of us Duvaliers, especially my mother. Doreen hated the world. But, she loved Charlotte. Charlotte treated her so kindly, accepted her for who she was, demons and all. It never bothered Charlotte that Doreen chewed those damn ice cubes.

My other wives, those fat cows who took me to the dry cleaners, they never missed a chance to criticize Doreen's upbringing, her drinking habits or her chewing habits. You would have thought those ornery second and third conniving wives of mine were from royalty. Why did I ever marry them? ... I was out of my mind from missing Charlotte. I started talking to myself, talking to the walls, finally, I started talking to Charlotte.

I said, '*Charlotte, you don't want me to be alone for the rest of my days on earth, do you? A man needs a woman to take care of him, his needs and his family.*' The next thing you know, I end up marrying two fat, money-grubbing, no-good, northern harpies, one right after the other; the two biggest mistakes of my life. Charlotte must have had a hand in those marriages. She knew I couldn't bear to be alone ... I still hate being alone.

Late at night, when I'm sitting in my chair, reading *Field & Stream*, thinking about Charlotte, my mind plays funny tricks on me. My heart beats so loud, it sounds like someone is knocking in my head, calling my name. 'Go to sleep, Winston,' it says. 'Don't be afraid, son. Go to sleep.'

I have got more money under my mattress than most people have saved in a lifetime.

SWAMP
(Atchafalaya)

You crazy ass Duvaliers carve your initials in the bark of my Swamp Cypress Trees; WD, CD, SD, WD again and again. Generations and generations of dishonourable carvings have created a nesting place for bugs and disease that have eaten away at the splendid trunks of my noble trees. You selfish rotters. This swamp, *my* swamp, the largest swamp in our country, holds each one of you accountable for your monstrous destruction.

I am one of the jack-o'-lanterns in the marsh, a sprite who burns by self-ignition, who lives underneath this glorious bog. As I float on fresh water, I watch you as you paddle your way to oblivion. I see you and your unconscionable doings undoing my wet world. You are my enemy; the enemy of this refuge, these grassy marshes with low-growing shrubs, the enemy of my wildlife, my wild things, all things that live in my wet world.

Before a hurricane hits land, instead of trying to protect my wetlands, you're busy chasing after the helpless crawfish that are trying their damnedest to escape the storm's surge. Those helpless creatures end up in your freezer, wrapped in plastic bags, thrown away in tomorrow's garbage. When you see a young grosbeak nesting in the green foliage of my cypress tree, you swoon with desire. And what is it you want from this frail creature? You want its blood. You want to rip its delicate wings from its body, broil the bird on a skewer and lick your fingers clean. You are a two-legged killer.

Look! Look! Look at that thing in the sky! The peregrine falcon flies high above you. What do you want? You want to kill it, you want to fly alongside it, fly above it, but you can't fly. You're just a human being who wants what you can't possess. You ask yourself how can you kill that '*thing*' in the sky? You have no idea what it means to *be* a beautiful warm-blooded creature gliding on air currents, circling the earth without fear. How could you understand? You see the world through cruel eyes. Your vision is marred by your destructive instincts; kill the bear, kill the gator, kill the buck, kill the raccoon, kill whatever you can, as long as you can kill, torment, destroy what you can't control. You can't control nature. You can't control the natural instincts that inhabit the wetlands inside you or anyone else.

You couldn't control the beautiful, hot-headed, wide-eyed woman who loved my peregrine falcons, loved my cypress trees, loved me, loved every one of my amazing natural elements with an appreciation I have never known since she left my swamp for that world without water. You couldn't control the boy you call *son;* the boy you criticized and tormented because he didn't understand your cruel nature. Your son understood the beauty of my wetness, just like his mother did. He doesn't visit me any more. You ruined him. You drove him away from those of us who loved his sweetness, loved his gentle nature.

Damn you, Winston Duvalier! Remember the day you dragged your son, Theodore, to my swamp? You said, '*Look at this, son. This here is an eight-foot alligator. Alligator Mississippiensis. That's what we call this lizard here. You know what she wants, son? She wants to crush your bones in that great big jaw of hers. That's why we are going to tie up her mouth; you and me, son. After we tie up her mouth, we are going to tickle her tummy.*' Then you screamed at Theodore. You screamed at the top of your lungs. You woke up every single jack-o'-lantern tryin' to get some day sleep in the swamp. '*Don't you run away! You come back here! Right now! I said, turn around, young man! Turn around or I'll come get you! And when I get you, you will wish you had never run away from your daddy!*' Poor Theodore pissed his pants. And what did you say? '*Stop that crying! If your mama were alive today, she would be mighty unhappy with your behaviour. She wasn't afraid of alligators. She and I came to the Atchafalaya on Saturdays rain or shine; every Saturday a picnic with the alligators, your mama and me. That was the sweet time. Your mama and me.'*

Winston Duvalier! You are a liar! Your wife hated coming to my swamp with you. She liked it better when she came by herself, leaned against the cypress tree, looked above, through the limbs and saw her future home. You made her life unbearable. That's why she died. And then, after she died, you had to make sure your boy would grow up to be a man ... like you.

Remember on that same day; Theodore hid behind the cattails. You were furious. Back then you were always furious. *'Come over here! Stop crying,'* you said. *'Come here. Take this rope. Take it! Now! Damn you! Be a man like your daddy! That's my boy. We got her. She's ours. Theodore Faulkner Duvalier, you are now most certainly a Duvalier; Winston Duvalier's son. How many times have I told you there is nothing to be afraid of except those things that go bump in the night.'* You laughed so hard you fell down. *'Look at her tail wiggling for you, boy. She likes you. Uh huh. She is a living fossil. She is a creature with her own special kind of reptilian brain. All she wants is to crush your bones.'* You were hysterical with laughter. Your son, Theodore, could not stop crying.

Shame on you, Winston! Look at what you have done to the woman who was the love of your life and the boy who is your son.

CHARLOTTE

'*Winston Duvalier! Don't you come in here! I don't want you near me!*'

'*But honey, all I want …*'

'*… What you want! What you want! It's always about what you want! Damn you and your dead soul!*'

'*Baby … You don't mean that. I love you. You're my girl.*'

'*I don't want to be your girl! I'm sick of it! Sick of you!*'

'*Honey, remember how happy we were; not that long ago?*'

'*You got me pregnant … Again … This fucking baby is going to be sucking at my tits! What the hell do you know about it!? You're never here. Busy man; so busy cutting open some poor fool's heart, making empty promises to his family. Lying bastard! You come into this room and I promise … I will kill you!*'

'*Baby! Open the door!*'

'*No!*'

'*I wouldn't do anything to hurt my darling Charlotte.*'

'*No!*'

'*Alice and me, we love you, honey. Lily loves you, Steven adores you, Doreen wouldn't get out of bed if it weren't for you. Your mama, your daddy, we all love our Charlotte. Come on, honey! Open the damned door!*'

'*Fuck you! I am getting out of here! You and your people are driving me crazy! You've been sucking the life out of me since the moment we met. No more! You hear me? No more! Mama's coming to get me. I'm going to kill this child growing inside me, then I'm going to kill you. After you're dead, I'll kill myself!*'

'*Baby. Please.*'

'I can't live like this any more! If I stay here, I'll die. Do you hear me! I've got to get away, away from you, Winston! Your kind of love is destroying me! Let me go! Please! Let me go!'

'If you don't let me in, I'm going to break down this door!'

'Break it down, you cheap son of a bitch! Who'll fix it? I'm the fixer around here. You don't fix! You just break!'

❉

I don't understand why these ancient memories are still with me. I can't get rid of the past. It plagues. It haunts. I work through this, that comes back to torment me. I work through that and something else appears like a tangled cobweb with no light shining through it. I cannot escape the intricacy of my history. No matter how hard I try, how far I run, my past catches up with me; no matter what I do. Look at me. I am as far away from living life as possible and I am still plagued with life's memories.

How many people did I hurt? How much wounding did I cause to those who loved me, those I left behind? Why did I forever have this unsettled feeling? Why do I still have this feeling? I heard voices then, I hear voices now. They whisper. *'You lived your life in shadow.'* What the hell does that mean? *'You lived your life in shadow.'* I need some real answers about my unrest. I don't need poetry.

First I was Charlotte Brickman, then I was Charlotte Duvalier. I felt like neither a Brickman nor a Duvalier. I found my refuge in the cypress tree, in the peregrine falcon. I found my soul in the wind, whether violent or tame. However it blew, the wind understood me. The rain, the thunder, the swamp, they understood me. They were my intimates. No person made me feel like I belonged to myself or to them. Nobody. Oh, but the world loved me, adored me, especially after I passed. I have been anointed in the minds and hearts of family and friends as 'one of the most amazing, magical, complicated women ...' How difficult it is to live up to my reputation.

My perspective has changed ... slightly. I feel an overwhelming delight for those who live, those who have not yet reached this Afterworld. I wish I were with them. At the same time, I feel the depths of their despair, their inescapable sorrow, as if it were my sorrow; a curse to feel the ache of so many weary hearts. I wish I could help, but what can I do? I most certainly can't give a testimonial about better times ahead. I don't know if there's such a thing as a positive outcome. What makes no sense to me and to many others in here, is how fate works. Life is a tug of war with some sort of purpose, a definite end. In Afterworld there is the same tug of war without an obvious purpose or an apparent end.

I spend quite a bit of time watching my life's movie over and over. I see it from many perspectives. I have judgements. One moment I feel this way, the next moment I feel that way; a life without answers. I'm not certain I remember the essential questions regarding the meaning of life. But, I do see moments, critical moments that changed many lives, mine was just one of them.

Lily, Winston's mother, was so sweet. She was convinced the Bible would save me. Convinced. *'I love them that love me; and those that seek me early shall find me.'* She must have said those words a thousand times. The truth is, if you don't have faith, the Bible doesn't do you much good.

'Charlotte,' she said, *'I know Winston is a difficult man. I know he suffers from melancholy, like his father, like his older brother, Steven, but he is your husband, honey. As his wife, it is your duty to bear this burden. Hormones have made women crazy since the beginning of time. That is the Lord's way. Hormones are a woman's problem.'*

'Lily. Do you love Carter?' I asked. *'How can you love him when the good-for-nothing disappears for weeks on end? And when he is home, which is practically never, he carouses till dawn, comes home drunk, acts like a mean fool, then treats you and everyone else like dirt. How can you love that kind of a man?'*

Lily laughed. '*Charlotte. You are such a child. Many years ago, when I was very young, still living with my folks, when Carter walked up those front steps, looking like a wild animal who needed some serious attention, the Lord looked down on me. The Lord said, I heard him say, "Do him good." And I did just that. When the Lord speaks, there is no other way but to follow.*'

'*I don't believe in the Lord, Lily.*'

'*Yes, you do, honey. You believe in him.*'

'*I have never believed in him or her or whatever it is or is not.*' I was certain about that, then. I still don't think much of the Lord thing.

'*Of course you believe. Otherwise, why would you have married Winston? You could not help but mingle with someone from another persuasion; two people from different faiths … getting married … It was the Lord that brought you two together. It was the Lord!*' Lily had a religious theory for everything that happened in life and death. I'd very much like to hear Lily's point of view about this bizarre world; she'd most likely be confused like the rest of us.

When I cried, Lily took me in her arms, stroked my hair, kissed the top of my head. '*Life is not meant to be easy. "A time to weep." You will get through this.*'

'*I'm not going to have this baby.*'

'*Of course you will.*'

I was angry. '*If it's a boy and I know it's a boy, he will be …*'

'*… Stop that talk right now!*' Lily didn't want to hear about my prophecy. '*I will not listen to evil thoughts. Take my hand, Charlotte. Take my hand! … Now! We are going to pray together. Our Father …*'

Lily took my hand in hers. We knelt on the floor. She prayed for the soul of my daughter, Alice, my future child, Theodore, for the soul of her son, Winston, for my soul, for Carter's soul, for her other son, Steven's soul, Doreen's soul. She prayed for what seemed like an eternity. I pretended I was praying, too, but my thoughts were elsewhere. I had to figure out the future. How could I escape? Could I leave my parents? Could I leave my baby girl? If I went back home to Atlanta and stayed with my parents, would Winston come and get me, would he bring me back to Louisiana, where I would surely die from acute unhappiness? While I was plotting and planning, Lily prayed and prayed ... and prayed; trying to pray away her own fears as well as mine. Ridiculous. No matter how hard she tried, she couldn't lift me up with her prayer, unless I wanted to lift myself. The truth is I didn't want to be saved. I wanted out of my untenable situation. I was tired of my moods, tired of those unbearable thoughts, tired of life.

Memory. Sixteen weeks into pregnancy. *'Knit one purl two. Baby booties. Knit sole. Soul. Ten rows running. Ten rows. Turn and turn and turn some more. Right hand needle upside down. Needle under, loop around. Needle ... Needle ... In through the front door, once around the back, peek through the window and off jumps Jack. In through the front door, once around the back ... Needle in the door; up and up ... and up it goes ... baby ... no baby ... up and up and up ... inside it goes ... and ... oh ... Got to kill this ... kill this thing that's killing me ... Help! Help! No more ... Baby no ... more ... baby ... Oh no ...'*

I play this part of the movie over and over. I look at the images. The past tense becomes present tense.

'Miss Charlotte! Can you hear me? Miss Charlotte! Oh dear God, what have you done?' Rheta takes me in her arms, rocks from side to side. *'What have you done? You crazy girl?'* Rheta runs to the bathroom. I hear her rummaging through the medicine cabinet. *'Shit! Ain't nothin' gonna save no one here.'* Rheta runs to the telephone with towel in hand. *'Miss Doreen.*

Come quick! Mr Winston's house … quick! Miss Charlotte she hurt herself real bad. Real bad!' Rheta hangs up the telephone, yanks the sheets off the bed, wraps me in her arms, wipes the endless stream of blood with her bare hands, wipes the endless stream of blood with one soft towel, then another soft towel, wipes the blood with the ripped white sheets. Rheta weeps. Rheta moans. Rheta sings a beautiful hymn about angels. Rheta prays. *'The Lord is my shepherd, I shall not want. He maketh me to lie down in green pastures, He leadeth me beside the still waters, He restoreth my soul.'* Rheta trembles. Rheta cries. *'Oh God! You hear me! Please restoreth this child's soul!'* Rheta, with me in her arms, rocks front to back, side to side. *'He leadeth me in the paths of righteousness for his namesake.'* Rheta rests my head on her knees. She raises her hands high above her head, pleads for my soul. *'Yea, though I walk through the valley of the shadow of death I fear no evil, for thou art with me.'* Through her sobs, she swears on her life, *'I swear to God I am with you, Miss Charlotte! God is with you! We are with you! Miss Doreen's gonna be with you soon. Hold on, Miss Charlotte. You are in the valley, but you will make it through. You will make it through. I will not let you go!'*

Doreen whispers. *'Charlotte. Listen to me. Look at me. Open your eyes. Oh, honey. Why would you do such a thing? Can't be that bad. Winston can't be all that bad, can he? He loves you, baby. Every single one of us loves you. I adore you, Charlotte. What would I do without you? … Don't talk. Don't say anything … just listen. Rheta and me are goin' to take you to a hospital, a hospital that Rheta knows real well. Nobody's gonna know where you are. Winston won't bother you. I'll make sure of that. We're gonna get you in the car right away, gonna get you to this hospital in Baton Rouge, where they're gonna take good care of you. When you get better and I promise, you will get better, you will come back home.*

When you come back home, Rheta and I will take care of you. Don't you shake your head no, miss thing! Your friend, Doreen, doesn't lie. You know that.' I try to speak, but I can't. Doreen says, *'I'm gonna call your mama now. Tell her what happened. She'll meet us at the hospital. We will take care of our Charlotte. You don't have to worry any more about anything. You're gonna be fine.'* Rheta B. weeps so loud, it sounds like nobody's going to be fine. *'Damn it, Rheta!'* Doreen loses her temper. *'Pull yourself together! Make yourself useful. Go downstairs. Make sure Alice isn't anywhere around the house! Make sure nobody's around the house! Go on! Pull the car up to the back door!'*

Rheta B. doesn't budge. *'I don't know how to drive, Miss Doreen.'*

'Well, learn!'

Somehow, Doreen and Rheta B. get me out of the house without a hitch. We end up at some hospital in Baton Rouge. I'm the only white girl in the whole damn hospital. Doreen takes such good care of me. She makes sure the Duvaliers leave me the fuck alone, for a little while anyway.

Mama flies down from Atlanta. She never leaves my side. She never cries. Every time I open my eyes, I see her smile through my blurred vision. Many weeks later, Winston arrives. He takes me back home. During the entire trip, Mama holds me in her arms. Most of the time I'm fast asleep on her lap in the back seat of the car. When we get back to Napoleonville, she helps me up the front steps, into the bedroom, tucks me into bed, like when I was a baby, whispers my name, *'Sweet Charlotte. My sweet Charlotte.'* She whispers my name all night long.

At the end of my life, all those I loved were with me. Of course Carter didn't show up. He was off somewhere, sleeping with someone, probably drunk out of his mind. He never could deal with grief. The truth is, I didn't miss him, not for a moment.

I blamed him for whatever ailed his sons, I still blame him for their misery.

I said goodbye to those I loved. I gave each one of them marching orders, even Winston.

'*Love yourself, Winston. Forgive me. Most important of all … forgive yourself. And love the boy. He is your son.*'

I had a heart-to-heart with Steven, who couldn't stop crying. I grabbed his hand, told him, '*Hush.*' I made him promise to take care of my boy. '*Promise me. Forever and ever. You will treat him like he was your own flesh and blood. Promise me … How lucky my boy is that you are his uncle. You make sure he grows up to be as good a man as you.*' He promised, then kissed me on my forehead. He was so upset, he left the room without saying goodbye. I didn't take it personally. By that time, the silver cord lit up the room. How could I take anything personally with all that light shining through me?

Doreen, Rheta B. and Lily prayed and prayed … and prayed. Lily forgot she hated Doreen. Doreen forgot she hated Lily. Then, after all that praying, those three women sobbed like mothers whose sons don't make it home from war. In my life on that earth and since looking at life from this Afterworld, I've never seen women cry as hard as those ladies cried on the day I died.

Lily cried so hard she forgot to pray. That was a miracle. At one point Lily said, '*I will love you and miss you for the rest of my life. If I ever, in this life or any other life, did anything to hurt you, please forgive me.*' I wanted to assure her she had been the kindest mother-in-law any daughter-in-law could have asked for, but I didn't have the strength to speak.

Doreen put a flower in my hand. '*You are my best friend. Thank you for your love. I will find you one day, Charlotte. Until I do, I will see you in every cypress tree, see you wherever the peregrine falcon flies … You will be there for as long as I live.*'

Rheta B. kissed my fingers, all ten of them.

Alice, my beautiful girl, sat at the foot of my bed. When it was almost my time, she sat on the left side of the big four-poster bed, lay her head on my belly and cried. '*Don't go, Mama. Don't go.*'

I whispered. *'Take care of your daddy and your baby brother. They will take care of you.'*

And then there was Melanie and Bud; my mother and father. My father kissed me goodbye, stroked my hand like I was a child. I was a child. I was *his* child.

Mama lifted me up, held me in her arms, whispered in my ear. *'I will take care of the boy. Don't you worry, my sweet girl. I will take good care of him.'* She wiped my forehead like mothers do when their child is sick. Once again, she didn't cry. She locked the tears inside her heart, so I wouldn't feel badly.

My child was safe. I was ready, ready to ride that ribbon to the stars. Something greater than myself called my name. *'Charlotte.'* I wasn't afraid to die. I had finished my worldly travels. Finally, it was my time to fly with the peregrine falcons.

I still don't understand why the past happened the way it happened. I don't know why the future will happen the way it will happen either. I see the future as it looms in front of those I've known, those I've loved, but I can't change anybody's future, so what good is knowing about it? And, who gives a damn about the past!

So, they're having a celebration; celebrate Winston's sixty-fifth, celebrate the great football hero's graduation. Steven's grandson, the party boy, graduates with honours. Alice has been planning this party for months. Theodore's coming home. Many a Duvalier and friend will attend. So much of the family is gone. They're here, somewhere in this Afterworld. I haven't been able to connect with any of the Duvalier clan, yet. It seems we're still living in different realms. Why should that surprise me? Nothing changes. Absolutely nothing.

LILY

'Love is patient, love is kind and is not jealous ... bears all things, believes all things, hopes all things, endures all things ...'

❋

Sermons: I have heard such magnificent ideas spoken inside the house of the Lord. Because of the many holy lessons I received under the roof of our Lord, I soared, without regret, above my personal grief. I lived my life according to the teachings of Jesus Christ. While I embraced most teachings easily, there were other teachings that tried my soul to its core. But, no matter what trials or tribulations confronted me, I embraced my hardships. I knew these hardships would prepare me for the arduous journey home to my maker. Throughout history, devoted believers have struggled against oppression, fought for the goodness of God in man and man in God. Fortunately, in my lifetime, I was chosen as one of the holy flock.

Recently, while sleepwalking in this unfamiliar world, in my somnambulistic state, I heard a deep disembodied voice call my name. *'Lily. Lily. Some who are still alive, others who have preceded you in death, judge your actions harshly. They criticize your behaviour.'*

Those who judge me harshly do not understand I had no choice but to make the decisions I made in business as well as in my personal life. Wagging tongues are the work of idle minds. Idle minds have too much time and envy. I didn't have the luxury of too much time, nor did I envy those who envied me. I pitied them. If I felt unkindly toward anyone, I prayed. asked the Lord's forgiveness for my petty thoughts. Even when the sting of wagging tongues burned my heart, I turned the other cheek. My faith never wavered. My heart hardened. I had to protect myself and my family from the outside world; protect my boys from Carter Duvalier's monumental mistakes. His mistakes could have destroyed our lives. As a dutiful wife, my role was to salvage, to clean up Carter's mess, to raise a family in peril, to acquire the land that rightfully belonged to the Duvalier family.

And there was the boy; my grandson, Theodore. Theodore needed a strong hand to guide him. I was that hand. I loved him like he was my son; taught him the importance of family values, faith and self-worth. I introduced him to sugar's world, sugar's beauty. Theodore played for hours in sugar's fields. Daphne and he played; they played in those fields until the sun set in the hazy early evening sky. Theodore was born from the womb of God's untamed, glorious creature, Charlotte, who spent as much time, though it was a short time, as was necessary for her soul's walk on God's great earth.

Whether I am in this unfamiliar, unusual world or that familiar, usual world, what truly matters is I can, in good conscience, rest in peace and look back on my personal history with a quiet humility. Humility found me late in life. When the weight of a family rests on your shoulders, there is no time for humility. You lift yourself up, lift others up, calculate the risk, focus, stay steps ahead of your feelings and most important of all, never stop fighting for what you believe is right in the eyes of the Lord.

When I finally stand before the eternal tribunal, I will inform the celebrated body of justice that I never surrendered. I fought God's holy battle. 'Oh,' I will say, 'I was more than a headstrong woman holding a family together, a business together, a husband together. I was unselfish and intrepid. When trouble darkened my path, I turned to God for answers. Do not judge my swift and accurate actions as harsh deeds. What else could I have done in a world of sin and shame?' The tribunal will applaud my tempered life.

✳

As a young woman, I was well read, well bred, well suited for marriage. I attended Holy Ascension private boarding school for women in Baton Rouge. I was studious. I was not interested in athletics or the arts. I found athletes and artists foolish, frivolous, unfulfilled beings. I preferred history, science and the law. When I wasn't studying for exams, I read books about America's history. I studied the Constitution. I believed in the Constitution as the supreme law of my country. I believed in its enlightened doctrines with every fibre of my heart. I loved my country as much as I loved my faith. From early childhood, my daddy and my mother instilled these two great loves in me, as well as the love and devotion of family.

My mother, Iris, taught me about the science of plant cultivation. She was a horticulturist for the garden club. Her area of expertise was the cultivation of dwarf gardenias. She taught me about raised beds, irrigation, pruning and potting. I learned everything I would need to know about pests, fungus and soil drainage from my mother. Because of her knowledge, I had an innate understanding about the vicissitudes of sugar-cane, which came in handy, especially after I took over Pine Grove's business.

✳

When I was seventeen, after a long undiagnosed illness, my beloved mother passed away. Daddy and I sat beside her during her final moments. I saw the divine's hand guide my mother's spirit away from the material world. It was a magnificent experience for both Daddy and myself.

After my mother died, I attended H. Sophie Newcomb College, Tulane's co-ordinate college for women. I commuted between Baton Rouge and New Orleans, so Daddy wouldn't have to live alone in Mother's house of flowers. I kept my mother's greenhouse alive. Her gardenias flourished. In my spare time, I took horticulture classes at LSU. In my sophomore year, I transferred from Tulane to LSU. I loved the campus; walked its lakes, strolled its walking trails. I graduated with honours in political science. I lived at home during those years of learning. I was content with my books, my plants and Daddy.

*

Daddy was William Duvalier's personal attorney. One night Carter, William Duvalier's son, showed up at our doorstep. When I opened the screen door, there he stood ... the most dishevelled-looking character with an unlit cigarette dangling out of the corner of his mouth, tobacco stains on his fingers, shirt unbuttoned to his navel; a downright mess he was. Carter had been sent over by his father, William, to thank Daddy for getting Carter off on bail for disorderly conduct and drunk-driving charges.

Upon leaving our house, Carter ambled down the front steps, stopped, scratched his head, turned around, looked me up and down in a most peculiar way; a way no man has looked at me since. '*Gardenias,*' he said, '*you smell like gardenias.*' As he walked away, he mumbled under his breath. '*I will never forget your scent, young lady. For as long as I live, your scent will be my heart's desire.*' He walked through the front yard, murmuring, '*Gardenias, love gardenias.*' That was my introduction to Carter Duvalier; the most foolish, imprudent man whoever walked God's earth.

Carter Duvalier was an atheist and an alcoholic. Of course he was an alcoholic because he was an atheist. I believed I could save him. How arrogant of me. There is only one saviour ... God. I believed all men were like Daddy; honest, considerate, faithful and good-natured.

Daddy convinced me that Carter's problems were temporary. '*The boy needs to sow his wild oats, honey.*' Daddy was certain about his hypothesis. '*Carter is just plain fed up with William's rules and by-laws. To tell you the truth, so am I. That man is a tyrant; a bully with too much money and too little conscience.*'

Carter's father made a fortune in the sugar business. Nobody understood how William Duvalier made that kind of money selling sugar. But, he did. He was shrewd. He was nasty. He was unforgiving. And, he was cruel, especially when it came to his only son. He beat Carter, locked him in a dark room for days on end with no food or water. Carter's mother cowered at William's temper, powerless to keep him from beating her pigheaded son. When Carter wasn't getting a beating from his father, he spent the rest of his days and nights begging for a beating, looking for trouble wherever trouble lurked.

Daddy spent enormous amounts of time getting Carter out of trouble with this cop or that pool-hall owner. Carter's antics tickled Daddy. For some reason, the young rascal amused him. I, to this day, cannot understand why Daddy encouraged our relationship. There I was, a serious student, an innocent girl who worshipped the Lord. There Carter was, a lost soul without a shred of common sense or decency. What was Daddy thinking?

When I was despondent, when I wanted to break off the relationship, Daddy talked me out of it. He believed I was in Carter's life for a reason; to help him find his true nature. Lord knows I tried. I read verse after verse about man's pleasure so I might better understand this tormented man that I ... loved; at least I thought I loved him.

My relationship with Carter was the most difficult test of my life. Taking over the business after he died was easy compared to the business of taking care of Carter while he was alive. It wasn't until many years later that Daddy admitted he might have made a mistake. By then it was too late for everyone involved, especially my boys.

Whenever Carter walked through the door drunk, I thought to myself, '*What doth it profit a man if he gain the whole world and lose his own life?*' But, there was no point in quoting

Ecclesiastes to a man who took the gift of life and family for granted.

Steven and Winston suffered terribly. More than anything on earth, they wanted the love of their father. They craved his attention. Carter tried his best to be a decent father. But, a drunk is unable to facilitate a child's need for parental continuity. One day Carter was sweet as sugar, the next day he was a mad man cursing us, cursing his father and of course, cursing the sugar for ruining his life.

Every now and then he would give the boys what he called life lessons. '*Boys, come on over here. The world is an unpredictable, topsy-turvy place. You best learn to look at the world from many different perspectives. Watch me. Spread your legs, clasp your ankles with your hands. Good boys. Pull your head down in between your legs. That's right. Look around. No laughing. What I am tellin' you is no laughin' matter … Listen to your father. He knows what's up. Knows what's down. If the sugar crop is destroyed durin' harvest-time, you best lean over, just like this and kiss your ass goodbye. While you're at it, kiss the good times goodbye, too.*' Carter's life lessons.

Steven hid behind my back. I grabbed his hand. Together, we prayed for Carter's soul. When Carter heard us praying, he staggered upstairs. Steven disappeared into the sugar fields. Hours later, he came back soaked in sugar-cane juice. Winston cut himself off from his feelings. He became sarcastic and sullen. He didn't know where to put his anger. I became his target. When I dragged Winston to church on Sundays, he kicked and screamed, cursed me out like a drunken sailor. I wondered where he learned such language? From his father no doubt. How many times did I have to wash Winston's mouth out with borax and castor oil? I hated Carter for what he made me. I tried, with the Lord's help, to forgive him. But, until he was killed in that hurricane, killed in an instant, when a manhole cover hit him so hard he died in an inhale, I was unable to forgive him … That's what Joseph said. '*He died in an inhale.*' Joseph is a good man.

He loved the sugar. Sugar loved him. I bet he misses cutting back those beautiful fields. He will be at the Gates soon enough. I will greet him with sheaves of sugar-cane upon his arrival.

There are so many memories. Rheta B. saved Winston's life. Steven let Rheta go. Even though he needed her help with Doreen, he gave Rheta away. Doreen was too far gone to notice. What happened with Doreen is a mystery; beautiful children, beautiful home, wonderful husband who shared the love of God with her. She drank herself to death, wasted her life. Foolish, foolish girl. I never understood her or her problems. Steven loved her, took care of her, took care of the children ... took care of me. My boy stood by me every step of the way. When I took over Pine Grove, he never wavered in his support. I said, '*What a good son you are ... My sweet boy. My best man.*' Without Steven all of us would have fallen apart. His kindness still lights the way for any stranger or friend he meets at home or on the road.

After Charlotte died, Steven took care of those who mourned her death. He took care of everyone, especially Theodore. He spent hours upon hours in the nursery with the boy. When Steven wasn't on the road, he looked after Theodore ... every single day. He prayed for the boy's soul. He prayed for Charlotte's safe journey home. He prayed for Winston and the family. What a good boy. I miss Steven. I didn't realize I would miss anyone or anything after I left that world behind.

I loved Charlotte like she was my own. I still love her. Her pain was my pain. Her eyes were my eyes. Her loss was my loss. Her love gave Winston life. For the time they were together, however many years it was, they shared a kind of love that illuminated Winston's world. I never saw a light like Charlotte's light. When it dimmed, the world suffered a profound despair. When Charlotte took her leave, I cried so many tears I thought I would drown.

During her last hours on earth, when she could barely speak, she whispered in my ear, asked me to take care of Winston, the girl and the boy. '*Lily. They need you. Take them in hand. Give them strength. Give them your love.*' Charlotte thought about everyone but herself.

I crossed my heart and promised Charlotte her last wish. I held myself accountable for Theodore's upbringing. Rheta B. and I took charge. Winston fell apart. He never recovered. Poor Winston.

Then there was Melanie, Charlotte's mother. Melanie lived in her own world, had her unique views about how to live her life, how to live other people's lives, how to make the world a better place. Religion, of any kind, did not resonate with Melanie. Her idea about marriage was peculiar and progressive, far too progressive for me. She and Bud, her husband, had an unusual arrangement. Downright strange! Until Melanie, I never knew a woman to commute between two lives. I still don't understand why she settled in Baton Rouge. Her second home should have been right there with Winston and the children in Napoleonville. But, Melanie did what suited Melanie. She was different. Jews are different. I hear they have a special place for Jews. I'm not surprised. Jews have always had a special place in time, space and history.

Melanie took control of the boy's life. She had Theodore commuting to Baton Rouge every other weekend, fed him weird foods, shared private thoughts, thoughts much too risqué for a little boy. She had him call her '*Melanie*' instead of Grandma. Have you ever heard of such a thing? Rheta B. packed his bags, walked him to the bus station, sent him on his way, but I know, for a fact, Rheta did not approve of the boy's travels.

After those avant-garde weekends away from home, when Theodore returned, he seemed changed, restless. Melanie put crazy notions about this and that in the boy's head.

'*Gonna travel, Grandma. When I grow up, I'm gonna see the world on a motorcycle. Maybe Melanie will travel with me. Maybe you. Maybe Uncle Steve.*' That's what the boy said whenever he came back from spending weekends with Melanie. Can you imagine such foolish notions?

How is it possible there is not a pew, not a kneeling bench in sight? Still, I feel I am in a splendid church of sorts, in a constant state of prayer and devotion. I made my crossing without a compass or a guide. There was a light, a thread of light, a silver thread, like spinning yarn; my soul's yarn. There was no maker at the gate. No gate. I made my crossing without wings. I saw flashes of seminal moments that shaped my life; moments of trials, tribulations, abundance and most of all ... faith. I saw flocks of birds that soared through an endless sky filled with an eternal sunshine. I was old in years. What I will miss no longer exists in that bankrupt world I left behind.

If only I could celebrate with my children, my grandchildren and my great-grandchildren; just one more time. From now on they will celebrate without me; celebrate my fine-looking, great-grandson, Steven Jr's graduation, celebrate poor Winston's sixty-fifth birthday, celebrate themselves for being alive. Theodore will come back home, walk the sugar fields, maybe stay in Louisiana longer than a weekend. Maybe he and Winston will finally embrace. Even if there are no pews or prayer benches in this unfamiliar Afterworld, I shall pray for that miracle. Pray indeed.

MELANIE

Thank God that bitch is dead! If I had to listen to one more 'Our Father, The Lord is my shepherd, love is patient, love is kind' bullshit, I would have killed her myself. I never have to see or hear another set of rosary beads working overtime. What a relief!

Hypocrites. The Duvalier clan is a thieving bunch of conniving hypocrites. *'Sugar is sweet. Sugar is power.'* Sugar my ass. If you think, for one moment, I wanted my little girl to marry that frozen man, you would be mistaken. Their marriage wasn't my idea. Bud came up with that beauty ... all by himself. I fought him every inch of the way. If Charlotte's future had been left up to me, she wouldn't have come within fifty feet of Winston Duvalier. Freaks, fanatics; the most dysfunctional family I have come across in all my many years and I have come across quite a few. Bud, being a top-notch accountant, has gerrymandered the books for many emotionally unstable, mentally disabled, revoltingly rich individuals. But, the Duvaliers take the cake.

Bud has what doctors call, in this day and age, erectile dysfunction. Simply put, Bud cannot get it up, has never gotten it up and at this late stage in life will, most definitely, never get it up. Nonetheless I love the man. Bud had an erection problem long before we met and married. If his mother was your mother, you, too, would have erectile dysfunction. The late Mrs Brickman was a ball-breaker.

Because of his inability to have an erection, Bud and I have a

... unique understanding. If I want to have sex with another man or another woman, I have Bud's permission; quite revolutionary for our generation.

Charlotte was not Bud's child. He raised her. He loved her like she was his own, he showered her with every kindness like she was his own, but Charlotte was another man's child. When I became pregnant with my little girl, I told Bud who the father was. I thought it was only fair that my husband know whose child he would be raising. We decided to keep our little secret between us for the rest of our lives. We made a pact that Charlotte must never find out who her blood father was for a variety of reasons too numerous to explain.

Even though Charlotte didn't have any of Bud's physical features, she had his charm, his warmth, as well as his delightful temperament ... on her good days. She had my love of nature, my love of life and my fair skin. Charlotte had the best parts of us. But, Charlotte had a rip in her heart; when she brooded, she was inconsolable. Inconsolable.

Charlotte asked a zillion questions; most of which had no answers, at least none that Bud or I knew. She asked questions like, '*Who or what were we before we were human beings? What comes after death? Why can't we fly like the birds?*' How do you answer questions like that? One day, when she was about twelve years old, I told her there were no answers to such big questions. She would have to figure out the answers by living her life. Do you know what she said? '*That's what I'll do. I'm gonna live a great big life. I'm gonna fly with the birds.*' That's what my little girl said.

✳

Charlotte's heart was wide open. Her open heart worried me sick. The littlest disappointment threw her into an uncontrollable rage. It took hours for her to cool down to a slow boil. I often thought, '*If only there were a way to protect my child from life's cruelties.*'

I didn't want Charlotte to become part of a family that couldn't possibly understand her unusual temperament; a family so far removed from her roots, removed from her heritage, removed from her familiar world. I was afraid my little girl would forget who she was, forget where she came from, afraid she would be unable to find her way back to where she truly belonged. That is, in fact, what happened to my baby.

Why, when I came to Louisiana, did I choose to live in Baton Rouge instead of Napoleonville? Why did I commute between Baton Rouge and Atlanta? Why didn't I live with Winston and those lovely grandchildren of mine? I wanted to live my life my way! That's why. I wasn't interested in living in a small town, where people pry into your personal affairs, where every person knows every other person's business. That kind of life didn't interest me. I needed to be near the boy, but I refused to spend any of my precious time in close proximity to the rest of the Duvalier family. I wanted to make sure that Theodore grew up with a healthy expansive world view; not a small-time, small-town, swamp-scape, sugar-coated, corrupt view of the world, but a view as expansive as the peregrine falcon's view, when he flies without a care, without restraint, above the earth, in a clear sky, full of sunshine, on a perfect fall day. That was the view I wanted for Theodore. I gave him that great big view. Every time Rheta B. packed his bag, every time he got on the Greyhound bus to visit his Grandma Melanie in Baton Rouge, his world view expanded just a little bit more. Today, when I spend time with Theodore Duvalier, I am proud of my brilliant accomplishment.

I required a private life. When I lived in Louisiana, if I had a guest, which I often had, I preferred our rendezvous to be a personal affair, no pun intended. I enjoyed flying, travelling back and forth between Louisiana and Georgia. It made me feel special. When I travelled from Atlanta to Baton Rouge, from Baton Rouge to Atlanta, it was a celebration of sorts. I created an abundant, varied life that, as Theodore would say, assuaged my inexorable grief.

I love Bud all the more for how he has loved me, how he has so generously let me come and go as I please. He would have preferred a regular marriage. But, he didn't marry a regular girl. Funny how things work out. Bud got tired of Atlanta. He sold our house for a small fortune. Now, he's full-time in Baton Rouge. No fooling around for me any more. We have good friends here. We belong to a temple. Bud prefers Louisiana's slower pace. He still does some accounting for the Duvalier family. It keeps him busy. At our age you need to keep busy. We take good care of each other. I like taking care of him. He has taken such good care of me since Charlotte died. He has prostate problems; it comes with the territory. I have a little bit of this and a little bit of that, nothing serious. No cancer, no Alzheimer's.

Rheta B. works for Steven and Winston. She works for us, too. We take good care of her. She takes such pride in her cleaning. 'How's that, Miss Melanie? Have you ever seen such a shine on a coffee table?' I hire another girl to clean up after she leaves. Rheta has no idea. I mess things up before she comes back. I owe that woman my life.

On her deathbed, when my baby asked each one of us in the room to take care of Winston, Alice and Theodore, we thought we were going to die from heartbreak. During Charlotte's passing, more tears were shed, more hearts were broken, more lives were changed than anyone could have imagined. The only time Lily and I came together, and had some sort of a mutual understanding, was during Charlotte's death. Lily loved my little girl. She understood her immense contribution to the Duvalier family. In those final moments, endless tears poured down Lily's lily-white cheeks. For the first time in her life, grief grabbed Lily by the heart and blew her mind beyond God's love.

Winston was a hollow man. Charlotte filled the crater in his soul. For the years she lived with him, she raised him up from his emptiness, gave him his humanity and filled his crippling void with her kindness. Charlotte was his magus. He was her curse. When Winston felt Charlotte's deep unrest, his behaviour became erratic, just like his father's. My baby longed for a different life. She wanted to be free.

'*Mama. I'm so tired,*' she said. '*I'm tired of taking care of Winston, tired of lifting him up on my shoulders. I want someone to lift me up with their love. I don't want to be pulled down by their need. I want my own life,*' she said, fretfully. As long as Charlotte was married to Winston, there was no way in hell she could lift herself out of his shadow or survive his obsessive neediness.

Winston believed having another child was the answer to Charlotte's unrest. He became fixated on the idea. Charlotte begged him to let her go. Winston knew better than to release his beloved genie. God forbid Charlotte should leave him. If he let Charlotte go, Winston understood he would surely die from emptiness. My baby had no choice. There was no way out, except for the ultimate escape. Charlotte had to die. That's all there is to it.

After Charlotte died, Winston's brother, Steven, spent an awful lot of time visiting Theodore. I knew he had promised Charlotte to look out for the boy, but it seemed weird to me that a grown man was spending that much time with a newborn baby. When Steven wasn't out on the road selling sugar or whatever he was selling, he hung out in the nursery ... with a baby. His children, Daphne and Carter Jr, never saw him. It was right around the same time Doreen started drinking. Doreen and her ice cubes; what was that about? Charlotte loved Doreen. I sure didn't understand their friendship. But, it was nice for Doreen to have a friend.

If I could have, I would have taken Theodore away from the Duvaliers. Lily wouldn't have allowed it. The truth is I wouldn't have wanted a baby cramping my style.

※

Years later ... I remember the day, as if it were today; it's a hot summer day. Theodore gets off the Greyhound bus with his cardboard suitcase in hand. He refuses to look me in the eye. Instead, he looks at the ground and kicks stones every which way. We get in the car. No words spoken. The boy chokes on his tears. He doesn't look left. He doesn't look right. He looks straight ahead at the road in front of him. He doesn't roll down the window, like he usually does, to smell the fresh air. He bites his lip till it bleeds on his best white shirt.

'*Theodore Faulkner Duvalier, what on earth is the matter with you?*' I reach inside my skirt pocket, hand him a tissue.

Theodore wipes his eyes. He blots his lip. He stares and stares … and stares. Until he says, '*Fire down there.*' He swallows hard. '*Fire in the fields. Body on fire. Shirt in the air.*' He sobs. '*Play in the field. Playing … Playing … Like we always play. That's all.*' And sobs. '*Run and run and run. Sun on my back. Shirt in the air.*' He shakes. He quivers. '*Fire in my body.*' He catches his breath. '*I'm on fire. Fire. Uncle Steve is on fire, too.*'

Oh no, no, no! I knew it … I … I am going to *kill* him. *Kill* him! First, I'm going to castrate him, then I'm going to hang his balls from a limb of the live oak tree in his backyard, then I'm going to kill him. I pull over to the side of the road. I look Theodore square in his young red eyes. I tell him it will be all right. It will be our secret. '*You will not do that again! If anything like that happens, ever, ever again, you will tell me and I will have a talk with your Uncle Steven.*' It won't happen again!

I hold Theodore, rock him like a baby. My baby boy. Charlotte's baby boy. '*It's going to be fine.*' Nothing is fine. Nothing is going to be fine. Charlotte is dead. Winston's obsessive love destroyed her. Theodore has been violated.

Steven's obsession could destroy Charlotte's boy. Over my dead body. You hear me? Whoever *you* are? Over my dead body!

❋

I can't wait to see Theodore. Of course, he won't let anyone else pick him up at the airport except his favourite grandma ... Melanie. Grandma. How I hate that word. What with Lily gone, I am his only living grandma.

Theodore loves the afternoon Jet Blue flight. He will most probably pick up a baggage handler, a pilot or a passenger at the airport. I hope he doesn't miss his flight like he did the last time he came home. Louisiana is his home; no matter what has happened, this is where the boy belongs.

I hope Winston acts, more or less, like a human being; half normal. Maybe he will finally hug Theodore. Now that would be a big step for old Winston ... He's younger than I am. I better watch out who I call old. It's not about numbers. What is it about? Point of view. I have a young person's point of view, therefore I am young.

Steven's off the road. Bud told me he got back last night. It is mind-boggling that Steven hasn't been arrested ... yet. Those college boys better watch their asses; between Steven and Theodore no sexual shenanigans are off the table. All these years. What I didn't say about so many things that were too painful to share with another living soul. Sometimes, I talk to Charlotte about the sordid details. I've been doing a lot more of that lately; talking to Charlotte.

It'll be nice to see Alice, Rob and their lovely children, Lily and Billy. The family is so damn happy when Theodore comes home. He is a people magnet. Everybody loves Theodore, just like they loved his mother.

Last night Bud mentioned something about Steven Jr having some personal problems; the brilliant football hero faces the impossibility of an unknown future. Faith and Carter Jr could drive any child crazy. I hope Faith leaves her knitting at home.

And please, God, please, let Carter Jr talk about something, anything but the Army Corps of Engineers. Boring. Maybe Theodore can give Steven Jr some good advice. I hope it's not a serious problem. I hope the party is a big success. This party means so much to Alice. It means so much to Winston. Maybe there's hope for that unfortunate man after all.

Bud says the harvest looks real promising this year. Soyabeans are growing well. No bad sugar blight. Sugar's selling for a higher price than usual. That's because the rest of the world is in such a mess. Down here, at least we have the possibility of a positive outcome. Possibility. That's what Louisiana is about.

UNCLE STEVE

'Forgive me Father for I have sinned.'

✻

My father, Carter Duvalier, was a difficult man, an unusual man who suffered from an unrelenting melancholy. He drank to disappear. Sometimes, he drank so much that, in fact, he would disappear for days on end. Sometimes, the days turned into weeks. Where he went, or what he did, we never knew. When he returned home, my mother refused to ask where he had been or what he had been doing. She acted as if it didn't matter one bit if he was home, away, in jail or in bed with another woman. That's how my mother acted; like nothing my father did mattered. I doubt that's what she felt. Winston and I couldn't figure out what our mother felt, if our mother felt. And, we were so afraid of our father, we didn't dare ask him any questions. How could we? When he was home, he was drunk more than he was sober. The man was so deeply unhappy. My parents were complicit in each other's misery.

I was the buffer between my mother and father; the son in the middle of their arrangement, the child who never had the opportunity to be a child. Winston had that privilege. Whenever my father went away, I was the son who took my father's place. I was responsible for protecting my parents from acknowledging their dysfunction, while trying to protect myself from acknowledging my own dysfunction.

✻

When my father was away, my mother raised *her* boys and ran the family business with an iron fist. She performed these tasks brilliantly. Even though my father clearly didn't appreciate my mother as a woman, he appreciated how well she ran our household and how well she ran Pine Grove Plantation's day-to-day business operations. Whenever he meandered, wherever he meandered, *she* was the woman *he* relied on to run the business and take care of *his* personal property.

When he died his untimely death, it was with good reason my mother demanded she take full and complete control of the Duvalier business. Doreen, my late wife, was furious with Lily's takeover. Unbeknownst to Doreen and everyone else, except for Bud Brickman and myself, my mother had been running the business for years.

❉

Doreen's father, Joseph, emigrated from Brazil to settle in Louisiana. For as long as I can remember, Joseph worked at Pine Grove plantation; the man knows as much about the life and death of sugar as any man in the business. Because he toiled in Pine Grove's fields from early morning till late at night, he had no time for his family. When Doreen was alive, she complained that when she was growing up, she only saw her father when he staggered home, late at night, drunk and exhausted. Sugar got the best of Joseph. Sugar got the best of us all.

Whenever I wasn't on the road, she got the best of me. Now, she's got the best of my son Carter Jr. I'm sure his wife, Faith, would love her husband to give up the business, stay at home, plant magnolia trees, travel and see the world. Maybe that will happen. Now that Steven Jr is graduating they don't have to worry much about anything any more. Maybe they'll spend more time together. I wish Doreen and I had spent more time together. I can't rewrite that history. Poor Doreen. Between her father and me, she didn't have it easy with men.

Pensioning off Joseph was difficult, but it was long overdue.

He would have worked till he dropped dead. The man loves sugar more than any Duvalier past or present. During hurricane season, Joseph always kept a watchful eye on the crop. Day and night, in the middle of the worst storm, I found him pacing back and forth in the office, worried out of his mind. Even as the wind blew out windows, pummelled the cane, Joseph stood guard over Pine Grove's fragile crops.

It is a fact that hurricanes usually occur right before harvest time; another example of our Lord's perverse sense of humour. I remember one particularly violent storm, a week before harvest. The wind was howling, rain pouring down like it was the end of the world. I was scared, scared for the crop. I ran out of my house, got into my car, drove through flooded fields, got out of my car, nearly got blown to the ground, ran into the office, only to find Joseph on his knees praying.

'*Please spare the crop this year. We have worked so hard. So much time and love has gone into the sugar's tender growth. Please be merciful,*' he pleaded to the heavens. Most of the time the heavens turned a deaf ear. The wind didn't give a good goddamn about Joseph's prayers. She just blew the cane as hard as she could. The cane's stalk bent to the ground like a half-broken body. The strong cane survived nature's beating. The weaker cane didn't have the strength to find its way to the sugar house. After the storm, no matter what was left standing, Joseph and his men cleaned up the mess. The next day Joseph reported the damages to my mother and me.

My father died during one of those storms. He died in New Orleans; a manhole cover blew out. It killed him on the spot. Joseph was the first to know about my father's death. He told my mother about the accident. My mother told Winston and me. I told Doreen. Doreen didn't care; by then she was too drunk to notice if my father was dead or alive.

One day, soon after my father's death, I overheard Joseph trying to console my mother. '*Lily,*' he said, '*I am here for you day or night. Whatever you want. Whatever you need. Please, let me help you in any way I can. Please.'* The poor man turned himself inside out trying to please my mother; an impossible feat.

I'm convinced Joseph was secretly in love with my mother. She didn't give him the time of day. She was too busy running the family business to pay attention to the murmurings of her heart ... or anyone else's heart.

✵

Doreen and I attended Saint Mary's public high school in Napoleonville, Louisiana. Even though we were the same age, I was two grades ahead of her. Doreen was not much of a student. Her parents tried disciplining her, but there was no disciplining Doreen. She was a party girl. Unbeknownst to her mother, Maria, and her father, Joseph, Doreen spent a great deal of time with a number of the more colourful boys in town down at the Atchafalaya. Even though Doreen was not much of a nature lover, what she was doing down at the swamp was more than natural for Doreen.

Doreen controlled her world and all of the boys in it by making herself sexually available. If she wasn't interested in you, she wouldn't give you the time of day. But if Doreen wanted you, you couldn't escape her spell. She was irresistible with her dark brown hair, grey-green eyes, olive skin and lovely curves in all the right places. She was a true beauty.

The first time I had sex with Doreen was the most arousing sexual experience I could have imagined. It scared me to death; like I had done something wrong, something indecent, something evil. But, after that night in the Atchafalaya, under the cypress trees on that hot June evening with the fireflies lighting up the swamp and the stars lighting up the sky, I couldn't stay away from her. I was hers. Doreen used her body to get anything she wanted from anybody she wanted. I was no exception to the rule.

On that sultry summer night, our first night *together*, Doreen wore the tightest skirt imaginable. I wondered how she got herself into it. When the sex happened, I didn't think about how she got herself out of it. All of a sudden, I was inside her. I don't remember taking off one article of *my* clothing. I didn't unzip *my* fly. Doreen beat me to it. I was out of control with desire. Doreen awakened my desire ... There's a part of me that wishes my desire had stayed dormant. But, you can't wish away desire. Desire follows its own circuitous course; no matter how hard you try to control it, it controls you. It controls me.

Because my mother was Doreen's father's boss, Doreen and I didn't socialize at school. When we began dating, we knew our parents wouldn't approve of our affair. Soon after we started seeing each other, Doreen got pregnant. I felt it was my obligation to marry her. I often wonder how she knew the child was mine. She said it was mine. I believed her.

My mother never believed Doreen. She called her a gold digger, she tried paying her off, she begged her to have an abortion. Doreen refused. She said it was against her religion. She had a point there. From then on the two of them were like alley cats in heat; yowling, howling and hissing at each other whenever they had the opportunity. Their hatred was palpable, especially for my eldest son Carter Jr. Whenever he heard them hollering at each other, he ran outside, hid in the sugar fields for hours and waited until my mother vacated the premises. Finally, after she had gone, he came back home, and without so much as saying a word to either Doreen or myself, he went into his room and locked the door. I heard him crying. I knew what he felt, but I didn't know what to do for him. I was torn between my mother and my wife.

Doreen tried being civil. When it came to Doreen, my mother did not give civil a second thought. Why bother taking hatred to your grave? It's bad for the soil, bad for whatever grows out of its hatred, bad for the members of the family left behind.

My children, Daphne and Carter Jr, loved Doreen. When Doreen was still herself, there was no better wife, no better mother, no better friend. I fell short as a husband and a father.

The business occupied the better part of my days and nights. Like Joseph, I spent many a sleepless night and a fretful morning worrying about the crops, the harvest, the pests, the storms, the books, the Bible. Back then there was much I worried about, especially the personal heartaches on the road; young, foolish heartaches in every town.

I no longer worry about *them*; my mother, my father or Doreen. They are gone. I miss them, each one of them, no matter how much they disappointed me or I disappointed them. Sometimes, when I go to sleep at night, I hear their voices. I see their faces in my dreams. I remember the many peculiarities that made them who they were, even if who they were was hardly who I wanted them to be. So few people are who you want them to be; I know only one person.

When he was too young to know that human beings get undone, Theodore Faulkner Duvalier was my undoing. As an infant, how could he understand that my spirit yearned for his spirit? As an adolescent, he had no idea how to control himself. Controlling your desire is an adult's responsibility. What saddens me most is that I understood my actions would unhinge Theodore for the rest of his life, but I couldn't control myself. I knew it was a sin, but I wanted the boy. What I saw in Theodore was the purity and goodness of the Holy Spirit. I wanted the Holy Spirit to bind us in every way possible, even if it meant I was a sinner. I have sinned. I have sinned. For this I will forever repent.

Charlotte gave birth to her goodness. To this day Winston doesn't understand that Charlotte gave the world a gift through her sacrifice for him. When Winston looks at Theodore, he feels nothing but uncontrollable grief and rage. Winston longs for the woman who beguiled him into believing he might have had a beating, feeling heart. Winston is a fool. Because of his stupid illusions, Theodore has been deprived of a father's love. A child without a mother is defenceless. That child must be protected, must be loved. When a mother gives her life for her baby, there is something sacred about the inexplicable exchange of energy. No one truly understands the trade. It is an even trade. Death brings life through the uncorrupted transmutation of the Lord's will. Amen.

We were in a field. It was summer. Life changes in the summer, the warmest, wettest season of the year. Theodore loved me, trusted me ... He trusted one other person; Melanie. But, I was his only adult male companion. And how I wanted to touch him, to feel his young skin against my body; his skin against my skin. That is, in this life, all I ever wanted.

Sugar is pure. It is 100 per cent natural. It is safe. The FDA says so. It is planted vegetatively, using the whole stalk of cane rather than seed. Each stalk consists of several joints. Each joint has a bud. The stalks are planted in rows during the fall of each year. The buds produce shoots the following spring. During late summer, the crops mature. In fall the crop is harvested. This is what we, in the sugar business, call the plant cane crop. Sugar-cane is like grass. Sugar-cane *is* grass. More than one cutting is harvested from its planting: two to four annual cuttings can be harvested; usually, there are three cuttings. The first two cuttings are the best. In the old days, when my father Carter was alive, we used machetes to cut the cane. Nowadays, the cane is mechanically harvested. At Pine Grove we use combine-type harvesters. We cut the stalks into small pieces. The tops of the cane blow away. The bottoms are left sweet and tender, ready to be processed in the sugar mills, after which time they will be packed and shipped across America, where they will sweeten coffee cups on kitchen tables in millions of households. Eventually, sugar-cane's land has to lie fallow before it is replanted. At Pine Grove we plant soyabeans in rotation with the cane. During the summer months the sugar-cane can grow an inch a day; a whole inch in one single day. By the end of summer the cane fields are the most glorious sight to behold. Sugar-cane has been my life for all the many years I have called Louisiana home.

✳

I remember the summer was a particularly beautiful summer. Theodore and I kept our bikes in the back seat of my car. Every other Saturday we biked for hours on the river road along the levee. Some days we biked so far, so long, we could hardly move. On certain Saturdays we motored part way, biked the next; back and forth and back and forth between motor and bicycle, until we reached the outskirts of New Orleans. Exhausted.

One Saturday we made it all the way into the city, parked the car and shopped on Canal Street. I would have bought Theodore anything his heart desired. Theodore never wanted anything. All he wanted was to look in the windows, press his eleven-year-old nose against the glass, maybe leave his nose mark for the next window shopper. We had good times that summer.

The sugar-cane was gorgeous that year. Beads of sunlight glistened on its long, lean stalks. When the wind blew, the cane danced; she moved with a heavenly grace. The boy and I were hypnotized. We sat on the edge of a golden field, a field less than one half a mile from my house.

I am, to this day, always on the edge of that field. '*Let's watch the cane grow, listen to the wind blow, listen to the summer sounds. Rest your head right here on my shoulder, boy.*' I ask Theodore, '*Do you mind if I massage your head?*'

He says, '*Not at all. Not at all, Uncle Steven.*'

We sit together for hours upon hours on the Saturdays in between his Saturday visits with his grandmother. When I touch him, I touch God.

I still live for Saturdays. I sit for hours at the edge of the field by myself. I watch the cane grow, listen to the wind blow, listen to the summer sounds. The sounds, the wind, that remarkable day is with me each Saturday.

When she was close to the end, Charlotte whispered in my ear.

'*Steven, take care of my boy. You take care of him. Do you hear me? Love him with all your heart, help him grow up to be as good a man as you.*' Theodore was to be my charge.

'*The Lord is my shepherd; I shall not want.*'

It is a hot summer day. The cane is taller than the sky. Theodore takes off his torn, grey T-shirt. He throws it a mile high into the air. He catches it in one hand. His skin glows in the summer sunlight. He runs and runs and runs in the field until he can run no more. He turns around. He runs toward me. His hands outstretched. I lift him up as high as I can. I hear Charlotte's voice. '*You take care of him. Do you hear me.*' I hear you, Charlotte. Every day of my life I hear you. He holds me. He runs away again. I chase him. I fall hard on the ground in that field full of longing. He runs back to where I have fallen. He wants to make sure I haven't hurt myself. His hair, which hasn't been washed for days, is plastered against his beautiful head. He jumps on top of me. We roll like bears in the mud, in the field; over and over the sugar-cane. He pulls up a stalk, sucks hard on it. He moans with delight. He screams with joy. I grab the stalk from his hand, shove it into my mouth. I, too, scream with complete abandon. We are children in the sandbox. I love him. He makes me feel alive. He loves me because no one in the world makes him feel more alive. I stroke his forehead, run my fingers through his hair. '*My cup runneth over.*' He grabs my hair. His skin is covered in cane juice and dirt. I am undone by the smell of him. I cannot control myself. I grab his beautiful adolescent penis. He doesn't resist. He's too young to know that we have come to a forbidden crossing. I unzip the fly on his torn khaki shorts. His penis is hard; young but hard. I hold him. I hold it. I help him come unglued. He closes his eyes, his head arches back, his chest arches back, his body trembles without reason. I have him in my hand. He is inside my soul. He will be with me ... forever. I will be with him ... forever. I will be his shame. He will be ... my shame.

Ever since that day, I pray for forgiveness.

'*And lead us not into temptation.*' I will *forever* live and die with my shame.

DOREEN

You couldn't pay me a truckload of cash to go back there. The place doesn't interest me one bit; so much bickering, money-grubbing, mean-spirited, back-stabbing, bullshit behaviour. Other than the kids and Theodore, who needs all the aggravation? While I'm at it, let me set the record straight. I am *quite* sure, quite sure, Carter Jr was Steven's child. I kept track of my swamp adventures. I might have been promiscuous, but I was very much a one-at-a-time kind of girl; a serial monogamist. There might have been one short period when that wasn't the case. But, when I got pregnant with Carter Jr, I wasn't sleeping with anyone but Steven. So help me God.

That first night underneath those cypress trees, staring up at the starry Louisiana sky, Steven was still a virgin. Can you imagine? I had a virgin! I did all the hard work. He didn't know where to put it. In fact, he didn't put it anywhere. I put it there for him. I have never seen anyone come so hard, so fast, in so short a period of time; not that I had had *that* much experience.

Those Duvaliers, especially Lily, figured I didn't know my ass from third base, figured I was trash, not worth keeping around their lah-di-dah fancy family. I knew the score. Lily didn't want anyone coming between her and her '*sweet boy*'. That's what she called Steven: '*My sweet boy.*' Bitch. They could have offered me all the money in the world, I still wouldn't have taken the bribe. I was going to have Steven Duvalier's baby, no matter what that hard-ass bitch said or did. A good Catholic girl doesn't abort what's living inside her.

When my father found out I was pregnant, he nearly beat me

to death. Fortunately, my mother, who was a reasonable woman, stopped him. He screamed. '*Garbage. You are garbage.*'

I'd heard those words so many times before, it didn't mean shit to me. When I told him who the father was, he put his belt away, spit on the floor, turned around, walked out the door into *his* beautiful sugar fields; *his* sugar fields, my ass.

Part of me thinks he was thrilled. He was desperate to be a member of the Duvalier clan. This would solidify his position, even if it was a very low-down way to get from sugar-cane foreman to father-in-law. If he weren't such an asshole, he probably would have admitted to being delighted; not for me, but for himself. I, to this day, wonder if he had an affair with Lily. Lord! I can't imagine why anyone would want to sleep with that cold bitch.

Pain in my ass! That there woman was the most conniving woman in the south ... north, east, west; the entire United States of America. I never saw anyone swoop down on a business as fast as she did after her husband died. Like it was hers and hers alone to make that decision. If Steven or Winston had any balls, they might have given her a hard time. But, when it came to Lily, those two boys rolled over, took it in the ass. And her husband; what the hell was he doing walking around New Orleans in the middle of a hurricane? That's right; in the middle of a hurricane, walking the streets of New Orleans. He was one crazy-ass, rich, drunken mess. Without a doubt, it was Lily who drove him to drink. She drove me to drink. There were a few other personal reasons as well ... I said personal.

Thank goodness for Rheta B. I hated when she left our family for Winston's family. Even though Steven explained why she had to go, I hated it. Steven was such a good man. He's still a good man. I wonder if he misses me? When I was alive, I missed him. Even when he was lying next to me, I felt like he wasn't there. I felt like he was still out there, on the road, selling his sugar.

He was forever somewhere else, just like his daddy. He wanted to be anywhere but where he was. It made me sad. Could be, if

Steven made me feel like I mattered, like I mattered to him, I might have stopped drinking altogether. Maybe, I wouldn't have hit the bottle at all. My children appreciated me. They worried about me. I bet they miss me. Shit! I've been gone a long time, haven't I?

❋

Crazy family that Duvalier bunch was. Then, there was Charlotte. I never met anyone like her. She was kind; not just kind. She didn't have it in her to say a mean word about even the worst person in the world. Nobody was like Charlotte. That girl, and she was more like a girl than a woman, that girl never raised her voice. She never got angry; not with me. Maybe with Winston. Believe me, she had plenty to get angry about, what with Winston's crazy-ass rules and regulations. He was a handful. For the most part she handled him with kindness. Charlotte's kindness; whenever something rubbed her the wrong way or she saw some injustice in the world, she smiled. It was a beautiful smile. It lit up the room. She had wisdom; like she knew something or felt something that none of the rest of us understood.

Charlotte lived in her own world; a world full of endless revelations. She was an angel without wings. I confided in her my most personal secrets, my deepest fears. She went to her grave with my pain locked inside her heart. Charlotte was my confidante. Charlotte was my best friend.

One memorable Christmas Eve, when I was crazy drunk, she wiped my forehead with a damp rag in one hand, held my head with the other, while I puked in the toilet bowl. Then, she rubbed my forehead with ice cubes. They felt so good. Ice cubes cool you down. They take away the fire. They take away the pain. She's around here somewhere, taking care of someone or another. I feel her. I hope we find each other soon. Maybe if I pray hard enough, it will happen.

❋

Every Christmas Eve was celebrated at our home. 'The Mansion.' That's what the locals called it. Our family lived in a beautiful Greek Revival-style house.

'*The great Thomas Jefferson introduced Greek Revival architecture to the United States of America.*' I can still hear Steven talking, walking arm in arm with a captivated Christmas Eve guest, most likely a politician or an important person from the Army Corps of Engineers. Steven loved his facts. I wonder whether some of his facts were fiction.

I loved the Mansion's beauty; very grand, enormous white columns in front of the house, many beautifully appointed rooms with high ceilings, windows that reached to the tops of the cypress trees, wide-planked wood floors covered with beautiful carpets from around the world, a winding staircase. That was my home; my home near the river. I spent a good deal of time in the parlour with my feet up, curtains drawn, chewing ice cubes, throwing ice cubes, talking to the curtains. Drunk.

Christmas Eve. All along the river's edge the workmen and their children built wooden teepees made from small tree branches, twigs and kindling. At midnight, each teepee was set on fire so Santa Claus could find his way home.

'*Follow the fire along the river.*' Steven said those words every Christmas Eve. There are no more parties at my house.

I have nothing against sugar-cane. I don't love it. I don't hate it. It fed me, clothed me, kept me in liquor. Sugar gave and took from my mother and father. Mostly, it took my father from my mother. It gave and took from my husband. Sugar's been kind and cruel. It kept a family together, tore it apart. Winston and Steven were spoiled, soiled and ruined by its juice. I've seen the best and worst of sugar and its familial by-products. Sugar's ruled the Duvalier family for as far back as their family tree extends.

If there was corruption of some sort or another involved in its acquisition, I didn't know of such a thing. I can only assume corruption was in play for at least part of the 8,000 acres owned, stolen or purchased by the Duvaliers.

I remember a hot summer's day when Steven came running into the parlour room. He was dazed; sweat pouring down his face, his shirt drenched, his pants filthy. He smelled like some sort of sweet syrup. Tears were running down his cheeks. His body shook, trembled. He put his head in my lap, grabbed me around the waist.

He said, '*Sugar is evil, Doreen. Sugar is evil,*' over and over. '*Sugar is evil, Doreen. Sugar is evil.*' Finally, he stopped crying. Then, without saying another word, he got up, walked into his study, closed the door behind him. He didn't come to bed that night. We never slept together again.

I remember nights when Steven read the Bible out loud. I loved it when he talked Bible talk. Steven loved the Bible more than anything in the world. He understood its deepest meaning, like he had written it himself. '*Doreen. To think the Lord says we can master sin. We can escape its clutches.*' Sometimes he shouted at the top of his lungs like a Baptist minister delivering his Sunday sermon. He often paced up and down, up and down. He ran his fingers through his hair, sweat poured from his forehead. Sometimes, he acted like he was possessed. '*Sin is crouching at the door! Its desire is for us, but we must master it! We must!*' Sweet, sweet Steven often wept uncontrollably. '*Oh Doreen. If we don't master sin, we will live the rest of our days fallen from the grace of the Lord. How sad for everyone.*' The man was inconsolable. How I wished I could ease his pain.

No matter what happened or didn't happen between us, Steven and I followed the Bible's teachings. We had a mutual love of Scripture. We believed in the genuine word of the Lord our God. While I was alive, Bibles lay on both of our bed stands. At night, before he went into his room, we read prayers and passages from the Bible out loud. Steven explained their meaning. The Lord's Prayer was his favourite, especially the line, 'Lead us not into temptation.' *The Lord doesn't want us to be led into temptation by our wants, our needs, our desires or by Satan's wants, needs and desires. If we can't resist temptation, how can we be delivered from evil?*

God bless you, Steven. You always had the ability to understand forgiveness.

My mother was a good woman, my father is an evil man. Even in this peculiar place, where I presume I'm meant to forgive ... everyone, I'm still unable to forgive my father. I should try to cleanse my thoughts from this all-consuming hatred; maybe then I'll walk where Charlotte walks. I'll find you, Charlotte! Before I'm called back into being, I will find you! Before I'm dreamed into form, I will be free! I'll be reunited with those who have gone before me, those who have come after me. We will walk hand in hand to the higher ground with Jesus by our side.

I'm beyond excited about the celebration; Winston turning sixty-five. Faith and Carter Jr's son, my only grandson, Steven Jr, the football hero, graduating from college ... with honours. That is going to be one damn wild party. I wish I could be there. Maybe I can sneak out of here for a couple of days. I wonder if they let you out if you still hate? A forty-eight-hour marathon; Winston's house the first day, second day everybody drives to Gran' Isle. That's a party I don't want to miss!

How the hell is Rheta B. going to get both places ready? I imagine she looks older than God. She can't hardly move, can she? She's been cleaning toilets too long ... Theodore's coming home. He's such a good boy. After all these years, with a father who treats him like shit, he's still flying down, showing up for the bastard's sixty-fifth birthday party. There's only one reason *he's* coming home; Steven Jr's graduation class. All those pretty boys. Theodore loves pretty boys.

Who do I talk to about getting out of here? I haven't seen a living soul for I don't know how long. It's a mystery all right ... And what about a drink? They served wine at The Last Supper.

SUGAR

I am your whore! Fertilize me, rotate me, lay me fallow, kiss the ground that keeps your lucrative enterprise growing. I am, without a doubt, a bona fide, sweet-talkin', swingin', sweeter-than-any-lady-you-have-ever-fucked, kind of gal. Yet, I have no rights. There is no such thing as 'Sugar suffrage'. Me and my kind live and die by your hand. Your machinery rapes my long, lean body, throws it to the ground, carries it away and burns it like garbage. I ain't garbage! You hear me?

You and your Jesuit priests brought me to Louisiana in the 1750s, without asking my permission. You don't have my permission! You don't own me. You need me. You want me to be your sugar baby? What the hell do I get out of this one-sided affair? I am soaked with rain, flooded with shame, torn down one harvest after another harvest, lousy bugs crawlin' all over me, eatin' my roots, suckin' my minerals, makin' holes in every part of me and you don't want to hear about it?

Tellin' your children stories about generations and generations of honourable sugar men and sugar women who came before you. You don't tell the truth! This land was stolen! Some bastard sued some other bastard and that bastard got a hold of me. Some government agency settled, out of court, so that you could own me. That agency got paid; under-the-table paid. Millions of dollars have exchanged hands, so you can live in mansions, have servants, reap the benefits of my hard work, my tireless dedication to the art of survival. I have endured your carelessness for as long as I have existed. Damn it! I am tired of being stripped of my self-respect. You, on the other hand, you are respected, because you have acquired 8,000 acres of my golden fields over the last one hundred years of my life. I am fed up with you and your progeny!

You bring that boy back here! Do you hear what I'm sayin'? I want Theodore! *He* is the only one in your family who respects and adores me. When he walks through my fields, he is in awe of my beauty. Bring that boy back and all will be forgiven. Or get yourself ready for all hell to break loose! And I am not just talkin' bullshit!

Then there's Joseph. I love him. Joseph worked harder than any man who worked my gorgeous fields. At the end of the day, even if he was exhausted, he didn't want to leave. He didn't want to leave me here in the dark, all by myself; leave his sweet baby. The man adored his Sugar, hated goin' home. He confided in me, told me secrets. Don't tell him I told you, but he had plans for a better future. His plans were destroyed by his daughter, Doreen. Let's leave it at that.

And now, what do those damn Duvaliers do to him? They pension him right off the books. How's that for gratitude? My poor baby has much, too much time on his hands. With Maria dead, who's gonna feed him, who's gonna take care of him?

In the old days, late at night, after he left me, he would go get crazy drunk. He missed his favourite girl. That's why he drank. When he got home, I heard him screamin' like a mad man. It worried me sick. It was awful. '*Garbage! You are garbage!*' He yelled at the top of his lungs. Joseph would never treat me that way. The man knows *I* am a lady.

BOOK II

CELEBRATION

Lily awakens! I should be overjoyed. Instead, I am deeply disappointed. She is frantic; continually searching for a pew, a prayer bench, as if such things exist in my realm.

I am heartbroken ... Doreen awakens from her stupor. I have lifted her up with my unconditional love and support, yanked her through a hideous psychological slime, freed her spirit and what does Doreen crave? A drink. A drink? I am heartbroken ... And Charlotte. Nothing *ever* changes with Charlotte. For thirty-five years I have lived through Charlotte's mood swings, frustrations, inability to cope, agony over a failed life, agony over an early death, agony over Theodore's well-being. What Charlotte refuses to understand is when she gazes at Theodore, foolishly attempts to make her presence felt, she hinders her son's emotional growth. Charlotte has insinuated herself onto Theodore's psyche for thirty-five years! I am at my wits' end ... Beings are baffling.

Theodore arrives at Jet Blue's terminal T5 at Kennedy airport. He travels with a carry-on bag that will easily fit under his fifth-row seat or stow away in the overhead bin. He is ready; ready for action, ready for whatever will come his way. If he wants to roam the corners of the terminal, check out the stalls in the bathrooms, hang out in the ticket lines, lean against those cracked walls in the baggage area or just cruise around Jet Blue's terminal, his lightweight carry-on bag will make it easier for Theodore to do so. The boy knows how to travel, how to escape from whatever is bothering him. He has mastered this skill. Call him a wanderer and you would be belittling his genius at escape.

Theodore doesn't feel at home in any given place, at any given time. He feels at home in and with his beautiful body.

He *feels* at home in and with other beautiful bodies. He *is* at home with nobody. The world around him is his observation deck. He has a flight plan at all times. He has detached. His smile covers his deepest longing. He prowls with bag in hand. He is on his way back to what Rheta B. calls '*your only home, boy, your only home*.' But that home, like all other homes since, makes Theodore slightly uncomfortable; uncomfortable in his body. This discomfort is problematic for a man who finds comfort *only* within his skin. The home he travels to is the very home he ran away from without ever missing a step. He hasn't missed a step since he left Louisiana. Certainly, the address has its memories; memories that began in a crib, developed in a field and continually develop in bathrooms and bars across the United States of America.

Theodore sits in a hard plastic chair attached to many other hard plastic chairs. He peruses the possibilities. People stare at him. He is a good-looking boy; a boy with a magnetic field that reaches to the stars in the sky where his mother lives. Travel safely, Charlotte's son. I envy you. You fly on wings that aren't yours. You have the wherewithal to love, even if you choose another way, you *can* choose. Sometimes, I wish we could trade places. I have been here so long, without touch, without taste, without the sound of feet running in hallways. I have been here forever.

Theodore straddles the toilet seat. He wears his blue Tod tennis sneakers, his feet planted securely on the toilet seat, his hands tightly clasp the sides of the stall. He looks something akin to a well-heeled sexual acrobat. As the stranger wraps his mouth around Theodore's penis, Theodore's head drops back, his eyes close, his body quivers. Charlotte has seen Theodore's head drop back, his body quiver many times before. I am sure, if she has her way, she will see it time and time again.

Because she is the boy's mother, Charlotte's maternal interest is somewhat distorted. She is utterly fascinated with her son's ecstatic state. She has been absolutely fascinated with Theodore's sex life for years.

The stranger, a well-hung black man, who has Theodore's penis in his mouth, reaches the same ecstatic state, at the same moment, in a different way. One of his hands grabs Theodore's beautiful ass, while the other hand slides up and down his very own large penis. There is something magnetic, animalistic between these two men. Their ecstasy interferes with the connective field between Charlotte and her son. The interference hurts Charlotte in a very human way.

How many times have I advised Charlotte to detach from Theodore? Unfortunately, Charlotte is incapable of liberating herself from the world and the boy she *chose* to leave behind.

I reiterate. 'Charlotte. When you feel the ache, turn toward the light. Listen to me! Your son is in good hands. He does not need your help! Let him go.' For a moment she turns away. As always, she turns back, again.

The black man asks Theodore about his tattoo. Theodore says, 'I told you no questions. But, because you are so pretty, I'll answer one question. My mother gave me this tattoo. On my twenty-first birthday she took me to a tattoo parlour in Baton Rouge. This tattoo was a gift for her favourite son; this heart on my ass.' For as many years as Theodore has been having sex with strangers, which is many, many years, whenever he has sex, he tells the tattoo fable. He talks about Charlotte, about why she left the room, about how she hated seeing her favourite son in such terrible pain. I find it peculiar that whenever Charlotte's son has sex he talks about his mother.

As far as Theodore being his mother's favourite son, he is her only son. Of course he is her favourite son. She has a wonderful daughter, Alice. Alice does not talk about her mother ... during sex. Alice most probably has not experienced the kind of ecstatic orgasmic release Theodore has experienced. I do not know, since Charlotte is not concerned with Alice's sex life. Alice is not the problem.

✻

It is June. It is hot. It is humid. It is Louisiana. Having gambled the entire evening and the better part of the day at Harrah's Hotel and Casino in New Orleans, Alice, Rheta B. and Melanie drive at a snail's pace down highway 10 to Louis Armstrong New Orleans International Airport. Theodore will arrive on his favourite Jet Blue flight from Kennedy International Airport; flight 119 due in at 5:03 p.m. At this pace, he will arrive long before his sister, Rheta B. and his grandmother. The drive is taking forever. It always takes forever. Because, without fail, some poor, unprepared person has forgotten to put coolant in his or her beaten-up car radiator. This time, that particular person wears a very, very, short skirt, smokes a cigarette, leans against her smoldering 1957 turquoise and white Chevy automobile, screams into her cellphone, obviously receiving no satisfaction from AAA, her boyfriend or whoever is on the other end of the line.

Alice is infuriated. As the designated driver, she has good reason. Because of Rheta's lack of driving experience and Melanie's poor health, Alice is forever the designated driver, especially when it comes to picking up Theodore at the airport.

'Damn. I hate this road. Aren't you exhausted?' Collapsed in the back seat, Melanie and Rheta B. nod without even hearing the question. 'For the life of me, I don't understand how you ladies do it; stay up all night. I need eight hours. Rob doesn't need any sleep. Oh Lord! Would you look at the traffic! Damn! If I didn't love Theodore so much, I would turn this heap around and head back to the hotel ... Damn it! The next time he comes home, he can rent a car.' Rheta B. and Melanie take a catnap. 'I am getting the hell off this lousy road. Insane drivers. I've got to get home! I have to pick Billy up at baseball practice, drop

Lily off at a sleepover date. How am I ever going to get home in time? The toll road. That's what I'll do; the toll road.' Alice swerves from the centre lane, nearly hits a beat-up red, white and blue pickup truck in the right lane and drives up the ramp onto the toll road.

Melanie and Rheta B. awaken. In unison they squawk, 'Alice! Don't! Don't take the toll road! We'll never get back on the highway! Never!'

Alice pretends to be as deaf as her passengers. She continues her unobstructed drive down the toll road.

The car pulls up at the passenger-loading zone. Theodore emerges from the baggage-claim area. The stranger follows. They head in opposite directions, wave goodbye. Theodore sees the car, smiles, saunters over to the vehicle. The older women wave and holler.

Alice mumbles under her breath. 'Wonder boy is home.' Theodore is glad to be home. Home is Louisiana. Thrilled to see the three women who love him, he runs toward the car. How he loves their sweetness. He even loves Alice's pouty kind of sweetness. 'Is that a friend of yours from up north?' Alice rolls her eyes. She gives Theodore a look of utter disgust.

'Nope. Never saw him before.' Theodore pops open the trunk, slides into the back seat, kisses Melanie and Rheta B., pinches Alice on her flushed cheeks. 'Looks to me like you girls barely got here in time. Too much gamblin', right? Bet you had to take the toll road. Gotta watch you girls like a hawk. We are goin' to have a good time this weekend, aren't we now?' Alice moves over to the passenger side, gives her brother a dirty look. Theodore gets the hint, slides into the front seat, takes the wheel. Melanie squeezes his shoulder. Rheta B. smiles from ear to ear.

Alice is annoyed about something ... again. She mumbles, 'The old man can't wait to see you.'

Theodore laughs. 'That is a bold-face lie and you know it.

He can't wait to see the football hero, Steven Jr. Thank the good Lord our father likes somebody in the family. Never thought that crazy kid would graduate from high school. Here he graduates with honours from my alma mater, LSU. Hard to believe.' Theodore smacks the steering wheel in excitement. 'I bet Uncle Steve is real proud of his grandson.' Theodore squeezes Alice's leg.

'Don't do that.' Alice says. She smacks Theodore's hand. 'You know how I hate that.'

'How is Uncle Steve?' Theodore winks at Melanie in the rearview mirror.

Melanie says, 'He's been spending an awful lot of time on the road lately.'

Theodore clears his throat. 'Hope the poor guy's not too lonely out there all by himself.'

Melanie clears her throat. 'The poor man, out there ... all alone,' Melanie says, sarcastically.

❋

Theodore will spend the night with Melanie. They will look at old photos; photos of Charlotte. Melanie will feed him well, love him well and ask no questions. Bud will talk Pine Grove business. The weekend will begin. It will end as well. And there will be so very much in between. There is no telling what might happen at a celebration of such significance; never any telling what can happen in the world of thoughts, feelings and family. Welcome home, Theodore. Perhaps, you will discover something new, when you walk through the sugar-cane fields you adore, when you walk inside the house where you were raised, when you walk around the world you left in such a hurry that you had mud on your shoes. Maybe the Gran' Isle sea will wash away your memories; memories that haunt you when you try to sleep at night, memories that whisper in your ear. '*If your momma were alive, she would be mighty unhappy with your behaviour, son.*'

Your mother is in Afterworld, son. She cannot let you go.

Maybe you can help her. You *do* understand *she* cannot protect you from those things that go bump in the night. *We* cannot protect any of you down there.

❋

Steven unpacks his suitcase. He throws his dirty clothes in the laundry basket. Rheta B. will get to those clothes at the beginning of next week ... after the celebration. He opens his dresser drawer. He returns his clean shirts to their rightful place. He retrieves a handsome blue and white pin-striped shirt from the drawer and places it on the old wooden chest located at the foot of his bed. He will wear the shirt tomorrow. It is his favourite shirt. He bought it on Canal Street on a Saturday, during a wild weekend in New Orleans; the same Canal Street he and Theodore strolled down many a Saturday long ago.

He opens the slacks side of his suitcase, unfolds his slacks, walks over to his walk-in closet, grabs a hanger, hangs the slacks on the hanger, gazes at the many hangers in his closet, thinks he ought to give away some of his clothes ... to the needy. He walks back to his suitcase, grabs another pair of slacks, walks back to his closet, grabs another hanger, looks at his many pairs of shoes, thinks he ought to give some of them to his son or his grandson; that is, if they want them. The boys might find his shoes a bit conservative. Steven is conservative ... in most areas of his life.

As he unpacks his socks, slacks and sundries, he finds a note stuffed inside his shaving kit. He reads it out loud. 'You are the best ball in Louisiana. I'm gettin' hard thinkin' about you. Love your aftershave. Reminds me of my father.' He crumples the note, then aims at the wastepaper basket. He misses, saunters over to the crumpled piece of paper, picks it up, walks back to his original position, takes aim and tosses. In it goes. He thinks out loud. 'Theodore would have slam-dunked it in one try. Theodore shoots hoops well, plays tennis well, runs like lightning and is the most wonderful man I have ever known.' Theodore is Steven's greatest joy, as well as his greatest regret.

Funny how one person imbues another person with feelings of both love and loathing.

Steven thinks about Doreen. He wishes she were alive. He misses her company. After all these years, her Bible still lays on the bed stand on what was once her side of the bed. Steven's Bible is no longer on his side of the bed. He has not been to church for many years; not since the priest talked about his sins in a way that made Steven feel like a criminal. It is hard enough to be unable to control your sexual appetite, harder still if you are condemned to hell because you have that appetite.

Steven no longer goes to the church, gives to the church or believes in its doctrines. Ever since that day in the field, in the hot summer sun, ever since he could no longer touch Doreen, because of that day, ever since Doreen became ill and he blamed himself for her illness, Steven has relinquished his religious rigours for libidinous adventures, fraught with momentary satisfactions, filled with the familiar melancholy of his father.

Steven is proud of his grandson, Steven Jr. He's such a fine young man. Faith and Carter Jr have done a fine job raising the boy. How many students graduate in three years, with honours, in science no less, from LSU and play varsity football at the same time? Winston graduated with honours. He worked like a dog, read his scientific books, scientific magazines, studied and studied, worked into the wee night hours. He worked so hard, he had no time to appreciate the many gifts around him. 'Winston was a fool, is a fool. My brother hasn't enjoyed one moment of his life. My brother is a sad man,' Steven thinks out loud. 'Maybe he enjoyed life when Charlotte was around. Maybe then?'

Let me tell you a secret, Steven. Winston did not, for even one moment, have the ability to enjoy anyone. When Charlotte slept in his bed, held him in her arms, when he fondled her breasts, when she wrapped her legs around his waist, shoved her fingers in his mouth, guided him inside her, woke with him in the morning, he still found little pleasure in their love. The poor man could not express emotion in any way that could be felt or understood by anyone close to him. How could he, Steven? He, like you, was Carter Duvalier's son. What Winston wanted was to possess what he loved. His children, Alice, Theodore, they were not good enough to be loved; like Winston was not good enough to be loved by his father, Carter. Carter was not good enough to be loved by his father, William. No one was ever good enough, never good enough to be loved. Winston's unrealized joy was trapped between his hate for his father and his fear of his mother. Had he been a different sort of man, Winston might have loved his children and Charlotte unconditionally, without bringing his parents into every moment of their married life. But, Winston was a hollow man, still is a hollow man. His emptiness is his only true companion.

Steven need not worry about his daughter, Daphne. She will survive. Since Chris, her husband, died last year in that terrible auto accident, she has not been herself. How could she be? The girl is mourning. There are no rules about grief, no timetable, no easy way to heal the fresh wounds of those left behind after a loved one's early death. Isn't that right, Charlotte? When a life is cut short in a tragic way, grief takes hold of the living with its all-consuming grip. Steven has no idea what Daphne suffers. He is too consumed with his shame and fear to understand his daughter's loss.

Daphne and Chris chose not to have children. They wanted freedom. They did not want to perpetuate the dysfunction from either side of their families. Chris's family is a back-woods, born-again, Bible-beating bunch. Daphne's family, as you know, was and is rife with alcoholics, depressives and degenerates; generations of degenerates and drunks; Doreen being but one of the drunks. Neither Chris nor Daphne knew about the sexual deviates on both sides of either family; Daphne's father being but one of the deviates.

The Duvalier family has known about Theodore's proclivity for years. Yet, nobody has once considered Theodore a deviate. 'He has made a choice.' That is how the family explains Theodore's sexuality to those who ask, why. 'He has made a choice.'

When they were children, Theodore and Daphne played in the sugar-cane fields. While Doreen was drunk, with the shades drawn, her feet on that ottoman, Daphne ran in the fields with Theodore chasing after her. When he caught her, *she* grabbed *him*; she held his hands, kissed his boyish fingers. They rolled on the ground. She pulled on his shirt sleeves. She tickled him until he could not breathe. Children at play are the sweetest sight in any world.

Nowadays, Daphne helps sort out Pine Grove's books. She keeps Steven company. He keeps her busy. Fortunately, Chris left Daphne with a large life-insurance policy, so money is not a problem. If it were, she would not be working at Pine Grove.

Listen to those beautiful voices; melody upon melody, perpetual vocal landscapes hidden in my world. No matter where they are, under clouds, inside walls of light, I see these hallowed beings. I hear their hallowed voices.

Lily has joined the choir. She is a welcome addition. We needed a full-bodied, bright, beautiful tone. Even during her illness, Lily loved singing in church, loved arranging flowers in church on Sunday; no matter what, Lily loved anything holy. My world will challenge her piety.

Charlotte hears Lily's unmistakable voice. I have not seen Charlotte this elated since she arrived. 'Look for me, Lily!' she shouts. 'If you look, you will find me ... if Afterworld allows it.' Silly child. I have no power over such meetings. If it is meant to be, it will happen.

＊

Winston opens the safe hidden behind Charlotte's portrait. Every day of his life, he opens the safe. When he is not out fishing in the Gulf, the man spends the better part of his days and nights counting his cash. Poor Winston. It has come to a small life, hasn't it? He had big plans, but his world veered out of control. After all these years, he has not recovered from Charlotte's death. He can open and close the safe as often as he likes, count his money backwards and forwards, put the cash in piles of tens, twenties, one hundred dollar bills on tables, chairs and beds throughout the house, but he finds absolutely nothing, especially money, replaces the bankrupt feeling he has lived with for an entire life, even before Charlotte died.

Charlotte is near. I feel her rage. She screams at the top of her vibration. 'What's that? A thousand dollars! Is that all the money the cheap bastard can part with? A lousy thousand dollars! Steven Jr is his only brother's grandson! Shame on you, Winston! Asshole!'

'Charlotte! Why don't you do something productive for a change.'

'The idiot has conveniently forgotten Steven Jr is his family favourite. Christ!'

'Let us not use that word. Please.'

'The boy graduated with honours, in science, in three years, played varsity football; quarterback with academic honours. Wouldn't you think he's worth at least $2,500, maybe even $5,000?'

'Charlotte! You are trying my patience.'

'The cheap son of a bitch! I hated that about him; his nickel and dime thinking. What was that line of his? *"You never know what might happen?"* That's it. *"You never know what might happen?"* What the hell is he saving it for? His old age?'

'That is sensible. It is very expensive living on earth.'

'Tell him to give it all away!'

'Charlotte! How many times have I told you, I cannot tell him or anyone else what to do, neither can you.' Charlotte leaves in a huff.

As if he had overheard our conversation, Winston, with a bewildered look on his face, counts out fifty one-hundred-dollar bills. 'That's too much. I don't want to spoil the boy.' He places twenty-five hundred-dollar bills back inside the safe. 'That's more than enough.' He closes the safe, he locks it. He swings Charlotte's portrait back in place. He sighs, 'I'm trying to make it right, Charlotte. I'm trying.'

You are doing a fine job, Winston. Keep it up. One day, I promise, you will have a supreme revelation. Right now, you had better get ready for your birthday party and Steven Jr's graduation celebration. Put the $2,500 in a box, wrap the box in some pretty wrapping paper and stick on a bow. You can do that, can't you? Stick a bow on a box? When you see Steven Jr, you give him the box. The boy you admire, more than anyone else in the family, has a gift for you. Life is about exchange, Winston. Life *is* an exchange. An exchange is *never* even. Soon you will understand.

Rheta B. does not sleep. She tosses and turns, kicks the sheets free from their hospital corners, turns the pillow around and around, so the open end faces right, then faces left. She asks herself the same questions she has been asking herself for years. 'Where is Cleveland Alexander? What does he look like? Does he know that he has a mother who loves him as much as the Lord loves those that follow his way?'

She talks to the cracks in the ceiling. 'How you doin'?' She watches the paint peel. Tomorrow she will ask her neighbour to fix the leak overhead.

Her mind spins. She cannot stop thinking. She pulls the

red and green wool blanket over her head; the same blanket she pulled out of Charlotte's bedroom closet and threw over Charlotte's shoulders the day she and Doreen took Charlotte to the hospital in Baton Rouge, to the same hospital where Rheta B. gave birth to Cleveland Alexander. She mumbles to herself. 'Wonder of all wonders is the gift of givin' somethin' to the world that you don't own, but comes from your womb. I have given the world a gift. I have a boy in this here world. I have two boys; one is probably lookin' at photographs with his grandma, the other has no idea who I am or where he comes from. Hope he was raised a good boy. Hope he has manners. Wonder if he's married? Hope he's happy. Works hard at somethin' he loves, like his mama does. Wherever he is, I hope he feels my love pourin' into him. Cleveland Alexander, even if you don't know my name, I'm your mother, son. You'll always be my boy.'

These days, more often than not, Rheta B. talks to herself. She looks old, older than her years, worn out from cleaning toilets, worn out from scrubbing floors, worn out from worry. The woman is tired. She is so tired that she *could* die cleaning Winston's house. It will take her the better part of a day to clean the finished basement – five hundred square feet of AstroTurf walls lined with more dead fish, foul and deer heads than in the entire Atchafalaya, piles of fishing and hunting magazines from before … Christ. Rheta B. will dust every feather, horn and gill. After cleaning, she will pass out on the mouldy orange and pink pull-out couch, in the far right-hand corner of Winston Duvalier's finished basement.

I wonder if Charlotte's boy will make it to church with the rest of the family? Why bother going to church? Devotion is nothing more than an over-rated exaltation that absolves *devoted* humans from the hapless world's shame. What world came up with that silly notion?

Who is going to help Rheta B. clean up the mess at Gran' Isle?

Maybe Daphne. Daphne is a good girl. Goodness is over-rated. Except for Daphne, nobody in the Duvalier family need worry about that condition. Look at Steven. Look at Theodore. Look at Steven Jr. Has he got problems? Why can't males control their over-stimulated libidos? Then there is Winston. Winston has no libido.

✳

Doreen is passing through. 'Charlotte. Smell the gratitude. What a wonderful scent, isn't it?' I ask.

Charlotte replies. 'Smells like frankincense; sweet, sweet smell. I know that scent, that sound.'

'Isn't it a beautiful sound, Charlotte?'

Doreen prays. 'Blessed are the poor in spirit, for theirs is the kingdom of heaven.'

Charlotte says, 'I recognize the voice. Who are you?' she asks Doreen. 'Who carries this familiar scent?'

Doreen prays. She pays no attention to Charlotte. 'Blessed are they who mourn, for they will be comforted. Blessed are the meek, for they will inherit the land. Blessed are they who hunger and thirst for righteousness, for they will be satisfied.'

'Doreen! It's Doreen! Can you hear me?' Charlotte shrieks with excitement. 'Christmas fires along the river road! Your house! My house! We spent precious time together, my friend. We were family. Don't you remember? Don't you remember me?'

Doreen is oblivious to Charlotte's shrieks. 'Blessed are the merciful, for they will be shown mercy.'

'Doreen. It's me. Charlotte. Can you smell me? Can you see me! Don't you remember me? I saved your life. You saved mine.' Charlotte tries explaining their past relationship. 'We were ... family.' Doreen's scent is as powerful now as it was when she sat with Charlotte while Charlotte was dying. 'Sweet Doreen. Don't tell me you've found God ... again, given yourself over to the Holy Spirit ... again? In here there's spirit beyond any asinine, identifiable icon.'

Doreen's mania is unstoppable. 'Blessed are the clean of heart, for they will see God. Blessed are the peacemakers, for they will be called children of God. Blessed are they who are persecuted for the sake of righteousness. For theirs is the kingdom of heaven.'

Charlotte is agitated by Doreen's old-time religion. 'Doreen! You can't believe this holy nonsense any more!'

Doreen moans. 'Blessed are you when they insult you and persecute and utter every kind of evil against you (falsely) because of me.' She screams at the top of her lungs. 'Rejoice and be glad, for your reward will be great in heaven!'

'You are dead, Doreen! You're in Afterworld; a place as close to heaven as we're ever going to get. Listen to me!'

Doreen moans, 'Heaven!'

Charlotte screams, 'You're free! *You* are free from all the organized religious crap!' Charlotte finds it impossible to contain her frustration. 'Can't you smell me? Damn it! I can smell you! I can see you ... sort of; it's a different *kind* of you, but it's definitely you. Definitely, Doreen. Come on, Doreen? It's me, Charlotte!'

Behind Doreen an enormous cross made of ash and light glows like a holy cinder block. Doreen's scent is within a breath of Charlotte. For the first time since death, Charlotte meets her past in my world. Charlotte is speechless.

Doreen wails. 'I have been to Jerusalem! I have seen him! When he fell to his knees at the Third Station, I was one of the chosen women who picked him up from the ground. I am his daughter! I am the daughter of the Son of God! Hallelujah! Jesus is everywhere! This is his cross.'

'What is the matter with you, Doreen? Look around you! Feel it. Feel the freedom here. Look at me! Here! I'm over here!' Doreen does not see Charlotte. 'If you can't see me, what can you see? Can't you hear me? Can't you smell me? I can smell you. *You* smell like frankincense. Why can't you see me? What's the matter with you!?' Charlotte turns around and around in a cyclone of emotion. 'If I had tears, I would cry,' Charlotte cries.

'I hear a mysterious voice.' Doreen whispers. 'I smell myrrh. God is here. What has happened to the Holy Ghost? Where are the angels who carried me from my misery? Where are the sainted beings who walk with haloed light? Where are they?' Doreen, in a confused state, has a revelation. 'If I am to walk amongst them, I must return to my humble beginnings and return to my unexalted life. Why aren't there any sainted beings here?'

'Sweet Doreen. We are the sainted beings.' Charlotte weeps. 'Nothing's as sacred as where we are right now. Nothing. Lay down your cross of ash and light. Trade your cross in for an unknowable recognition without any strings attached. We are in a phenomenal place.' Charlotte clarifies some of the most important rules she has, somehow, absorbed during her tenure in my world ... 'I've been told that we *can* re-enter that world. When we find the thread of someone who has crossed over without regret, we can go back for a little while ... with purpose; always with purpose. We are the angels without wings.' Charlotte has been listening after all.

Steven Jr stares in the bathroom mirror. He sticks out his tongue, wiggles it around, presses the tip of his tongue behind his upper teeth, looks at the purple veins underneath. He opens his mouth wide, notices the dry whiteness caked on his tongue, caked on the corners of his mouth. He looks deep into his eyes, observes the reddening in the whites, the decreased intra-ocular pressure. He touches his face with his right hand, places his left hand directly over his heart. He feels his increased heart rate. Although his heart rate has increased, the rest of the muscles in his body have relaxed. For the first time, in as long as he can remember, those overworked muscles that have been running on football fields for the better part of his life are relaxed. He will never play football again. No one will chase him down a field, tackle him, throw him on the ground, pull at his helmet or yank his head in the wrong direction. He has come to the end of his football career. He is overwhelmed with relief at the prospect of giving his exhausted body permission to fall apart. He will miss the team, but he will not miss the gruelling practices, the summer football camps, the muscle cramps, the broken bones, the highs, the lows, the locker-room antics, the stress of living up to his heroics on the field from one game to the next, the fear of letting his teammates down and most of all, the fear of letting his family down, especially his father.

Steven Jr walks from the bathroom into his bedroom. Next to his bed is the red Volcano, a vaporizer that for years has heated his cannabis to the perfect temperature, so his lungs of steel could, without fail, breathe effortlessly as he ran down the field into the end zone with nobody near him. Steven is fast as lightning. His mind is fast, his body is fast, his metabolism is fast. That is why he likes to smoke. It slows him down. It slows down his brain; the brain that got him through college with honours in three years, the brain that has him being head-hunted by the finest laboratories and research companies in America. One of these companies will keep him in the finest quality cannabis with the highest amount of THC, north, south, east or west of the University of Mississippi's Potency Monitoring Project; one of the few schools in America specializing in research into the significant increase of THC in dope, as well as the multiple psychotropic effects cannabis has on its growing number of users.

Three years ago, when Steven Jr was applying to colleges across America, had he known that the University of Mississippi had a science department dedicated to the study of ganja and its effects on the brain, he would have gladly enrolled and played football for LSU's rival without a blink of an eye. It would not have mattered to Steven Jr what football team he played for, as long as he had a hand in buying, selling and manufacturing the most perfect herb known to man.

Steven Jr inhales the vapours from the Volcano, leans his handsome head against the wall, closes his eyes and sees electric circles spinning in his head. He is proud of his new batch of seedless, female cannabis. In the world of weed cultivation, the male seed is quite unnecessary. He wonders about the world of sugar. In fact, he could care less about the world of sugar. That world is his dad's world and his granddad's world; his granddad who likes the boys in Steven Jr's locker room. His second cousin, Theodore, also likes the boys in Steven Jr's locker room. His great-uncle, Winston, does not like anyone. From what Steven Jr has been told, Winston loved only one person; his late wife, Charlotte.

The young man worries. He has read numerous articles about the Gateway drug theory. It is possible that cannabis users will eventually use harder drugs. He hopes never to cross that bridge. 'Ridiculous,' he says. He opens and closes his mouth, grunts like a bear, beats against his chest like an Indian and laughs like a hyena. 'I haven't been this high in a fuckin' long time.' He rolls off the bed, cuddles his pillow, yowls like a dog in heat.

The last thing Steven Jr wants is to spend the entire weekend with his family; his unbelievably dysfunctional family. Why should he have to celebrate his twenty-first birthday, his football victories, his early graduation with his crazy great-uncle, his gay second cousin (whom he adores ... but), his pervert of a grandfather (who is sleeping with one of Steven Jr's teammates) and the rest of the rednecks on both sides of the family?

'Why me?' he asks, as he rolls onto his back, notices a crack in *his* ceiling, closes his eyes, thinks about his gorgeous Aunt Daphne and imagines the unimaginable; being inside her. Touchdown.

Aunt Daphne is the most beautiful woman Steven Jr has ever known. It kills him to see her so unhappy. Ever since her husband, Chris, died, she has been lost in grief. She no longer regales Steven Jr with stories of the family; her difficult childhood, her mother's drunken binges, her twisted father's sexual habits, her parents' religious fervour, her gay cousin Theodore's wildness as a child. She no longer talks about her summer escapades with Theodore in Pine Grove's sugar fields; their time of play, their sexual dalliances, the cultivation of their souls. She finds it impossible to recite the lyric to the Celtic song 'Lakes of Pontchartrain'. With an Irish brogue Steven Jr recites the last stanza of the song to his feather pillow:

So fare thee well me bonny ol' girl I never see no more
But I'll ne'er forget your kindness and the cottage by
the shore
And at each social gathering a flowin' glass I'll raise
And drink a health to me Creole girl from the Lakes
of Pontchartrain.

The song will forever be Chris and Daphne's song. With Chris gone, the lyric has an even deeper meaning. Steven Jr's heart tightens. He understands, all too well, when Daphne holds his hand, it is a familial hold. Nothing more, nothing less. But, considering the predisposition of the family, any aberrant behaviour is probable.

The young man's mind drifts to his great-grandma Lily's final days. He wishes he could have convinced her to smoke weed. The weed would have helped. 'Why suffer from chemotherapy?' He has no idea who she was praying to at the end, but she was praying. 'What the fuck good did it do her?' He misses Lily.

At the end of her life, Lily spoke Charlotte's name. '*Charlotte.*' When a dying person utters somebody's name, it is a blessing for the one who is named. Whether here or there that principle is a benevolent rule of thumb.

Steven Jr wonders how Bud and Melanie are doing these days. He likes them. They're different from the rest of his family. He is right about that. The boy is right about many things, but he has no idea how to paint his future. Most of his friends are clear about their future. Steven Jr is not clear about today or tomorrow. He needs time to process the last three years and all the years before college. For as far back as he can remember Steven Jr has been a star. He is tired of the role.

Steven Jr's father, Carter Jr, would like his boy to take a high-paying job. It is unlikely that Steven Jr will take his father's advice. As far as he is concerned, the only man in the family worth taking any advice from is his cousin, Theodore Faulkner Duvalier. They have promised each other to spend time together over the weekend. Steven Jr looks forward to that; so does Theodore.

✳

Doreen and Charlotte have become reacquainted. Doreen remembers the Christmas Eve parties in a beautiful house, the fires along a river road, the birth of Theodore. She remembers Steven, the man who read the Bible, the man who fathered her children. Doreen remembers her children, especially Carter Jr. She knows nothing about her grandson's accomplishments. Somehow, Charlotte knows *almost* everything there is to know about the football hero's success both on and off the field. How could Doreen know anything about Steven Jr? She drank herself to death long before Steven Jr was even an idea.

Doreen reminisces about a particular afternoon in June, a hot, tortured afternoon. 'Life took a U-turn. From then on ... everything changed between Steven and me. I don't know how to explain it. Life hurt worse for the rest of my days down there.'

Unfortunately, Doreen feels as if she is still living in a body; skin, bones, heart, hate and the rest of it. There is a quiet despair to Doreen's remembered world. After all her living and dying, what Doreen still craves is not the husband, the son, the grandson, Christmas or the beautiful house. The only craving Doreen has is a craving for the booze. She would kill for a drink, she would die for a drink. She has died from the drink.

Charlotte reminds Doreen ... 'You were an alcoholic, honey.'

Doreen recalls her past. 'I remember. I remember chewing ice cubes, throwing empty glasses. I remember that the drapes were pulled shut in a dark room. Terrible.' She admits to a chronic, mythological hatred for her father, Joseph. 'Pig!' Doreen realizes she has some serious work to do on herself.

✻

A heavenly scent approaches. 'Gardenias.' Charlotte sniffs. 'Has there ever been such a sweet smell in any world?'

Doreen sniffs. 'Mmm. Luscious.'

For the first time since she arrived Charlotte seems serene, intoxicated by the scent. 'What a beautiful smell! It makes me feel good inside.'

From somewhere within my world without directions enters a feminine force surrounded by a field of filtered light with a southern accent and a power as unstoppable as a pre-hurricane wind. 'There is not a pew to be found here! How does one kneel without a pew? How do I pray without a pew to rest my ethereal knees upon? I require something soft, something cushioned. Velvet would be lovely. Essential ... I have wandered aimlessly. Years. Lifetimes. I remember a sea in a desert land with trees. They could have been bushes. I'm not sure any more ... It has been a long, long time. I cannot remember many of the important details of that remarkable time. But, I know, since that time of wandering, I have lived many other lives. None of them mattered except for that one glorious lifetime. The rest of my lives got me here, so I could work for my Lord and work for the holy man who was the Son of God. I have seen God's son.

'Long ago I asked God if I could be of service to something larger than myself. Soon after I asked to serve, I saw this man. He was not a large man, not a small man, just a man. He had many male disciples, running here, running there, taking care of his every need, tending him as if he were a god. Somehow, I knew he was the Son of God. But, he was just a man, a man who worked miracles. I saw him work miracles.

'The man needed help organizing a crowd of people gathered

at his feet by the sea ... What sea? It was such a long time ago, I cannot remember ... What *was* the name of that sea? ... Oh well. His disciples helped him to implement miracles; real miracles. He took five loaves of bread, two fishes, turned them into enough loaves and fishes to feed 5,000 people; flocks of people seated on the grass by the sea were fed by the man who made miracles. Then he waved goodbye, walked up a mountain and disappeared into the clouds. It was miraculous!

'His disciples left in boats. The others, including myself, dispersed with full bellies and an undying faith in the man. Since that time, I have been his servant. I will always be his servant. I must find a pew! I have to pray! It is an absolute necessity that I pray! Now! I know the man's soul is going to resurrect ... soon. All of his disciples, those who shared in the feast of the multitudes, will resurrect beside him. We will see miracles again! Miracles!'

Lily has holy-rolled her way into Charlotte, Doreen's and *my* world.

I observe Charlotte. She is busy watching Melanie and Theodore. They are seated on the living-room sofa, leafing through pictures in a frayed family album, looking at pictures of Charlotte ... Three-year-old Charlotte in a pink dress swinging on a swing. Melanie pushing Charlotte on the swing. Charlotte with her funny face, wearing a smile as wide as the sky. Theodore turns the page ... Four-year-old Charlotte beaming and screaming. As she pushes the swing, Melanie's face is flushed with joy. She smiles at the camera. Charlotte is five, six and so on into her teenaged years; dungarees, T-shirts, college years, binoculars, bird-watching, peregrine falcon years. Pictures trace time, but they do not explain how time exists, why time exists, why man exists in time's world.

Melanie carefully turns one page at a time; a pony ride, a Ferris wheel. Charlotte is high in the air at some fair.

'I don't remember. Why don't I remember?' Charlotte tries to recall the time, the place, but she cannot remember either time or place. There is a photo of Melanie running toward the camera with her arms outstretched. She is flushed with excitement. It surprises Charlotte to see her mother so full of life. 'My mother never acted that way.'

There is a picture of Winston, a picture of Charlotte, a picture of Charlotte with Winston before they were married. 'He was handsome, he had a glint in his eye.' Charlotte never noticed the glint in Winston's eye before now. She wonders what else she failed to notice about Winston. 'Why worry about missed opportunities? What good will it do me now?'

'Charlotte!'

'Shh. I'm busy.' When Charlotte is engaged in either gazing at her mother or gazing at her son, there is no distracting her.

Theodore turns the page; Charlotte's wedding day. Charlotte thinks out loud. 'Look at Lily. She's the most beautiful woman alive. Carter's drunk ... for a change. He is a handsome no-gooder. Look at him dancing with me, hand on my ass. Shameless. There's one with Carter and Lily dancing together ... for a change. Oh my! He's got his hand down Doreen's dress in that picture. Shame on you, Carter!' Melanie turns the page ... 'There's one of Steven dancing with Doreen. They look happy. That certainly was a long time ago. Look at Doreen's parents; Joseph and Maria. Maria just passed away, didn't she? I haven't seen her here, yet. I guess she'll be passing through. I wonder if everyone passes through?'

I answer Charlotte's question. 'Some of them do, some of them do not. It depends on where they *need* to go.'

'Oh ... Joseph looks uncomfortable in a suit and tie. He looks angry. Even though they pensioned him off, I bet he shows up at the party. That man drinks and drinks, just like his daughter. That's where she gets it from, except Joseph is a mean drunk, Doreen is a sad drunk. It's no wonder she's still working out her hatred for her father.'

'Charlotte! That is *quite* enough!'

'I'm not *quite* finished. Please leave me alone! Would you look at her: wonderful Rheta B. wearing a black straw hat, yellow dress, white gloves. Back then, she was working for Steven and Doreen. That picture was taken before Doreen started drinking. Maybe she was drinking a little bit.'

I give up.

'Hold on! Don't go! Look at this picture of my baby girl, Alice. She's so beautiful. When she was a little girl, she was the prettiest girl in the state of Louisiana. Oh how we laughed at Winston, especially when we drove to and from Gran' Isle; Winston and his women.' Charlotte bursts out laughing. 'He didn't have a clue how to handle his girls, but he did know how to dance. Will you look at that picture! At least the roof hasn't blown off ... yet.'

The last page; the last picture is of Charlotte, at home in bed. It is nearly the end of her life. She is beautiful.

Melanie closes the album, kisses Theodore on the top of his head. 'Wasn't my little girl beautiful?' She swallows hard.

Theodore kisses Melanie on her cheek. 'Uh huh. Just like her mama.' As he imagines his mother, he says, 'Just like her mama.'

'I'm here, Theodore! Can't you see me? I'm right here!'

'Charlotte. How many times have I told you? Look away. If you let him go, it will be better for both of you.'

'I won't let him go. Never!' She turns and stomps her way back to Lily and Doreen.

Lily and Doreen, two women who at one time hated each other more than the devil hates forgiveness, have mended fences. They have bonded. The Bible is their glue. When they were alive, they had a commonality of interest in the Bible. The problem was they had enormous differences in how they translated the Bible's teachings. Lily followed the good book in order to find purpose and meaning in her life. Doreen followed its teachings to overcome her feelings of inadequacy. Neither tolerated the other's personal interpretation of the good book until now.

Lily recalls her biblical death. 'I heard the voice of God. I heard Gabriel's trumpet. Gabriel's trumpet played for me and me alone. God's voice roared. "Hasten your step. Travel to another world!" God promised he would show me glorious things, things I had never seen, things I was meant to understand. He promised I would come back to Earth's Kingdom when I was needed. Finally, after a long rest, I would be of service.' She sighs. 'At last. *Service.*'

Trying to one up Lily, Doreen describes her exit. 'I not only saw an eagle, I heard the eagle, held the eagle, climbed on the eagle's back while it flew through heaven with wings wider than the sky. The wings carried me home. Have either of you seen or heard an eagle mid-flight in mid-heaven?'

Charlotte recalls how, at the end of her life, a peregrine falcon circled in the sky without a care. '*His* wings were wider than the sky. In fact the sky disappeared into his wings. It was ...'

Doreen interrupts Charlotte, '... flying in mid-heaven, saying with a loud voice, "You, who are on your way to another world, take heed. There are three angels. They are yet to sound their golden voices, their resonant tone. The grace of Lord Jesus Christ will be with these three angels."' Doreen is overcome with emotion. 'I believe *we* are those angels!'

Charlotte wonders whether they are, in fact, the angels without wings. She has no idea why three Duvaliers would come together in *my* transient world under the watchful eye of that which builds man up, breaks him down, plucks him from the world he has come to call 'home', then, perhaps with some purpose, starts the process over again, not once, but many times. Just like Charlotte, I wonder about the hows and whys of being and non-being. Although I have my place, I am but a small part of a large design.

✳

I have been advised that the three Duvalier women will attend the party. Melanie, Bud, Rheta B., the LSU football team, living members of the family and untold others, will take part in the celebration. Charlotte will be in the same room as Theodore. She will smell him. She will want to touch him. She will not touch him. She cannot touch him. When they are in the same room, it will be extremely difficult for Charlotte to turn away. I hope she remembers what I am forever reminding her. 'Turn away, Charlotte. Turn away.' This time I won't be there to remind her.

Hopefully, Doreen will forgive her father, come to know her husband better, see her grandchildren, watch them play dress up and enjoy their troublemaking. Doreen will adore seeing those children for the first time in her afterlife. If she needs to, she can have a drink, chew on some ice cubes, maybe figure out what went wrong during her life. There are many reasons for Doreen's return.

And Lily. She will find a pew, visit the family mausoleum and look for Carter. If she finds him, she will give him hell. He might already be there. No. That is impossible. *I* forget it does not exist. She might scold Winston for his bad behaviour; lecture Steven about working too hard; hold Daphne in her arms; tell Daphne to take care of her father; kiss Steven Jr on his forehead and finally she will ask Carter Jr to take care of his precious family. '*Please, please* take care of the family business in case anything should happen to Steven.'

There is bound to be grief, there is bound to be joy. As the three Duvaliers wait for the thread, they wonder whose thread will carry them on the ride of many lifetimes. How long will it take to get there? Charlotte is ready to go. She has been ready for years. As soon as I am given instructions, I will give the Duvaliers their instructions. Life won't be the same without Charlotte. At least I know she will be back ... When her work is finished, Charlotte will return.

❋

I receive my instructions at dawn. How do I know it is dawn? In Afterworld, in every passing moment, the light changes, the smells transform, the atmosphere becomes thick during this time, thin during that time. In my world nothing is static. In that regard, there is no difference between life here and life there. Dawn is a sweet-smelling, diffusely lit, low-toned time. Dawn is a precious time. One becomes aware of a new beginning in the other realm. When dawn breaks, I am thankful.

✳

Doreen, Lily and Charlotte are delighted to spend their first dawn together in Afterworld. They await my orders. They await the way back to those they love, those they know, those they wish they had never known.

In a hushed but firm tone I alert them to their miraculous mode of transportation. 'Duvaliers! You have been given a rare opportunity. Your family needs your help. You must leave immediately! There is an outstanding, *outstanding* man who has offered his thread as your means of transportation.'

'A man!' I was sure it would be a woman. 'He must be quite a guy,' Charlotte says to the others.

There is a subtle shift in density inside my world of in-betweens. The shift thrills Charlotte. 'I'm ready!'

Doreen and Lily feel the shift. They pray. 'Our Father, who art in Heaven ...'

'Here is the thread of a man who has fostered such great work in so many. Here is a man who has fathered many distinguished children, preached thousands of sermons, lifted the spirits of those who believed they could not continue on life's path. Here is a thread strong enough for three powerful beings to descend upon with ease ... together ... to help a family in need. Ladies, I present Minister Cleveland's colossal cord.'

'... I'm not travelling on *his* co-los-sal *bullshit*!' Doreen flies into a rage. 'That prick ruined Rheta B.'s life on the pulpit, in God's holy temple. He's a fornicating sinner. Get someone else to go in my place!'

Being the more genteel of the two, Lily expresses her disapproval with less vitriol. 'I think there might be ... there could be ... a serious error in judgement. We, each one of us, have our personal reason for resisting *his* particular mode of transport.' Ashamed to refuse, Lily apologizes. 'I am so very sorry, but I must deny your generous offer. I will render my services at some future date. Surely, there will be many important family functions – weddings, scandals, funerals, trials.'

I am furious. 'Ladies, you will go! You will do the work! Most are not given the wherewithal to return to the terra firma! You have the opportunity to assist those less fortunate than yourselves. End of discussion!'

The dawn light thickens with a dense, impenetrable fog. There is a foetid smell in my world followed by a deafening, cacophonous tone. 'I am disappointed in the three of you. Minister Cleveland has been through numerous trials and tribulations. True, he has failed in certain, sexually inappropriate ways, but he has overcome multitudinous obstacles, so that you ingrates can safely travel to your family during its perilous time of need. He has *pleaded*, he has *begged* for the job. His thread is as strong as any thread I have seen.' I wait for any *one* of the Duvaliers to make the first move. Nobody budges. 'Get-on-it!'

Lily resists the ride. 'Why don't you let the others go without me?' With a newfound humility, she says, 'Clearly, I have more work to do on myself before I can serve Christ.'

'Get-on-it!' I command.

Lily surrenders. 'Just one moment, if you please.' She does not budge.

Doreen sulks. 'I intend to drink myself into oblivion; absolute oblivion.'

Lily chides Doreen. 'One of your least attractive coping mechanisms, dear.'

I agree with Lily. 'It certainly is.' Doreen ambles toward the cord.

Charlotte is ready to travel. She is amazed at the idea of going between two worlds on the thread of the man who impregnated Rheta B. long before Charlotte even knew Rheta B. existed. To think the man she believed a complete and utter scoundrel is the only man who has the wherewithal to transport Charlotte back to her beautiful boy.

The way in or out of any situation is unknowable. Just when you are certain you know what lies ahead, there are surprises in store.

Charlotte grabs the cord. She is first in line, then Lily, then Doreen. They slide, shake, rumble, fall like stars in a meteor shower, zoom through light, darkness, centuries, millenniums, cells, oceans and memories.

I shout. 'Hold on! Hold on tight! Don't let go of Minister Cleveland's colossal cord!'

Charlotte asks herself whether she should tell Doreen that Steven is having an affair with Jason Stickley, LSU's wide receiver? Should she tell Lily the business is in trouble? Should she tell Rheta B. she got back on Minister Cleveland's cord? If Rheta hears that, she will, for sure, faint dead away.

Lily sings a hymn. Doreen harmonizes. Charlotte listens to the words; something about angels, something about angels.

❋

Charlotte asks herself, 'Why am I so anxious to get back to Louisiana? I couldn't wait to leave. Sure. I've wished I could be in the same room as Theodore, but if we're in the same room, what will I do? How will I feel? To be that close to him without touching him will hurt so much.'

I murmur, 'Turn away, Charlotte. You can turn away.'

'What if I don't want to turn away? What if I *can't* turn away?'

'When you are beyond my domain, I will not be able to protect you.'

❋

During her many years in Afterworld, instead of spending precious time participating in productive activities, Charlotte has spent the greater part of time following the day-to-day dramas of the Duvaliers. She is terrified by what Doreen and Lily could discover. 'They don't have the vaguest idea. If Doreen finds out that Steven likes boys, what will she do? It's quite possible Steven's sexual preference was the reason Doreen drank herself to death. What's the worst that could happen? She'll drink. What if Jason Stickley's at the party? ... If, if, if ...' Charlotte is preoccupied with ifs and ands.

'What if Steven Jr puts the make on Daphne? What a mess; Doreen's grandson, the drug addict, hitting on Doreen's daughter.' Charlotte prays. 'Please! Please can we turn this fucker around!' Praying has never been Charlotte's strength. She pleads sotto voce. 'Lily. Pray for us. Get us off the ride.' She cogitates. 'How's Lily going to deal with Carter Jr's problems with the lawsuit and the land mess? I wonder if she's figured out her older son is gay? I wonder if she'll notice her younger son is *still* a misery? If Joseph does show up, I guarantee he'll be drinking. I hope Doreen forgives him. He's her father, for God's sake. It's time she stopped hating him. Did Lily have an affair with him? If she did fuck him, I don't blame her. It's doubtful she got any from Carter. Carter. He ruined everybody's life; one way or another the bad blood can be traced back to Carter and his mean-ass father, William.'

Charlotte continues her introspective inquiry. 'I hope Winston gives Steven Jr $5,000 instead of $2,500. Sometimes, I forget Winston knows I'm watching him. I hope Afterworld got Winston to up the ante. Duvaliers make me crazy. The only time I enjoyed being part of their family was when I was dying. My death brought out the best in all of us. It certainly brought out the best in me. I enjoyed those last few minutes of life when the world disappeared, when there was nothing but sound and filtered light around me.' Charlotte continues her silent monologue. 'Before Doreen and Lily showed up, it was dandy in Afterworld; unfinished family business can ruin the best of times. I can't see a damn thing! Zero visibility. I'm having a terrible journey. Terrible. Minister Cleveland's colossal cord! Really!'

Charlotte worries herself into a frenetic state. 'What if Doreen *does* get plastered? How's that possible? How's this possible? I don't see any peregrine falcons; not one! No eagles. No eagles blowing trumpets on the way down. I don't see any eagles. Where are we going to land? *How* are we going to land? In the cane fields? That's crazy. Sugar-cane will be growing like wild fire. Honestly, I don't want to see another sugar-cane field. Sugar *is* the root of all evil.'

Charlotte gags. 'What's that? Smells like fear. It must be Lily. Maybe, it's Doreen. It could be me. Fear. What a negative ride this is turning out to be.'

I console Charlotte. 'Charlotte. If you want, you *can* turn around.'

Charlotte asks, 'When we're finished down there, how are we going to get back in?'

I laugh. 'We will worry about that when the time comes.'

'But ... !'

'When the time comes.' I watch as the Duvaliers descend beyond my reach, beyond my control, but within my vision.

※

The three Duvaliers arrive in the sugar-cane field where, many years ago, a family legacy began. They land in the first field purchased by William Duvalier's father. It has rained. The mud-soaked sugar-cane field moves, undulates like a soft bed at the bottom of a warm stream. The soft bed steams with images from the past. Many feet have walked through this field of memory.

The cane field remembers when Carter took Lily for her first walk around the family property. It has taken Carter weeks to get Lily on a date. In order to get her on a date, Carter has promised Lily's father, Daddy, he will stay out of trouble for good, if

Daddy insists that Lily go on a date with him. Even though Daddy knows Carter's good behaviour will be a temporary aberration of his true spirit, against Daddy's better judgement he insists his daughter goes on a date with him. He insists, not because of a fondness for Carter or a belief in the young man's empty promises. He insists because he has made a deal.

One hot, wet, June night, after a hard day's fight over some property rights, William Duvalier calls Daddy on the telephone. They talk business. William says, 'Tell your little girl to go out with my crazy boy. I'll make it worth your while. Something tells me it'll be good for both of them, good for us and good for the business.'

William was right. If it weren't for Lily, the business would have sunk beyond saving. Who knew on that night, when Lily and Carter kissed in the sugar-cane field, Lily would eventually be the driving force behind Pine Grove's survival; certainly not William Duvalier. From his point of view a woman was nothing more than a man's slave. And from what the locals said, Mrs William Duvalier did nothing but serve her husband. He was her master, she was his slave. Until her dying day, he treated her like dirt.

I imagine that William and his wife tried, but never succeeded in having another child. When Carter was growing up, if he only had a sibling to bully, if he only had someone other than his poor mother to torment, if he only had someone other than his cruel, ruthless father to hate, Carter might have turned out to be a different kind of crazy, mean-spirited 'no-gooder', as Charlotte calls him. It is hard to imagine the man any other way, but it is possible there was some goodness in him, even if his behaviour was positively abominable. I often speculate how someone that good-looking could be all bad.

※

When Lily takes over the business soon after Carter dies, she does not mention his name. Neither does Winston. Steven, on the other hand, visits Carter's tomb in the family mausoleum every other Sunday. He says the Lord's Prayer, forgives Carter his many trespasses; his father who committed so many trespasses against Steven and his younger brother Winston. Winston tells Charlotte shocking stories about his father. Charlotte weeps. Winston weeps. There comes a day when Winston stops crying. He stops laughing. He gives up feeling altogether. It is hard for a woman who feels as much as Charlotte feels to live with a man who refuses to feel. Maybe, that is one of the reasons why Charlotte had to die.

✻

The wind picks up speed. The sugar stalks bend. Sugar remembers the night Steven and Doreen lie on the field's soft earth. Doreen is pregnant. This particular sultry June night is when Doreen tells Steven she is going to have his child. She knows the child is his child, because she hasn't slept with anyone but him, she says. He knows the child is his, because he is so much in love with Doreen, it must be his ... because that is what happens when two people are in love. Even if he is frightened by Doreen's passions, even if he believes sex is evil, he has found someone who loves him. Without a moment's hesitation he asks her to be his forever. They pray for the soul of their unborn child. They will name the child Carter Jr. By naming him Carter Jr, the boy will heal the wounds between Steven and his father. He *will* be a boy. Doreen knows it to be true. They are ecstatic at the idea of bringing new life into the world. Without a care in the world, they roll with laughter, crushing the cane beneath their wet bodies, in the damp field, where another kind of legacy presents itself. They celebrate themselves and their future child.

Later that evening when Steven tells Lily he intends to marry Doreen, it is hell on earth. Lily threatens Steven. '*I will have that no-good gold digger run out of town!*' She refers to Doreen as '*that rotten conniving low life tramp*'. She yells, '*Over my dead body is that slut going to marry my boy! You fool! You stupid fool!*'

Steven runs out the door. He finds his way back to the field where he and Doreen celebrated their good news. He sobs. Then, with great clarity, he rethinks his desperation. He shouts to the heavens. '*I will marry her! Do you hear me, Lord! We will have a good life together! We will have a family! She will be a good wife. I will be a good husband. I promise! I will follow your path for as long as I live! I swear on my life!*'

The Lord listens. Unfortunately for Steven and Doreen, Steven is unable to keep his end of the bargain.

✳

When Doreen arrives home, she tells Maria the news. Maria sends Doreen to her room. She will break the news to her husband. Maria waits for Joseph to return. That is usually what Maria does. She waits for Joseph to return late at night.

At two a.m. Joseph falls through the screen door. He is drunk. '*Where's my dinner?*' He yells at the top of his lungs.

Maria brings his food and drink to the table.

He plays with his machete. The machete is covered with cane juice. He runs his fingers over the blade. '*This is my blood, Maria. The sugar-cane owns my soul. One day she will be my slave! One day!*' He devours the rice and beans; two helpings. After he has eaten, he notices Maria's silence. '*What? What?*' he asks.

She tells him their daughter will marry Steven Duvalier. She tells him his daughter is pregnant with Steven's child.

He takes off his belt, storms into Doreen's bedroom, beats the living daylights out of her, spits in her face, calls her '*garbage*', bolts out the door and runs into the hot night screaming at the top of his lungs: '*My daughter is a pregnant whore.*'

Joseph drives his truck into the field of legacy. He shakes with a familiar rage; the rage of drink. He thinks of the many ways to kill the baby, to kill his daughter. His daughter has ruined his future. He will be nothing but the hired foreman on a sugar plantation for the rest of his life because of Doreen. Although Lily wants him, she will never let him touch her. Not now. Now he will become a member of the Duvalier family in the most demeaning manner imaginable: a shotgun wedding, like his shotgun wedding. History repeats itself. When that happens, there is no way to change one's station. Even if Lily wants him and he is certain she does want him, she will never let him be her lover. You can sleep with the hired help, but you cannot sleep with your son's father-in-law.

❋

Sugar whispers. 'Bring the boy back and all will be forgiven or get ready for all hell to break loose.'

Charlotte wishes she could make promises for her son, but she can't. Theodore's busy, busy making his fortune in Manhattan. He buys properties, fixes them up, sells them for a sizeable profit and lives his life of helter-skelter. As soon as a deal closes, he packs his bags, boards a plane and leaves the din of Manhattan to those who thrive on its noise. His business partner takes care of the boring details.

Theodore hates business, but he understands its monetary importance. One of these days he will amass enough money to get himself back to the place that makes him feel like life is worth living. He would like to settle down in Louisiana, before Melanie dies, before Steven Jr becomes an irretrievable drug addict, before Steven Sr sleeps with one too many boys and ends up in a Duvalier ditch, dead with a nine-year-old by his side. Theodore wants to go back home so he can hang out with his sister, his niece and nephew (Lily and Billy). He wants to tickle Daphne on the spot that always makes her laugh so hard she wets her pants. He wants to go fishing with Winston. He doesn't want to talk to his father about anything in particular, he just wants to be with the man. Theodore wishes he could figure out a way to right their chronic misunderstanding.

The only state where Theodore gets a good night's sleep is his home state of Louisiana. In between visits he catches up on his sleep in armchairs, on sofas, in movie houses, even in the bathtub. But, he cannot fall asleep or stay asleep in his bed in

New York City. He does all sorts of unimaginable things in that bed, but he hasn't slept through one night in his super-duper designer bedroom with blackout shades on the thirty-second floor of his high-falutin' apartment building.

When Theodore is stuck in New York City for long periods of time, he looks forward to getting back to Pine Grove's office. He looks forward to spending time with Joseph. He likes Joseph. Theodore is the only member of the family who gets along with him.

When Theodore was a young boy, Joseph taught him how to run the sugar-cane harvester, the combine. Whenever Manhattan gets him down, he relives that memorable day. It is a hot summer day. Theodore is ten years old. He sits next to Joseph. Theodore's feet do not touch the vehicle's floor. Joseph drives the combine, the combine rolls over the cane, chops the tall cane and spits out the unnecessary pulp.

'Isn't the cane beautiful, boy?'

Theodore looks out the window to his future. He dreams about the day when he will run the family business. He will not be like his father. He will work in the fields, get his hands dirty in the fertile soil, get his feet dirty, get his whole body dirty. Theodore longs to be covered in mud. He imagines himself all grown up, laughing in the rain with the workmen in the field. He imagines himself drowning in a mud-soaked field, walking on its drunken paths of cane that have been bent and broken by nature's whim. Instead, on his first ride on a combine, he is clean as a whistle. Rheta B. made Theodore take a bubble bath that morning. *'I smell like a sissy,'* he mutters to himself.

After the bath, Lily drives him to the field house. Lily is unusually nice to Joseph. It is unusual for Lily to be nice to anyone. *'It's the boy's first ride, Joseph. Don't take him out for too long or he won't ever want to come back. You know how it is?'* Lily smiles.

'I do.' Joseph smiles at Lily. *'Don't worry. I won't keep him in the cane fields too long … not his first time out. He will never come back. Look at what happened to me.'*

At the end of the ride, Theodore begs Joseph. '*Just one more time. Please! One more.*' When Joseph drives the combine back to the field house, Theodore suffers a sudden sadness. '*I don't want to be anywhere but right here. This is where I belong.*' With tears in his eyes, Theodore jumps off the combine.

Joseph catches him. He gently lets him down. He tousles his hair. He gives Theodore some good advice. '*Don't let the sugar get in your blood, boy. Once she's in your blood, you won't love anything else.*'

No matter what has happened to Theodore in those fields, no matter how his life was written and rewritten in that one particular field those many years ago, he has never loved anything more than sugar. He knows he would *love* his mother, but he has never known her except through faded photos inside a family album.

As the three Duvaliers move through fields of memory, they do not comprehend the purpose of their return. Have they come this distance to celebrate with those they left behind? Maybe they have returned to make peace, yet again, with the notion that they are not missing anything in the world of day and night. There is nothing anyone can do about the missing. It is the way of all worlds; longing for what was, reaching for the unattainable, looking backwards and forwards to find meaning in life, in death, in that which comes before and after the definitive beginnings and endings of what human beings call life and death ... They will attend a party. That is reason enough.

Winston is a man who is as likely to celebrate himself or anyone else as the man in the moon is likely to give out free tickets to tourists, who will undoubtedly trash the unfettered moonscape with obsolete electronics and twice-used Trojans. The party was Alice's idea. Alice loves the art of celebration. She should have been a party planner, but that would have taken the joy out of her being a party giver. She will throw a party for anyone at anytime. Many years ago, long after Charlotte was gone, Alice gave a 'welcome to Louisiana party' for a stranger from up north, whom she met while taking her morning run on River Road. The girl was lost. She was sunbathing on the side of the road. She had a map of Louisiana underneath her head. The girl told Alice, 'I can't read a map, but I can get a tan, even if I can't figure out where the hell I have to go,' which, by the way, was only three doors away from Alice's home. Alice offered the young lady her services as Bayou tour guide, Gran' Isle tour guide and New Orleans restaurant guide. Alice has taken many visitors to many notable Louisiana locations.

Alice will throw a benefit for any Republican or Democrat who runs for local office. She feels public service should be honoured, no matter what party. If her candidate wins, she will throw a blowout victory celebration. Because she is so goodnatured, Alice extends a warm invitation to the loser, who inevitably shows up no matter how big the loss. Alice is famous for her shindigs. Louisiana looks forward to Alice's soirées. She has thrown at least three gay pride parties for Theodore, as well as wedding banquets and baby showers for Daphne and Carter Jr. A few years ago she threw a wild bash for her husband, Dr Rob, when he got his fly-fishing licence. Alice has lit more candles on more cakes for more children and adults than anyone, anywhere in the United States of America.

Alice adores Winston. Since Winston is unable to celebrate himself, Alice will celebrate for him. Besides, Charlotte's daughter knows Winston's biggest secret. He wishes he were Steven Jr. Winston has forever dreamed of playing college football. The poor man did not even make his high school football team. He could not throw a ball if his life depended on it. He has convinced himself otherwise. *'If only I hadn't become a surgeon, I could have been a football hero.'*

Winston will enjoy celebrating his birthday with his alma

mater's football team and their star quarterback, his great nephew Steven Jr, who Winston loves almost as much as the $2,500 he *might* be giving to the football hero.

Since the day he was born, Theodore has been taken care of by Alice. She has protected him from those things that go bump in the night during his fairly charmed life, albeit a life without a mother.

As far as Alice is concerned, if you searched the world over, you could not find a better brother, uncle or friend. The problem is Theodore's attitude toward his father. The ultimate problem is his father's unforgiving attitude toward his son. When Winston looks at Theodore, he blames Theodore for Charlotte's early departure. There is no reason to blame anyone for Charlotte's passing. Winston might as well point a finger at fate. Fate is above blame.

Even after Charlotte's time on earth, Winston and his two children have had her almost undivided attention. Just because Charlotte was and is unable to cope with her unrest does not mean she has not concerned herself with her family's well-being. Although Theodore is her major concern, she worries about Winston and Alice. From her point of view they were a family, they are a family, they will continue to be a family. Whether in her present formless form or in her past customary physical form, Charlotte considers herself a mother. She considers herself Winston's wife. As far as Charlotte is concerned, those two women he married were fill-ins; fill-ins for something Winston could never replace. Winston's hunger has forever had him eating crumbs off an empty plate.

The ladies of the sky do not have to make up, dress up in party clothes, put on high-heeled shoes or brush out their hair. What they have to do is show up. Will anyone know they are in the room? Someone might smell them, but since there will be so much liquor flowing, whoever smells them will assume it is the booze or the bagasse blowing from the sugar mill.

If Doreen drinks, some savvy person might notice an unusual drop in the Jack Daniels. But, if Doreen is as smart as I believe she is, she will replace the liquor in question. Lily will most probably fuss over the floral arrangement. She will add her genteel touch to the floral design. Rheta B. will be too busy cleaning the AstroTurf to notice Lily's perfectly placed flowers. Rob will be late. He will be stuck at the hospital sewing up some athlete's ripped shoulder or placing pins in the athlete's ankle. Alice will be busy with food, drink, Lily and Billy. Lily and Billy will walk the cane fields like Daphne and Theodore did so many years before them. Steven's son, Carter Jr, will ramble on and on about the stupidity of the Army Corps of Engineers, about how New Orleans could be washed away in the next hurricane if the Corps doesn't fix the levees. Faith will be knitting Steven Jr a fancy button-down cardigan sweater. Steven Jr will be stoned. His Aunt Daphne will have spent the day crying. She will try her best to smile for everyone, especially for Steven Jr. Daphne's father will try his level best to get the wide receiver into the bedroom closet. Winston will talk football and politics. Eventually, Rheta B. will pass out from overwork in one of the pink bedrooms. In order to survive the evening, not to mention the weekend, the football team will consume copious amounts of both liquor and marijuana. Melanie and Bud will make polite conversation with Steven Sr, so as to keep him from making a fool of himself with the wide receiver or any other age-inappropriate male. Theodore will have his heart-to-heart with Steven Jr. Theodore will try tackling at least one member of the football team. Joseph will drink what Doreen does not finish. Charlotte will spend as much time as possible gazing at Theodore. No matter what I say. Hopefully, after the weekend, Charlotte will bring back a morsel of her boy's essence; back to my world without walls, back to my eternal world that reflects the whole of humanity.

❋

It is Friday night, June 24th. The year is 2005. The moon is waning. On June 22nd, two nights before, she was full. There is a slight rip in her lower right-hand corner. Clouds shaped like mythological creatures glide in front of the early evening's broken moon. The sight reminds Charlotte of a splendid memory, long ago with Winston and Alice. *'Look at the creatures. Look at those mythological, magical creatures in the beautiful Louisiana sky.'*

❋

It is a hot, humid Louisiana night. At six p.m. the heavens open wide. It pours buckets, which means those attending the party have a perfect excuse to be late; those except Rheta B., who is fast asleep in the pink bedroom upstairs. Winston has spent the last two hours agonizing over whether he should up Steven Jr's ante by five hundred dollars or just forget about it.

Winston obsesses over Billy Cannon; Billy Cannon who led LSU to its only national college championship until the last decade. He remembers the October day when he and his father, who was, as usual, inebriated, attended the thrilling football game when Billy returned an 89-yard punt, broke seven tackles and beat Ole' Miss. Sadly, that was the most exciting day of Winston's life, that day forty-six years ago. Tonight, for an entire evening, he will talk about Billy Cannon's Halloween Run.

Winston opens the safe, again. 'Hell! Billy won the Heisman trophy. He was inducted into the College Football Hall of Fame. Steven Jr wasn't even considered for the Heisman. Why should I give him any more money?' What Winston has conveniently forgotten is Billy Cannon was arrested for printing millions of dollars in counterfeit money. The man was a criminal who went to jail. There is nothing new about criminals in the state of Louisiana. Winston closes the safe.

❋

The three Duvaliers are caught up in the notion of history; how history shapes the individual, how the individual shapes history, how everyone *tries* to shape that which cannot be shaped. Charlotte asks Lily, 'Lily, if you could change anything in your life, the life before your most recent death, what would you change?'

Lily hesitates. 'I guess I would change my relationship with Daddy. If I hadn't loved him so much, I wouldn't have gone out with, no less married Carter. It was because of Daddy's working relationship with that bad-tempered, controlling brute, Mr William Duvalier, my life was stolen. It was Daddy's fault. He compromised my future. When those men decided Carter and I should get together, they ruined my life. Do you think I wanted to go out with Carter? Why would I have wanted that? The man was an incorrigible drunk. I was furious at the very idea. I wouldn't speak to Daddy for days. But, what could I do? My future was sold out from under me. I was traded like chattel.'

Sugar whispers. 'That is one hell of a bad deal; like selling sugar short.'

'I can't change anything!' Lily says, angrily. 'If I hadn't married Carter, I wouldn't have given birth to Winston.' She changes her tune. 'Which means, I wouldn't have known Charlotte.' Lily has a revelation. 'If it weren't for knowing Charlotte, I wouldn't have been anointed by her blessed memory, which inspired me for the remainder of my life on earth. It was because of my love for Charlotte that I learned forgiveness.'

Charlotte is touched by how Lily remembers her. Charlotte asks Doreen the same question.

Without a moment's hesitation Doreen says, 'I wouldn't have gotten pregnant with Carter Jr. We were too young. I should have said "no" when Steven proposed'. She remembers how happy she was the night in the sugar field. 'I loved him. But, if we had waited, if I had gotten married *before* I got pregnant, things would have been different. Lily would have been a lot nicer to

Carter Jr and me. Aren't I right, Lily?' Lily does not respond. It could be she does not know the answer, it could be she does.

Nobody asks, but Charlotte says, 'If I could change anything, anything at all, I wouldn't have been born. It never felt right. Living never felt comfortable. There are times, even now, I feel like I'm still human, I'm still suffering. I guess there's no getting around the human condition.' As Charlotte prepares for the party, she feels like she felt when she was flesh and blood; she is filled with wild, erratic emotions. 'I'm frightened by the world.' Lily reassures Charlotte. 'You are not alone, honey. You are not alone.'

Doreen agrees. 'That's for sure.'

I reiterate. 'You are not alone, Charlotte. You have never been alone.'

Sugar sighs. 'No, you haven't.'

Swamp sings. 'Certainly not.' Cattails sway in the wind. Mosquitoes buzz in the sultry, summer night. Birds swoop down. They catch mosquitoes mid-air and fly away. The natural world reminds Charlotte ... she is not alone.

Daphne sits at her desk; an old oak relic piled high with unpaid bills, love letters from Chris (before they were married), recent love letters from Steven Jr (professing his undying devotion) and letters of a different matter altogether. She examines a black and white photo hanging on the faded yellow wall of her office/study/bedroom, a photo of a beautiful couple; Doreen and Steven on their wedding night. Doreen wears a long white lace gown, her dark hair shimmers in the light, her eyes sparkle like newly polished gemstones. Steven wears a handsome black tuxedo, a white bow tie and a red carnation in his lapel. 'What the hell happened to the two of you?' asks Daphne. 'I would really like to know how you made such a fucking mess of your lives?'

Daphne picks up a crumpled handwritten letter from the

top of the pile. She reads. '*To whom it may concern. Your father, Steven Duvalier, is a faggot and a paedophile. He's been fucking underaged boys for years, destroying their childhood, ruining their adulthood. Your grandfather, Carter Duvalier, was a drunk and a fornicator. He ruined many a lady. He ruined whoever or whatever he touched. You've got incest in your family. I know that for a fact. And, your great-grandfather, William Duvalier, the snake, lied and stole the land out from under some of his best friends. He pulled the wool over their eyes while he stabbed them in the back and made millions for himself. He was a no-good bastard! Your family has led more innocent people down the road to ruin, more than you could possibly imagine. I know. I'm one of them. And I will have my say. You tell your faggot father he is finished. Nobody will miss him when he's gone, especially me.*'

Daphne rereads the letter, picks up the telephone and dials her father's number. It rings a few times. Steven Sr is in the bathroom applying make-up to his almost seventy-year-old, weathered, weary face. He hears the telephone. Hoping to find the wide receiver on the other end of the line, he rushes to his bedside table and grabs the handset.

'Hello,' Steven says, with an unfamiliar sparkle to his voice.

'Daddy. It's Daphne.' Because she is crying so hard, Daphne is all but incomprehensible.

'What's the matter, baby? Oh honey, you've got to get over Chris. Get on with your life. It's time. You are breaking my ...'

Daphne interrupts. 'Daddy. We need to talk ... tonight. Alone. It's very ... important.'

'Of course, honey. Whatever you want, whatever you say. You and your daddy will take a walk through your favourite fields; the two of us.' Although Steven has other plans, he will take time out from his sexual pleasures to listen to his daughter's problems. 'I promise.' He waits for Daphne's reply.

'It'll be nice to take a walk with you. It's been such a long time. I hope it doesn't rain.' Daphne blows her nose. 'I hate the rain.'

'It won't rain, baby. Don't worry. We'll have some private

time together. But right now, I had better get off the phone. I have to spruce up for my favourite girl.' Steven needs to get off the phone. 'Honey, do you feel a little better?' He needs to get ready. 'Come on, Daph. No more crying.' He needs to get off the phone right this second, so he can spruce up, look his very best, his very best for Jason Stickley; the ripple-chested, redneck, wide receiver. 'Is my favourite girl okay?'

'I'm fine, Daddy.' Daphne hangs up the telephone. She rereads the letter. She shoves it in her pocket. She rereads one of Chris's love letters. 'Damn you, Chris! Why aren't you here when I need you?' She doubts that she will ever get away from Pine Grove, from her family, from the never-ending secrets that keep her tied to the family's past. How is she going to get to New York City, so she can help Theodore get his financials in order, so he can figure out where and how he would like to spend the next thirty-five years of his life? Family affairs have a unique way of ruining an individual's future.

✻

Melanie washes the dinner dishes. Even if it was not entirely heart healthy, she is proud to have cooked another fabulous pulled-pork dinner for Theodore. She figures, 'Better eat at home in case the food at Winston's is inedible, which it usually is, and probably will be tonight.' Theodore is sprawled out on the sofa staring at his favourite photo; Melanie pushing Charlotte on a swing in some playground during Charlotte's childhood years. He wonders why Melanie's face is flushed with excitement. He wonders who is behind the camera. He doubts it is Bud. Bud is not a man who makes a woman flush with excitement. He is not the kind of man who makes *anyone* well up with excitement. He is a numbers man; a numbers man with a big heart. Bud is sound asleep in his recliner. The *New York Times* business section has dropped to the floor. The phone rings.

Melanie yells. 'Somebody get it! My hands are covered in grease!'

'Got it.' Theodore answers the telephone. 'Hello.'

'Hey ... when ... are ... you guys leavin' ... for ... ?'

Theodore interrupts Steven Jr, 'If it isn't our favourite football hero.'

'Who is it?' Melanie yells. She sticks her head out through the kitchen doorway.

Theodore says, 'Our favourite football hero and scholar; the party boy himself.'

'Fuck you, too.' Steven Jr says, sarcastically. 'You, my friend, are just a ... jealous ... horny ... gay boy.'

'Don't get smart on me.' Theodore knows, by the halting rhythm of his words, that Steven Jr is stoned. Theodore keeps the conversation light. 'I know you love me. You can't live without me. Kiss. Kiss.'

'You're ... crazy ... like your ... old man ... crazy.' Steven Jr cracks himself up 'Crazy like, like ... the rest of our family. Crazy.'

Theodore loses his temper. 'Listen, kid! You're as perverted as your grandfather, who, by the way, is fuckin' the wide receiver on your lousy, fucked-up football team!' Steven Jr does not respond. 'Just kiddin'. Kiddin' around, kid.'

Melanie yells from the kitchen. 'Is that Steven Jr? Tell him we're running a little behind schedule, but we can't wait to see him tonight.' Melanie walks into the living room, motions for Theodore to wrap up the call. She walks back into the kitchen.

'What's on your mind? You all right?' Theodore teases Steven Jr. 'A little bit high, maybe?'

'I've got a problem. I ...' He loses his train of thought.

Theodore realizes the boy is in trouble. 'What's up?'

'Listen ... tonight ... we ... need ... to talk ... private.'

'Didn't I promise you we'd have our private time? I'm pretty positive we've got a meetin' scheduled. Let me check my calendar.' Theodore loves Steven Jr. The young man reminds Theodore of himself when he graduated from LSU. Theodore did not have a clue about what he wanted to do with his life. He is still searching for that answer. 'Hey. You worried about what's next?'

'No.' Steven Jr chokes up. 'I ... have to ...' He starts to hang up the phone.

Theodore stops him. 'Wait a second. Don't hang up ... Talk to me ... What's wrong with you?'

From inside the kitchen Melanie yells, 'Bud, get your ass out of the chair, get dressed, get ready, let's go. Theodore. Get off the phone! Tell our football hero you will see him in a little while. We had better get a move on here, boys! If we are one minute late, Winston will be pissed off.'

Bud wakes up from his nap. 'Winston will be pissed off no matter what time we get there.'

Theodore whispers into the receiver. 'Let's take a walk in the sugar-cane fields; you and me. Promise me you won't have another hit before the party.' Steven Jr does not respond. 'Damn it! Did you hear what I said?'

'I promise,' promises an already high, almost monosyllabic Steven Jr, who after dazed deliberation concludes, if he is going to the party, he had better call upon the driving skills of someone less stoned than himself. Steven Jr cannot say another word. His desperate need for one more hit of the psychotropic concoction that has created the hum inside his head, the hum that is as loud as a buzz saw cutting through a steel rod, occupies his complete attention. When Steven Jr realizes he has left Theodore hanging on the other end of the phone for an indeterminate amount of time, he stammers, 'Don't worry ... I'm ... fine ...'

Melanie yells 'Theodore Faulkner Duvalier! Get your ass off that phone! Now!' Melanie is dressed. She is ready to go. 'Bud! Get your ass into the bedroom! Get dressed! Now!'

'You and me. We'll figure somethin' out. Don't worry.' Theodore is worried about the fair-haired football hero, stoned out of his mind, without a feasible plan for his uncertain future. 'I promise you,' he says, 'we'll figure somethin' out.'

When Lily, Doreen and Charlotte finally make it through the

door, they are met with a glorious sight; the drunken LSU football team minus Steven Jr singing the stately LSU alma mater:

Where steady oaks and broad magnolia
Shake inspiring halls
There stands our dear old alma mater
Who to us recalls …

'Will this song ever end?' Charlotte asks Doreen.

'Probably not.' Doreen discovers the booze on the dining-room table.

'Football players should be prohibited from singing.' Lily says, as she rearranges the flowers on the dining-room table. Charlotte emphatically agrees with Lily.

… we pray to keep it true …

Inspired by a nostalgic college moment, Theodore joins in on the last line.

And may the spirit live in us forever L-S-U.

Winston applauds. Steven applauds louder than Winston. Melanie and Bud are seated side by side on the orange couch. They are taken aback by the football players' vocal mediocrity. Melanie with mouth agape, with wine glass dangerously tilted and wine dripping like water onto the already stained AstroTurf, wipes her glass. Appalled that she is responsible for the most recent flecks of red, she groans, 'Shit', takes the heel of her shoe and mashes the spilled wine into the carpet, creating an exciting collage. She tilts Bud's glass back into an upright position. When Bud realizes the better part of his drink has disappeared beneath his feet, he says, 'Thank you, honey.'

Alice bravos. She requests an encore, which fortunately for

everyone in the room, is declined by the Tigers. Instead, Jason Stickley, *the* wide receiver, sings a solo version of another LSU favourite, 'Hey Fightin' Tigers'.

When Jason begins, Doreen saunters to the drink area. Lily, once again, turns her attention to the flowers. Charlotte finds her way between a transfixed Winston and a transported Steven. The brothers are astounded by the undiscovered genius of Jason Stickley.

Jason's rendition of LSU's fabulous fight song, set to the music of 'Hey Look Me Over', has several obvious connotations.

> *Hey, Fightin' Tigers, fight all the way.*
> *Hey, Fightin' Tigers, win the game today.*
> *You've got the know-how,*
> *You're doing fine,*
> *Hang onto the ball as you hit the wall.*

When young Jason sings this line, Charlotte imagines, without much imagination, the inevitable. The song continues.

> *… and keep the goal in view*
> *Victory for L-S-U!*

'Who knew the young man had so many hidden talents?' Doreen consumes the bourbon.

Following the performance, Jason and Steven share a not-so-subtle wink. Fortunately, Doreen misses the flirtation. Joseph enters the room. He says hello to Winston, heads toward the drink area, stands next to Doreen and pours himself a stiff drink from Doreen's nearly empty bottle. Joseph looks around the room. He acknowledges the many guests he knows intimately. He grudgingly toasts his son-in law; the son-in-law who recently sacked Joseph.

Lily spots Joseph. She thinks, 'What happened to him? He looks so old.' No longer the strapping man Lily remembered, Joseph looks worn and frail. As he drinks himself into a stupor, Doreen studies the craggy lines on her father's face, the lines around his mouth, the lines around his eyes. She notices the dazzling dark colour of his eyes, the aquiline shape of his nose, the firm grip of his fingers around the glass. For the very first time, Doreen *sees* her father without contempt. Finally, she understands what her mother saw in this strong man, this man of few words, this man of many disappointments. Joseph, who is uncomfortable in social situations, stands alone in a corner. Lily stands next to him. She watches him. She listens to his shallow breathing. She smells his manly scent. His smell reminds her of the night he came running, running into the house, covered in sweat, to tell her Carter had been killed. She would never forget that night; neither would Joseph.

Winston senses Charlotte is in the living room. He mumbles under his breath, 'Two thousand five hundred dollars. That's more than enough, Charlotte.' He marches to the drink area, pours himself a stiff one, stands next to Doreen, mumbles again, 'More than enough.' He says, 'Hello Joseph.'

Joseph raises his glass. 'Happy birthday, Winston.'

'I am so sorry about Maria. She was a wonderful woman.'

'Thank you.' Joseph drinks. Doreen pours herself another drink.

Lily, who never drank before, pours herself a stiff drink. She toasts Winston. 'Money locked inside a safe is worthless, son. Spend it. Give the boy *more* than you think he deserves.'

With almost empty glasses Bud and Melanie toast the young gay tenor. Hoping to find his very own tackle, tight end or wide receiver before evening's end, Theodore cruises the football team. Carter Jr and Faith are on the lookout for their son, Steven Jr. They keep an eye on the front door.

Faith feverishly knits Steven Jr's cardigan. 'Honey. Let's call him.' Carter Jr is busy watching the flirtation between his father and Jason Stickley. 'Honey!'

'Stop worrying about him!' Faith pulls a face. 'I'm sorry. I have so much on my mind.' He waves to Joseph across the room. 'I wish Joseph were still working for us. He was the best man we ever had at Pine Grove. I hate the sugar business. While Daddy is gallivanting who knows where, the business is falling apart. He doesn't give a damn. Daphne doesn't know the first thing about bookkeeping. The damn Army Corps of Engineers is killing us: "This ain't right, that ain't legal, that's our land!" They are trying to screw us any way they can. Lazy lying bastards! It's not worth it, Faith. Without Lily the business is sinking fast.'

Faith puts away her knitting. She takes Carter Jr's hand in hers. 'It's going to be fine, honey. In the end it always turns out right. Things have a way of working themselves out when they're good and ready.'

Carter Jr shakes his head. 'Why bother. Where the hell is Steven Jr? Our son, the great football hero!' Faith picks up a stitch. She continues to look out for Steven Jr.

Rheta B. kisses Theodore. 'You look so handsome tonight.' She notices Melanie and Bud's empty glasses. She offers them a refill.

Melanie says, 'Don't bother, Rheta.'

'How you two doin'?' asks Rheta, as she wipes tiny beads of sweat from her forehead with an old, faded, white embroidered handkerchief.

'We're just fine.' Melanie takes hold of Rheta's shoulders.

'You look as if you've been working much too hard, young lady.' Rheta shrugs. 'Haven't I told you a thousand times you can't do that any more. Rheta, you have been taking care of our families for years. It's about time you started taking care of yourself. Do you hear me?'

'Oh what I must look like?' Rheta runs her fingers through her grey, matted hair. 'Long day. Daphne didn't show up, so I did most of the cleanin' and cookin'. An awful lot to do in this house. I'm not complainin'. You know how I love gettin' a house ready for a Duvalier party.' Bud hugs Rheta. Rheta hugs Bud.

She continues her walk around filling empty drink glasses.

Melanie clutches Bud's hand. They sit. 'Where do you think Daphne is, honey?' Bud shrugs. 'Grief has got that girl by the short hairs. She's been an emotional mess for too long; another screwed-up Duvalier. Why did we ever get involved with this *meshuggeneh* family?' Melanie peers at Bud. If looks could kill, Bud would be a dead man.

Alice walks over to Theodore. 'Do you believe that guy?' she whispers in Theodore's ear. 'He is the gayest tight end I've ever seen.'

Theodore corrects her. 'Wide receiver. But, I'm sure he has a tight end.' They roar with laughter.

'No doubt.' Alice says, sarcastically. 'You ought to know.' She winks, as she pinches Theodore's cheek.

'I hate that.' Theodore pushes Alice.

'Now you know how I feel.' Alice laughs. 'Where the hell is the football hero ...'

Theodore interrupts his sister. 'Where the hell are your kids?'

'They'll be here. They'll be here.' Alice gets huffy. 'When you were a teenager, were you ever on time for anything except a football game?' Alice looks at her watch. 'Where the hell is my husband? Maybe there's been an outbreak of typhus in New Orleans.'

'It could happen.' Theodore pokes Alice. 'It could happen anywhere.'

Alice loses her patience. 'We are not living in a Third World country ... yet. But, anything could happen, anytime, anywhere.' Alice rants. 'Why am I always in charge of these parties!?'

'Are you upset about somethin'?'

'Sometimes you ask the stupidest questions. Of course I'm not upset!' Alice walks toward the drink area, which is fast becoming the place to be.

'Then why are you always angry?' Theodore shouts across the room. 'Why!?'

'Christ.' Alice mutters under her breath as she pours herself a glass of white wine. She screams at Theodore, 'You don't understand anything about throwing a party! You're too busy being everybody's pride and joy!' Theodore does not comment.

As Charlotte watches her children interact in the familiar big sister, little brother way, she is reminded of a moment, many years ago on the beach at Gran' Isle. It was at that moment Charlotte realized, even though she was no longer alive, she could watch the world beyond her reach. Winston was off fishing in the Gulf. As far as Winston was concerned, it was time for his children to be on their own for a couple of hours.

Theodore and Alice were off building sand castles. Theodore built the most beautiful sand castle imaginable. The walls were at perfect right angles to each other. They were tall, beyond a bucket tall, at least two buckets tall. Theodore was proud of his design. In sheer delight he jumped and jumped around his castle. Suddenly, he lost his balance, fell on the towers and in an instant destroyed his wondrous design. He cried so hard, Alice thought his bones would shatter into hundreds of tiny pieces, leaving nothing but a heap of dust in the sand. No matter what Alice said or did, she could not calm down her younger brother. Finally, Alice, with hands on hips, screamed, *'Stop bein' such a big baby! It's only a sand castle!'* Theodore, stunned by his older sister's indifference, said, *'Why are you such a meanie?'* To which Alice replied, *'I am not a meanie. I am honest.'* After which Alice helped Theodore rebuild his sand castle.

Soon after the LSU song tribute Lily and Billy arrive dressed in baggy pants, short-sleeved T-shirts and flip-flops.

Lily, who was often offended by the twins' get-up when she was alive, is still offended by their attire. She mumbles. 'It is disrespectful. You children look like a couple of hoboes! When the Duvaliers give a party, you dress your best. What is the matter with children nowadays!'

Lily and Billy run upstairs as fast as their legs can carry them. They disappear into Winston's closet. While rummaging through the closet, they find Winston's shabby, unfashionable, hunting gear, fishing gear, camouflage clothing and a few guns from his gun collection. The twins dress up in Winston's paraphernalia. They guzzle bottles of beer, brilliantly hidden in the pockets of their baggy pants. 'Dad doesn't own a gun, does he?' asks Billy, as he tries on Winston's black rubber fishing boots.

'Très chic,' Lily says, as she tries on Winston's orange hunting jackets, a yellow pair of fishing boots and a wide-rimmed, worn-out, khaki sun hat that she pulls over her eyes. 'How do I look?'

'Stupid.'

'No more stupid than you, stupid.' Lily throws a boot at Billy. She takes off the hat, looks at Billy for a long, long time before she says, 'Do you think Great-Uncle Steven is gay? For real?'

'Don't be stupid. He just likes wearing nice clothes. I'm bored. Let's go downstairs. Let's talk to Uncle Theodore. One day I'm gonna live in New York City like Theodore.'

'He's gay.' Lily acts like this is new news.

'You are so silly. Everybody knows that.' Billy says dismissively, being the older twin by one full minute. 'I smell gardenias. Do you? It smells like Great-Grandma Lily before she got sick.'

'She smelled pretty bad at the end. Ugh. I don't want to smell like that when I get old. I don't want to get old.' Lily sighs. 'I don't want to get married either.'

'Don't worry. If you look like that, no one's gonna marry you.' Billy, who adores his twin sister, takes a good look. 'I promise, even if you look like a crazy person, I'll take care of you, no matter what.' Billy sniffs the air. 'I smell Great-Grandma.'

Lily and Billy imagine Great-Grandma Lily, as she was, when she was near the end. They turn up their noses, fast as greased lightning take off Winston's paraphernalia and beeline it for the stairs, yelling, 'Mom! Mom!'

❋

Downstairs, young Lily notices that most grown-ups at parties act like idiots. She waves to Melanie and Bud, kisses Rheta B., kisses Winston on the cheek and wishes him a happy birthday. She avoids making eye contact with any of the *disgustingly* drunken members of the football team. She looks for Uncle Theodore, who is cackling in the corner with some of the LSU boys. She waves. 'Hi, Uncle Theodore.'

Theodore sees Lily. 'See you guys later.' He hugs Lily. 'Hi, honey. Love the outfit. You sure dressed up for the occasion.'

Lily is ecstatic. 'You like the baggy look?'

Theodore gives her the thumbs-up. 'Love. Love. Love it.'

'Why don't you come back home?'

'I will. I promise.' Lily gives him a quizzical look. 'Honest. I miss you and Billy, your mother, your father, but a man's gotta make a livin'. The fastest way to make a fortune in New York is ownin' and sellin' property.'

'Dumb answer,' says Lily. 'Have you seen Billy anywhere?'

'Last I saw him he was runnin' back upstairs without you.'

Longing to get back to the huddle, Theodore convinces Lily to find her twin brother. 'You better find him before he gets himself in some real trouble. Go on.' Lily bounds upstairs. She screams. 'Billy! Billy! Billy!'

Winston notices Lily running upstairs. He worries she might disturb important objects in his bedroom or his bedroom closet. She could find the safe. She could steal his money. He asks himself, 'Why is she running upstairs? This could mean trouble. There's always the possibility of chaos. I hate parties. I hate them. Where the hell is Steven Jr? That boy needs some discipline. Carter and Faith are lousy parents!'

Winston's mother overhears her son. 'No worse than you were, son.' A puzzled Winston looks over his shoulder. The smell of gardenias fills the air.

＊

Daphne is parked outside Steven Jr's redbrick apartment building. She is parked in her new red Jeep Grand Cherokee. She has been anxiously waiting, for more than fifteen minutes, for her drug-crazed nephew. Daphne picks up her cellphone and dials his number. She places him on speakerphone.

Steven answers, 'Hellooo.' He has fallen asleep. Daphne says, 'Where the hell are you?'

'In ... my apartment ... Why? Where ... are you?' He sounds dazed.

'I'm parked outside your building. Remember? You called?'

'I did?'

Daphne screams. 'Steven! You are so fucked up! I don't know if I can deal with you! I'm outta here!'

'No! Don't!' He yells into the phone. 'Don't go anywhere! I'll be right down. Wait! Wait ... right ... there! Where are you!? Front ... side?'

Daphne grabs the phone off its cradle. She shouts. 'I–am–in–front–of–your–fucking–goddamn–door–Steven! Right where you told me to be! Jesus!'

'I'm sorry. I'm on my way down. Give me two seconds.'

Steven hangs up the phone, lights up his bong one more time, takes a deep inhale, grabs his vest, looks under his couch. 'Shit.' He looks behind his couch. 'Fuck.' He throws the couch pillows on the floor. 'Damn!' He opens his bedroom closet, swipes the sweaters off the closet shelf. 'Fuck me!' He looks under his bed. 'Fuck you!' He turns around, walks back into the living room. 'Asshole!' There on the living-room table is Winston's gift. 'Fuck everyone!' He grabs the gift, runs down three flights of stairs, trips on his laces. He catches himself on the banister. He laughs. He tries to straighten himself out before he gets into the car. He opens the door, looks at Daphne, goes to kiss her on the cheek. She pulls away. He says, 'Nice seein' you, too.' She does not say a word. 'I'm sorry ... I said, I'm sorry.' He folds his arms, slumps down in his seat, looks out the front window. He does not say another word.

Daphne turns on the engine, hits the accelerator with a heavy foot, drives like a maniac through the winding roads of LSU's campus. 'You are always sorry. Always. I'm sick of you and your drugs, sick of you expecting me to help whenever you're in trouble, which is most of the time. I'm sick of you, Steven! Chris was right. You're never going to be anything but a dead-end football hero.' Daphne sobs. 'I don't want to go to this party. I just want to die. Right this second.'

The car veers out of control. Steven Jr grabs the wheel. 'Pull over! Damn it, Daphne! Slow down! Pull the fuckin' car over! Here! Right here!' The car swerves on the wet road. It skids to a halt. Steven looks at Daphne. She is hysterical. Steven Jr does not know what to do. Finally, he pulls himself together. 'I don't want to make you unhappy. I would do anything for you, Daph. You know that, don't you?' He smiles his beautiful toothy smile. She nods. 'I'm sorry Chris felt that way about me. It's not true. You know it's not true. I won't be like that. I just don't know what I *am* going to be, what I want, what's happening ... to me.' Steven Jr begins to cry. 'Oh Daphne. I am so confused.' The football hero falls apart in Daphne's red Cherokee.

Daphne reaches over. She strokes the short hairs on Steven Jr's neck. 'Don't cry, honey. I shouldn't have said that. It's not true. It wasn't nice. Forgive me. Please. Chris loved you. He loved you like a baby brother. We all love you. You are the great hope for this family, young man.' Daphne continues to stroke the back of Steven Jr's neck. Steven Jr nuzzles Daphne's hand with his cheek. He takes her hand in his. He kisses it, gently. Daphne quietly says, 'Honey, don't do that.' But, she does not stop him. 'Please don't do that.' Steven Jr takes Daphne's hand, places it in his lap. 'Oh honey, please don't do this.' She feels him get hard. He feels so good in her hand. She forgets who he is. She forgets who she is. She forgets who they are to each other in the family tree. She unzips his fly. He turns toward her, he takes her face in his hands, he kisses her lips. She tries to take her hand away from his cock. He takes one of his hands and presses it hard, on top of her hand. He grabs her tits, he begins to bury his face between her breasts. He pulls off her sweater, he undoes her bra. She gently pushes him away. She reaches around his seat and pushes the recline button. She bends over him, slowly wraps her mouth around his penis. He grabs her head and shoves it into his body. He pulls her on top of him. He pulls up her skirt, pulls down her underpants, shoves his young prick inside of her.

As if they had been together a thousand times before, they move with a familiar grace and ease. They fall into each other's gaze; slowing down, speeding up, always in sync, without saying a word. They run their hands up and down each other's body. They feel like children on a beach letting grains of sand run through their fingers on a hot June day; another hot June day. They sweat, they moan, they hold on tight like it was the end and the beginning of all life. They reach orgasm at precisely the same moment. And so it goes; another Duvalier interpretation of how love works.

The red Jeep Grand Cherokee pulls up in front of Winston's house. The party is in full swing. Daphne and Steven Jr sit motionless in the car. 'The Lakes of Pontchartrain' by Paul Brady plays on the CD player:

I asked her if she'd marry me, she'd said it could never be
For she had got another and he was far at sea.

As the song plays, Daphne turns off the engine. She drops her head back on the headrest. 'I don't want to talk about this. Okay?'

'Okay.' Steven Jr realizes something has happened that will alter their relationship for the rest of their lives. He is afraid he has lost the only woman he will ever love.

'I don't want to talk about this *ever*. Do you understand?' Steven Jr does not answer. 'Do you understand?' Daphne takes the keys out of the ignition, throws them in her bag, zips the bag, opens the car door, abruptly swings her torso around, places one foot on the ground, then the other. She gets ready to vacate the vehicle.

Steven Jr grabs her hand. 'I'll do whatever you want. You know how I feel, Daph.'

Daphne yanks her hand out from Steven Jr's grip. She slams the door shut, she turns, she glares at her nephew with utter disdain. In a monotone voice she says, 'That will never happen again. Do you understand?'

'Uh huh.' He does not want to understand. He looks through the passenger-side window. 'Looks like a party to me.' He opens his door, slowly gets out, closes the door, stands perfectly still. He shoves his hands deep inside his pockets.

Daphne makes her point undeniably clear. 'Do you understand?!' Again, she opens her door, slams it shut, looks over her shoulder, points a finger. 'Your shirt is unbuttoned.' Steven Jr fumbles around. He fixes the problem. 'Don't forget Winston's present.' Steven Jr opens the rear door, grabs the orange package from the back seat. Daphne rushes toward the house.

As he watches Daphne from behind, Steven Jr recites two lines from 'The Lakes of Pontchartrain':

So fare thee well me bonny o' girl I never see no more
But I'll ne'er forget your kindness and the cottage by the shore.

Steven Jr walks toward the house. He carries Winston's present in one hand and a merciless grief in the other.

Daphne opens the front door. She enters. She looks around the room. She wishes she were anywhere but in the room. She spots

Theodore on the other side of the living room. Theodore stops talking. Dumbstruck, he looks at Daphne. He can tell she has been through some life-shifting experience. He sees it in her eyes, he sees it in her body language; after all, he knows Daphne inside out. When they were children, they rolled in the sugar fields, they played doctor in the muddy trenches on hot sticky afternoons. He remembers the day he confided in her. *'I did something naughty. I think naughty thoughts.'*

Daphne laughed and laughed and laughed at him. *'Don't be such a silly boy, Theodore. Silly boy.'*

He tickled her. She screamed so loud, Sugar said, *'Hush.'*

Daphne jumped up and down at least one thousand times. *'We are bad. You and me, baddest, bad, boy and girl. Let's be naughty. Run away! Break the stupid grown-up rules! Promise me! Promise me! Break the silly grown-up rules. Theodore and Daphne … forever and ever! Promise! Promise! We will stay together … forever and ever!'* At that moment, in the same field where Theodore discovered what he did not understand, except as a wrongful desire in himself, Daphne pulled up her skirt, pulled down her underpants and danced in the sun. Forgetting his shame, Theodore jumped up and down with a feverish delight. That was the day they made a promise neither would forget.

※

Steven Jr enters, a vacant look on his face. Daphne glares at him. He points to the back door. She turns away, walks toward the drink table. Theodore comes between Daphne and the drink. He realizes what has happened.

Theodore grabs Daphne's arm. 'What's goin' on with you? You got this weird look in your eyes, Daph. Somethin' you want to tell me?'

'I need a drink, Theodore. That's what I want to tell you. I need a drink really bad.'

She shakes him off her arm. He grabs her, drags her into a corner. Lily overhears their conversation. 'Did you just fuck your nephew, Daph? Did you?' Daphne turns away. 'Look at me! Damn it! Did you?'

'I need a drink. Let go of me! I have got real problems. Have you seen my father?' Daphne looks around the room.

'He's probably upstairs in my daddy's closet or outside in the sugar fields, maybe in one of the bedrooms havin' a gay ol' time with Jason Stickley. You know Jason Stickley? The wide receiver? Don't worry about it, Daph; fornicatin' with inappropriate young men or relatives runs in the family. Let's just say you're followin' in your father's inimitable footsteps. Sure, I was once the naughty boy, but you are one naughty, stupid girl.' Theodore lets go of Daphne's arm. 'Foolish, foolish girl!' Theodore tries to reason with Daphne. 'He loves you, Daph. He doesn't know any better. The kid's stoned out of his mind. How could you?'

'Fuck you, Theodore!' For the first time in their lives, Daphne turns her back and walks away in the middle of an argument. She pours herself a double shot of bourbon. If only she could walk away, run away from her screwed-up family.

'Not you, Daph?' Theodore stares at Daphne. 'Not my favourite girl.' He fights back his tears. He hopes no one notices he is falling apart. Charlotte finds Theodore's disappointment unbearable. For the first time since I have known her, she turns away. *She* turns away.

Lily does not know what to think. 'My poor boy. My poor sweet boy. Poor girl. Poor family. What has happened to all of you? What don't I know?'

Gardenias permeate the air. Theodore whispers. 'Grandma? Lily? Lily?'

Lily is at her wits' end. She might as well be human. 'Please help me, Lord. Help them for they cannot help themselves.'

※

Young Lily and Billy run into the living room. They surround Theodore, who has, somehow, pulled himself together. 'We smell Great-Grandma Lily! We smell Great-Grandma Lily!'

Theodore hushes the twins. 'Shh. Not so loud. I'm gonna tell you a secret.' He bends down, pulls them close to him. 'Promise you won't tell anybody what I'm tellin' you?'

'We promise! Promise!' The twins can hardly contain their excitement.

'I smell her, too.' Theodore's eyes sparkle. 'Let's not tell anybody. It'll be our secret.'

'Cross our hearts.' The twins jump up and down, hug each other and scream with delight.

Winston walks over to Theodore and the twins. 'What's going on here?'

Theodore and the twins giggle. Theodore says, 'Nothin' much. We're just havin' ourselves a good time. How 'bout you, Dad?'

'If you kids are having a good time, I'm having a good time. That's quite a football team, isn't it? Fine young lads. I'm glad Steven Jr finally showed up.' Winston whispers to Theodore. 'The kid doesn't act normal. He acts like he's somewhere else.' Winston talks hunting, fishing and Louisiana politics with the twins. The twins roll their eyes. 'What a party! The whole world has shown up.'

Theodore nods. 'Sure has, Dad.' The twins giggle.

'I wish your mother were alive. She loved family celebrations. I can't wait to get to Gran' Isle. We are going to have a fantastic time!' For the very first time, Winston hugs Theodore. Winston *hugs* his son. Lily and Billy hug Winston. 'Alice outdid herself tonight, didn't she, son? I am a lucky man. Even if the government steals half of my hard-earned money and doesn't give me anything in return, I am a very lucky man.'

Theodore agrees. 'You certainly are.'

'Have you seen my brother anywhere?'

'No. I haven't, Dad. Must be somewhere close by.'

'I'll find him.' Winston walks away. Theodore hopes his father does not find his uncle, who is otherwise engaged, somewhere on the premises ... in Jason Stickley.

✳

The black man waits outside Winston's house. He reads the piece of paper, looks for a number on the mailbox. 'Nice place.' He looks at the surrounding sugar fields, listens to the night sounds, listens to the loud voices. He does not feel comfortable barging into a family celebration. He hardly knows Theodore. But, he said he would show up if he was still in Louisiana. He walks up the stone path, walks up the front steps, hesitates, knocks on the front door. He waits a few moments. Nobody hears him knocking. He opens the door, peeks inside, sees Theodore engaged in conversation with two children. He wonders who they are. He wonders if he has done the right thing. He rarely attends family functions of any kind.

Theodore sees the black man standing inside the doorway. He kisses the twins, excuses himself, walks toward the man, grabs his hand, hugs him, says, 'How are you?' Before the man can answer, Theodore whispers in his ear. 'I haven't been able to get you out of my mind. Been hard for days just thinkin' about you. Awful glad you made it.'

'Is this where you grew up?'

'It is.'

'Beautiful place. If I had grown up here, I never would have left.'

'If my father was your father, you would have.'

'Where's your father?'

'Over there with my sister, Alice.' Alice waves. 'Fortunately, I spent a lot of time in Baton Rouge visiting my mother's mother, Melanie. She's over there on the couch with her husband, Bud.' Theodore waves to Melanie.

Melanie gives Bud her empty wine glass, ambles over to Theodore and his *new* friend. 'Melanie, I'd like you to meet Cleveland.'

'Haven't we met before?'

'No, ma'am. We certainly have not.'

'Are you sure? I never forget a face.'

Theodore interrupts. 'Cleveland is a new friend. We just met before the weekend ... in New York.'

'Oh, I see. A *new* friend.' She winks at Theodore. 'Lovely to meet you, son. Enjoy the party.' As Melanie ambles back to the couch, she says, 'I never forget a face.' She mutters under her breath. 'Never.'

'She remembers you from the airport.' Theodore grins. 'That woman doesn't miss a trick.'

'She seems like quite a character.'

'If it weren't for her ...' Theodore stops mid-sentence. 'Let me introduce you around. When you've had enough of my family, just tell me. I won't be offended.' The two men walk toward the drink area. 'By the way, what brings you to Louisiana in the first place?'

'Wasn't it you who said, "I don't want to know a damn thing about you"? I'm pretty sure those were your exact words, unless I'm confusing you with somebody else.'

'I had no idea you were payin' such close attention.' Theodore introduces Cleveland to the rest of the family. Nobody asks too many questions; polite, well-mannered hellos are exchanged. Theodore forgets about the football team. The man on his arm has his complete attention.

Doreen follows Joseph into the sugar fields; the fields that shaped and defined their lives in different ways, at different times. Joseph gazes at the sugar-cane.

Sugar whispers. 'Welcome home, Joseph. I miss your gentle touch, your tender care.'

There was a time, not long ago, when Joseph believed the sugar was his sugar, the fields were his fields. He did not own them. They owned him. He loved, hated, needed the sugar, like sugar needs rain, like rain needs air, like man needs love. The sugar gave him purpose. When he walked through the fields, when he harvested the crop with his men by his side, he felt as mighty as a god, as a god who needs no other. Joseph was mistaken.

He misses Maria. He realizes how he took her love and her kindness for granted. He does not understand the emptiness inside, the sadness that wells up in his body every single night. Maria was always there at night. She loved him, even when he came home drunk, even when he beat Doreen, even when he loved Lily, even then, she loved him without question. Maria was the only constant in his life.

Sugar was not constant. She did not love him. She did not feed him, clothe him, kiss him, open her arms or fold her arms around him. The sugar was his life, but Maria was his one and only faithful love. This painful realization comes at a time in his life when there is nothing to replace either Maria or the sugar; nothing to live for, no one to come home to.

'Maria, I miss you. Forgive me. Wherever you are, please take me with you! Take me home. *You* are my home!' Joseph sobs. He gazes at the passing clouds. The clouds race in front of the devil moon.

Doreen is touched by her father's vulnerability. If only, if only she could hold him in her arms, stroke his hair, tell him she forgives him, she loves him, she finally understands him. But, she cannot. He is deaf to her unearthly language.

Two mud-soaked male figures walk through the field toward Winston's house. They laugh, stumble, fall all over each other. When they reach the middle of the field, they laugh so loud Sugar whispers, 'Shh. Someone is aching.' The men stop, listen to the night, wonder whose voice they hear. They continue walking, hand in hand, toward the edge of the field. One of the men, the older of the two, sees Joseph in tears on the ground. He unclasps his hand from the young man's grip. He runs toward Joseph.

'Joseph. Are you all right?'

Joseph looks at the man. 'Is that you? Is that you, Steven?'

'What is it, Joseph? What's the matter? What's the matter with you?' Without hesitation, Steven takes Joseph in his arms.

'I miss them. I miss all of them. What will happen now?'

Jason Stickley quickly walks toward the back door. As Doreen mulls over the image of the two men in the field, holding hands, she remembers why she drank, why she chewed ice cubes, why she talked to the walls during those lonely Louisiana afternoons.

❋

Carter Jr and Faith have cornered Steven Jr in the kitchen. Carter Jr bombards his son with unanswerable questions about the boy's future. 'What are you going to do, son? You have got to make up your mind! If you don't hurry, all the good research jobs will be scooped up by those smart ass Ivy Leaguers.'

'We want what's best for you, Steven. That's all we have ever wanted.' Faith knits with a vengeance. 'You know that? Don't you?' She realizes Steven Jr isn't listening to either one of his parents. 'Honey. Son, we are so very proud of you. Your father and I couldn't be happier. We just want you to make the right decision about next year.'

'What the hell is the matter with you!? Are you listening? Are you listening to me!' Carter Jr interrupts himself. 'Who's that package for, son?'

Steven Jr has forgotten to give Winston his birthday present. 'Damn. Have you ... seen ... Winston? Have you seen him?'

'Are you paying *any* attention to what we are trying to tell you? Sometimes, I'm convinced that you are not with us, you are not here. Are you with us, boy? You can't dream your way through the rest of your life, son. Can he, honey?' Carter Jr is annoyed. 'Would you put down that damn knitting of yours! We are having a serious discussion with *your* son!'

Faith puts her needles and yarn in her bag. 'Sorry, honey.' She chastises Steven Jr, 'Your father and I are truly concerned. We believe it's time you made some decisions regarding your future.'

Barely audible, Steven says, 'I will. I promise.' He cannot listen to his parents for one more second. He would rather die. He walks away. 'Got to find Winston.' As he walks out the kitchen door, Daphne walks in front of him. He jumps in front of her. 'Come on, Daph ... let's go walkin' in the fields. We need to ... Daph ... Please.'

Carter Jr wryly says, 'I hope she can talk some sense into that boy of yours.' As he storms out the kitchen door, Carter Jr says, 'That boy is driving me crazy! I need some fresh air.'

'It takes a good woman to make sense of any man,' Faith says to herself.

Upstairs in Winston's den, Theodore's old bedroom, Lily and Billy drink copious amounts of beer. Lily wears Winston's orange hunting hat. Billy sports all sorts of hunting paraphernalia; boots, jackets, vests and mud-soaked overalls. The rest of the family is where they need to be. Doreen is with her father. Lily is with Winston. Charlotte is in the living room with her son and his *new* friend, Cleveland.

Rheta B. refreshes empty drink glasses, cleans out ashtrays, throws out paper napkins in the oversized trash can, replaces dips, chips; every dishful with another dishful. The football team drinks vats of beer. They can barely stand.

Theodore spots Rheta B. on the other side of the living room.

He yells. 'Rheta! I've got somebody I want you to meet!' Rheta puts down a dish filled with pecans. She reluctantly walks over to the other side of the room. 'Rheta. Meet Cleveland Alexander.'

Rheta B.'s face turns ashen. Her eyes roll back inside her head. She passes out. Cold. Theodore tries to break her fall. Rheta lands with a thud on the living-room floor. Theodore yells for help. Cleveland Alexander holds Rheta's head. He fans her face with an old *Sports Illustrated* magazine. Rheta comes to, looks into Cleveland Alexander's eyes. She cries and cries. Because she cries so hard, Swamp weeps never-ending tears that turn into a brand new bayou, Sugar grows a foot taller and in an instant, Joseph, who rests in Steven's arms at the edge of the field, comes to believe in miracles. And for one moment, the worlds of here and there breathe a sigh of relief. When you find your long-lost son, there is no mistaking him.

When Rheta B. is pregnant with Cleveland Alexander, Minister Cleveland is well aware Rheta is carrying his child. He has impregnated many in his congregation, but none are as vulnerable as the young woman who will not say 'no' to the Minister, because he *is* the Minister in the house of her Lord. Rheta is the last in a long line of fallen women in Minister Cleveland's house of the Lord.

Her pregnancy brings shame to Rheta's family. Her mother and father disown her. They come to Minister Cleveland for counselling. During one of their weekly meetings Minister Cleveland realizes that he has destroyed a family, that he is responsible for the birth of a bastard child. Finally, Minister Cleveland reforms from fornicator to Lord's good and noble man.

His good friend, Minister Leroy Jones, ministers in a church in Port Fourchon in Lafourche Parish, which is located on the southern tip of Louisiana. On the way to Gran' Isle with oil wells pumping day and night, Port Fourchon is an important oil town in the great state of Louisiana. Minister Cleveland calls upon his good friend Minister Jones to place the future child with a good family in Lafourche Parish. Leroy never questions why his friend has taken such an interest in the case. He assumes the man is doing the Lord's work. After all, Minister Cleveland is a good and noble man.

Cleveland Alexander is placed in the home of Norma and Jordan Hicks. Jordan Hicks works at an oil refinery. He dies early in the boy's life; an accident at the refinery. Norma is given enough insurance money from the company, which will remain nameless, to raise the boy without sacrificing any material needs. Cleveland Alexander has little need for material possessions. He finds his fulfilment in the teachings of the Bible. He loves spending his days and nights studying with Minister Leroy Jones.

Norma Hicks is proud of her son. She encourages him to attend seminary in Baton Rouge, where he meets the honourable Minister Cleveland. Minister Cleveland takes the boy under his tutelage, treats him like a son, encourages him to find his unique way in the glorious world of ministering. The young man becomes Minister Cleveland's protégé. It is decided that Cleveland Alexander will take over for Minister Cleveland at the appropriate time.

On his deathbed, after a long illness, Minister Cleveland tells his son, Cleveland Alexander, who he is and where he comes from. He does not tell him Rheta B.'s name. Cleveland Alexander discovers that piece of information on a hot, June Louisiana night, in a house filled with family; a family that has been taken care of by his mother, Rheta B., since the day he was born.

Winston walks upstairs, walks into his bedroom, repositions Charlotte's picture, again, opens the safe and removes fifty hundred-dollar bills.

'The boy deserves it. He deserves it!' Winston is bowled over by his immense generosity.

He closes the safe, he locks it, he moves the picture back to its appropriate position. 'How's that, Charlotte? How's that?'

Lily whispers. 'It's the right thing to do. I am proud of you, son. I am so pleased to have made it to your celebration.'

Winston sits on his bed, money in hand. 'Mama? Mama?' As he looks around, as he takes in the room with all of his senses, it seems to Winston, the non-believer, that he and the room should engage in a mystical, albeit macabre, conversation.

'Where's Charlotte, Mama?'

'With your son, Winston.'

'Why are you, what are you doing ... here?' He looks for something recognizable. '*How* are *you* here?'

'It's wonderful to see you, son.'

Winston smells gardenias. 'I don't see how you're ...' He pauses. 'Charlotte's with Theodore?'

'She is. And Doreen is with Joseph. They're in the field together. What a beautiful sight. You should see them.'

'Doreen?' Winston bites his thumbnail. 'Why are you here? Why isn't Charlotte here?'

'Charlotte is busy with Theodore, son. Stop that! A sixty-five-year-old man should not be biting his nails! It's unseemly.'

'It is, isn't it?' Winston wrings his sweaty palms.

'How is your older brother, honey?'

'I have no idea.' Winston wipes his forehead with his sleeve. 'He keeps himself busy. He's always on the road. I really don't know how he is.'

'Take care of him. He needs your help, son.'

Winston begins to pace. 'He needs a different kind of help than I have to give him.'

'Winston!'

'Yes, Mama.' Winston begins to cry.

'Don't cry. Your mama's right here.'

'I need to speak with Charlotte.' He cries harder.

'Talk to me.' Winston covers his ears. 'You can talk to me. I have learned how to listen. Help your brother, Winston. He took such good care of us. Now, we need to take care of him.' Winston looks at Charlotte's picture. Lily says, 'I wish I could hold you. I wish that more than anything in the world.'

'You smell so sweet, Mama. I love that smell.'

'So did your father, son.'

※

Winston hears peals of laughter coming from his study. He

scurries from his bedroom, opens the study door, stands perfectly still, folds his arms and clears his throat.

As fast as they can, the twins tear off Winston's hunting attire. As if he could care less that two reckless teenagers have violated, possibly ruined, his irreplaceable possessions, without so much as moving a muscle or saying a word, Winston watches the commotion without feeling even a smidgen of contempt. Even if his world has been invaded, even if his house rules have been broken, for the first time in his adult life Winston does not raise his voice, does not register any concern, does not give the usual speech about playing with guns, trespassing on private property or damaging irreplaceable hunting equipment. Instead, Winston is mesmerized at the sight of two children at play in his study.

After having undressed down to their underwear, Lily and Billy try to get dressed as quickly as possible. With one sleeve in and one sleeve out Lily says, 'We smell Great-Grandma.'

'It smells like gardenias, especially in your bathroom.' Billy makes a funny face. 'Really weird.' Winston does not say a word.

'We were just playing around. Honest.' Lily looks terrified.

Billy notices Winston's strange behaviour.

'Sorry about the mess,' he says, apologetically.

Lily notices the unusual smile on Winston's face. She smiles.

'Don't worry. We'll clean up the room.'

'Don't bother.' Winston picks up the bits and pieces of hunting gear from the middle of the floor. Methodically, he places each item back inside the closet. Engrossed with the task at hand, he does not see the twins sneak out of the room.

After the youngsters exit, Winston rediscovers his ancient rubber boots. 'I hate to throw them out. They don't make boots like this any more.' He tosses them over his shoulder. 'What a shame.' He opens the closet door, looks inside the closet and sees a beaten-up box on the top shelf. He reaches, but he cannot get a hold of whatever it is. He grabs a chair from the corner of the room. He places the chair in the closet, stands on the chair, grabs the object from the top shelf and steps down with

Theodore's old suitcase in hand. He opens the suitcase. It is empty. He closes it. He steps back onto the chair. He returns the suitcase to the top shelf. He steps down from the chair, returns the chair to its corner position. Winston sits on the chair. He sighs. 'I did the best I could, Charlotte. I did the best I could.'

❈

Rheta B. lies on the four-poster bed in the room that, long ago, was Alice's bedroom; the bedroom where Theodore and Alice played circus games. Of course, Alice was the ringmaster. Young Theodore was the flying young man on top of the bottoms of Alice's feet. Usually, he ended up on the floor in tears. Whenever Rheta heard his cries, she hurried up the stairs and rescued Theodore from the circus.

Theodore and Cleveland Alexander sit at the foot of the bed. They rub Rheta's feet. With an overabundance of love in her heart and a flood of tears in her eyes, she looks from one man to the other. 'How did I get so lucky? The Lord has given me both my boys ... feast my eyes on ... both of you ... at the same time ... in this house ... this house that took me in, when I had nowhere to go; this house where I learned how to take care of myself, how to take care of others, how to cook, how to clean, how to sew and vac. A miracle! So help me God! My boys! My boys are with me! My heart is full with God's great love! I am overwhelmed with God's great and almighty goodness!' Rheta sobs. 'Overwhelmed by a holy grace given me, given *me*, right when I had stopped believin' my heart would ever heal.' Rheta reaches for Theodore and Cleveland. She grabs them. She squeezes them to her bosom. 'When I think about the heartache, the restless nights, the shame, the shame over givin' away my son, my boy, and now, now seein' him all grown up, so handsome, ready to serve God himself, I wanna jump up and sing more praises to the Lord than the Lord has heard in his many lifetimes! And then I see the boy I raised with my two hands, the boy whose mother gave her life, so she could give that boy, my other son, the gift of life, I say,

"Praise be the one who gives us life and takes it away! Praise be him! The Lord our God!'" Rheta catches her breath. 'Let me tell you both somethin'. Whatever happens from here on out makes no difference to me.' Rheta cries once more.

When Cleveland Alexander asks Theodore Faulkner Duvalier, 'What about the tattoo parlour? I thought your mother was with you? "She didn't want to see her favourite son in any pain." I'm pretty sure that's what you said.'

Theodore replies. 'Let's talk about it later.'

'What are you two boys jabberin' 'bout now?' asks Rheta B. 'Nothin',' reply both Theodore Faulkner Duvalier and Cleveland Alexander.

Theodore says, 'Absolutely nothin'.' The two men continue rubbing Rheta B.'s worn-out feet. 'Nothin' at all.' Theodore winks at Cleveland Alexander.

❋

Daphne runs into the sugar fields. Steven Jr runs after her. Daphne shouts. 'Leave me alone! LEAVE ME ALONE!'

'Come on, Daph!' Steven Jr yells. He runs fast. He runs like he has run a thousand times before. But, this time is different. This time he is running *after* someone. This time he is running after Daphne. 'Stop! Goddamn it!' He runs so hard, so fast, but he cannot catch her. She will not let him catch her. Even if he is the fastest man alive, she is going to give him a run for his money. 'I can't let her get away! I can't let her. If I ... keep ... at this ... pace ... I'm ... gonna ... pass ... if I keep ...' He gasps for air. 'I ... can't ... can't ...' He doubles over, tries to catch his breath. '... Can't breathe. Can't brea ...' The air inside his lungs has been sucked into the damp Louisiana night.

Daphne keeps running. 'Leave me the fuck alone, Steven! Go away!' She pleads. 'Please!'

'Daph! Daph! I ... I ...' His knees buckle. He falls in the mud, in the mud-soaked sugar field, like so many have fallen before him.

When he stops, when he falls, Daphne stops. She turns around. She sees Steven on his knees gasping for air. She runs toward him. She runs faster. She gets to him. She falls on her knees. She grabs his hair, smacks his face. 'Get up,' she says. 'Get up!' She grabs his shoulders, shakes him hard, smacks him again and again. She beats on his chest. She screams. 'Get out of my life!' She rips his shirt, digs her fingernails in his face. 'What do you want from me?' she yells. 'What! What do you want from me?!'

Steven Jr tries to speak; his mouth wide open, his words inaudible. He moans. He groans. His jaw goes slack, his body trembles, his face twists in agony. Finally, he passes out in Daphne's arms.

Daphne shrieks. 'Oh no. No! Somebody help! HELP!'

❋

Sugar shouts. 'Help!' Swamp shouts. 'Help!' Jack-o'-lanterns and the many spirits of the night galvanize into unseeable action.

'Get ready!' I holler. 'Everybody! Get ready!'

Sugar chants. 'Bring the boy back! Bring the boy back or all hell will break loose!'

Swamp echoes. 'Break loose!'

I roar, 'Nobody is going back! Somebody is coming home. The boy is coming home! Get the cord ready. Help the boy come home! Get moving. Get moving fast! Make yourselves useful!'

Daphne cries. 'Help! Somebody help me!' She grabs Steven Jr around his waist. She rolls on top of him. She pleads. 'Don't die. Please don't die. We need you! I need you! You are the only hope for this family!'

I holler, 'We need all the help we can get! Doreen, get over here. Now! Charlotte, leave your son! Bring your light where it needs to shine. Lily! Stop throwing your scent around the house. It is time to come back home!'

Daphne kisses Steven Jr on the lips. His lips are stone cold. 'No! No!' She yells at the top of her lungs. 'Somebody!

Anybody! PLEASE!'

Lily finds Winston in the study. 'Daphne needs you, son. I know she's not your blood, but she is your family. Go to the sugar field where we walked together on that night when I told you your father was gone. Go on.'

Winston gets up from the chair, walks down the stairs, walks through the living room into the kitchen. He does not say hello or goodbye to any of the guests. He walks out the back door into the fields. He walks by Jason Stickley. He hears the boy say, 'Hello Winston.' He does not reply. He walks. He walks past Steven. Steven is holding Joseph in his arms. Winston does not see Steven or Joseph. He sees only what is in front of him; acres and acres of sugar fields.

Sugar murmurs, 'They're back here. Right through here.' Winston walks the paths from one sugar field to another.

Sugar sways in the wind. For the first time in his life, Winston notices Sugar's beauty. But, this is not a suitable time for his newfound appreciation. He can only glance at the cane for a moment. He has somewhere to go. He is needed. It *is* an emergency. Winston realizes he is not alone. Lily is beside him. She guides him through the fields. The fields look like oceans upon oceans, waves upon waves, swaying from side to side. A male spirit emerges from the stalk of the cane. The spirit walks toward Winston.

'Carter Duvalier? Is that you?' asks Lily.

'It certainly is, my dear sweet Lily.'

'Don't you my dear sweet Lily me! What the hell are you doing here?'

'I thought I might help.'

Lily laughs. Sugar laughs. Swamp laughs. I do not laugh.

'When have you ever helped anyone but yourself?'

'There's always a first time, even for a dead man.' Carter burst out laughing.

Sugar, Swamp and I say, 'Let him come. Let his spirit come. We need all the help we can get.'

Winston finds Daphne. She is rocking back and forth. Steven Jr is wrapped in her arms. Winston separates them. He takes one look at the young man. He knows the young man is gone. 'Come on, Daphne. Let me take care of this.' He takes her hands in his, kisses them, looks into her eyes. 'Sometimes, we can't help those we love the most.' Winston cries. He remembers his last moments with Charlotte. He remembers how he prayed and prayed to some great unknowable force, even though, at that time, he was a non-believer.

Swamp knows, Sugar knows, I know how difficult these passings are for those left behind, how difficult it is for the body and the soul that are being wrenched apart by the ultimate force. These things of life transforming into death are not easy. These things are not easy for Lily, Doreen and Charlotte. They feel the pain; their own pain, as well as the pain of every single member of the family; each member of the family, who for his or her individual reasons, will not be able to accept Steven Jr's shocking death. If there is a God, why would God do such a horrible thing to them, to him, to those who know and love him? If there is a God, why would God snatch their hero from his heights, take him far away into some world beyond their grasp, beyond their gaze, beyond their adoration? If there is a God, damn him and his band of angels for their ferocious appetite that eventually devours those who worship the Lord and its messengers.

As if nothing unusual has happened, the party continues. Rheta B. talks with her boys. Joseph confides in Steven about his heartache, about his guilt. Steven confides in Joseph about the heartache he has endured since Doreen's death. His guilt does not enter into his side of the conversation. He will never confess his sexual trespasses to his father-in-law. Confessing would be unthinkable. The football team is feeling no pain. Alice sits at the piano like she has done so many times before. She plays 'Lakes of Pontchartrain'. She dedicates her performance to Chris and Daphne. Carter Jr and Faith talk with Melanie and Bud about the numerous problems at Pine Grove. Lily and Billy walk around upstairs trying to figure out where the gardenias are and how is it possible that Winston's house smells like Great-Grandma Lily? How is such a phenomenon possible? It is definitely a family affair, save for a few football players who, unbeknownst to them, have lost their star quarterback.

❊

Eventually, someone tells someone, who tells someone else about Steven Jr's death. People weep, sob and scream. Faith and Carter Jr run out the back door into the fields. They run as hard and as fast as they can run, running toward the most unbearable sight, running to mourn the death of their only son. Faith falls. Carter Jr picks her up. He holds her tight. He whispers. 'We will get through this. We will get through this, together. I promise. I promise.' As he strokes her hair, caresses her cheek, he prays for guidance from the unknown forces that have taken his son.

Everyone gathers in the field. Winston stands next to the body. Theodore walks toward the body. Winston steps aside. Theodore leans over Steven Jr's limp body. Theodore kneels. He holds Steven Jr in his arms. He says, 'We will have that talk one day.' Theodore kisses Steven Jr's hand. 'I love you, boy.' He asks himself, 'How could this happen to you? Why couldn't I stop it?' He chokes on his tears. 'I hope you will find ...' He stops crying just long enough to murmur, 'I know you *will* find some peace. Somewhere.' After a long moment, Theodore stands up. He walks over to Daphne. 'I'm right here, Daph. Not goin' anywhere.' He takes her in his arms, kisses the top of her head. 'Not goin' anywhere.'

'You promise?'

'Cross my heart and hope to ...'

Daphne gently places her hand over Theodore's mouth.

'Don't.' Theodore kisses her hand.

❋

The forces of birth and death work to ready the soul for its journey. Spirits gather around the body. Sugar, Swamp and I direct the proceedings. Sugar, Swamp, nymphs and spirits release the young man's physical body from its spirit body. Though Steven Jr is dead, his beauty is not diminished. His spirit body is free. His spirit is ready for the long journey ahead.

I ask Lily, Doreen and Charlotte to wrap a fine filament throughout the spirit body. Charlotte remembers how she felt when she passed from this world to my world; an indescribable feeling. She remembers it well.

Carter Sr whispers something to Winston. Winston walks over to Faith and Carter Jr. Winston says, 'There was nothing anyone could have done to save your boy. Nothing. Your boy had a weak heart.' Winston breaks down. 'I'm so sorry, so sorry for your loss.' He does not mention the drugs. He embraces his nephew, embraces his nephew's wife. What else can he do to help them through their unbearable despair? Winston embraces his brother, Steven. Steven embraces his son, Carter Jr. Carter Jr embraces Faith, strokes her hair, kisses her moist eyes, while Faith endures the greatest sadness of her life.

Carter Sr watches over his flock. For the first time in his many lives, he feels the pain, the suffering of a family ravaged by misfortunes; many of those misfortunes caused by him. But, it is too late to worry about that now.

❋

I direct Lily, Doreen and Charlotte. 'Ladies, get ready for the ride back to Afterworld. Remember, you must hold onto the filament wrapped around the boy's body.' Because of the family's grief, the ladies beg to stay behind. I clarify what they were not aware of before their visit home. 'This is how you help your family. You help Steven Jr on his journey. That is why you came back. That is why you must go.'

'I don't want to go!' Charlotte releases the thread.

'There was a time you would not stay. Things have progressed, haven't they, Charlotte?' I place Charlotte's translucent hands on the filament, on the filament of light. 'Lily, please read from *The Book of Wisdom*. Lead the prayer for those of us who make our home in the spirit world. You know the prayer. You have said the prayer so many times before.'

As the three Duvaliers leave the weary, wondrous world behind, as they travel with Steven Jr's spirit in their divine hands, Lily recites the verse.

> *But the just man, though he die early, shall be at rest.*
> *For the age that is honourable comes not with the passing of*
> *time, nor can it be measured in terms of years.*

As Lily continues her prayer, Charlotte looks back. What she sees and hears is beyond her understanding. What she recognizes is the beauty in all things done and undone.

❋

Winston, who has never recited this or any other verse, leads his family in prayer. He recites: '*Having become perfect in a short while, he reached the fullness of a long career …*'

Winston continues to pray. He continues to support his family and his brother's family long into the night, long into the next day and beyond.

❋

Carter Sr watches from afar. Before dawn, when the spirits begin to disappear into the swamp, Carter Sr disappears into Sugar's fields. He understands that his bereaved family will soon bury their hero. They will weep endless tears. Questions will be asked. How did it happen? Why did it happen? What could we have done? As the family asks these unanswerable questions, Carter

Sr leaves the world of family behind. Once again he becomes part of Sugar's natural world; the world he nearly destroyed those many years ago.

It is early morning. Winston stands alone in the sugar field. To his amazement he *still* finds the field beautiful. He takes a good long look around him. He notices an orange package lying in the field. He picks it up. It has his name on it. '*For Winston*'. He unties the bow, opens the package, peeks inside. As if he hasn't cried enough, Winston cries some more. When he sees Steven Jr's football jersey, Winston cries like he has never cried before.

BOOK III

END OF DAYS

Charlotte, with a melancholy as vast as the universe, gazes at the many moons in the many skies. 'More than sixty some odd moons, more than sixty some odd suns, millions upon millions of shooting stars, thousands upon thousands of orbiting planets, hundreds of high tides, just as many low tides, stillness, commotion, nothingness and everythingness; all this has come and gone and come and gone, again and again in the last lost period of time. Why haven't I seen another soul? Why hasn't Afterworld uttered my name, paid me a visit or even sent a request for my services? Where's Steven Jr? Why can't I help in his healing? There must be a rule forbidding me from searching for a soul, until that soul is ready to find me – or until our meeting serves some greater purpose, which is the reason why Lily, Doreen and I found each other. We found each other for the *greater purpose* of getting Steven Jr into this godforsaken place. So why, why when the purpose was served, why couldn't the three Duvaliers still be together? Stupid rules! Damn you Afterworld! Damn you and your rules!'

Oh dear me.

'I haven't caught a glimpse of Theodore, not once since my return. I can't focus. I can't stop thinking about how fabulous it was being with him. I would rather see him than witness all these changing days and nights, shooting stars and orbiting planets. There was a time, not long ago, I loved shooting stars. I loved feeling the changing tides. I loved watching the many universes as they danced in the sky like drunken fireflies on a hot Louisiana night in the bayou. But, if I can't see my son, why should I care about these countless universes and their mysterious ways?'

I shout! 'Tropical depression in the southeastern Bahamas! *Ferocious trajectory*! We have six days. There will be massive destruction. Victims of the storm will enter through a designated portal. Those of you who will be called to serve, please follow the rose scent. The scent will lead you into the service entrance. Duvalier women reunite! Your rest is complete. Your work will be arduous. You will witness death, grief and untold fear in many you love. Many souls from my realm will return to Louisiana. Unfortunately, Duvaliers are needed here. There is no going back for any of you. I am terribly sorry about the catastrophic situation. When it comes to Mother Nature's erratic ways, nothing, in any realm, can change her feckless, fickle behaviour.'

Charlotte, Lily and Doreen enter from parallel paths. Thrilled to smell each other again, they cherish the finite time they will have together.

The tropical depression strengthens into a storm. The storm lands in south Florida, where it becomes a category one hurricane. It twists and turns, it doubles in size. It lands in the Gulf, where it gains major hurricane status. The wind speed reaches over 170 mph. When the storm hits Gran' Isle, nobody is dancing. When you need to evacuate an island, dancing is the last thing on your mind.

At eight a.m. on August 29th the hurricane lands in New Orleans with wind speed over 125mph. And the walls come tumbling down. As a result of three levee failures, at one point eighty per cent of New Orleans is under water. New Orleans has been under water before; she will be under water again. Whoever heard of building such a beautiful city ... below sea level?

Lake Pontchartrain overflows. Listen. Someone is singing. *'Through swamps and elevations my tired feet did stray.'* Someone is singing about the lake. They will write songs about this disaster. That is what they do in Louisiana; make music out of misery.

Because of a storm surge caused by onshore winds, parts of

New Orleans are under twenty feet of water; bridges under water, roads under water, Interstate 10 leading east under water, covered with debris. Travel is impossible; no getting in or getting out of New Orleans. If you have not left, you are stuck in hell. Those poor black people in the Ninth Ward are stuck, hanging on rooftops. Hundreds of citizens are washed away in polluted waters. They make their sudden crossing into my world, where magnificent souls assist in their hour of transition. Desperate hands reach out to unseen angels. Victims scream, moan, gasp, until finally they take their final breath.

I yell. 'Lift them! Carry them! Wrap them in a web of light! Bring them to the portal! Bring them home! When they arrive, they will be healed!'

As the blues comes to roost in God's hallowed halls across the city, parishioners wail. They grieve for the sudden loss of loved ones. There will be no goodbyes. There will be sorrow for years to come. Once again, New Orleans will be a deeply wounded city.

Oil rigs in the Gulf are sucked under by an unforgiving current. Enormous barges float loose in Lake Charles. Wherever the eye can see, there is destruction for miles and miles. This natural disaster is beyond man's measly comprehension. Many Bible-beating zealots shout, 'End of Days! The End of Days!'

Forest land destroyed, beaches and shorelines eroded beyond repair, breeding grounds for birds decimated, turtles washed away, fish washed away, a world washed away inside nature's tears. Hospitals flooded, windows blown out, glass flies through the air, torrents of water filled with shards of glass strewn in all directions.

Her name is Katrina. Her name will be officially retired from the book of records at the request of the government. Amen.

Lily, Doreen and Charlotte stand at the service portal. They guide many lost souls through their sudden transition. They guide them from that world of walls, that world of familiar structures into my world without walls, my world without the familiar reminders of what they left behind.

I invite the newcomers into their unfamiliar surroundings. 'Smell where you are. Smell your way into the infinite. Do not be afraid. Let my guides take you to your resting place. Rest well. Soon, *you* will lead others to their resting place.'

At eight a.m. on Monday, August 29th, 2005, when Katrina hits the Gulf Coast, Joseph grabs his retired machete from underneath his bed. He throws open the screen door, staggers into the sugar fields in the pouring rain. He is naked. His body is covered with bedsores. The rain pelts against his skin. Soaked to the bone, he gazes at the sugar.

Sugar sways. She swoons, she bends, she breaks in the wind. 'That hurts.' Sugar says, 'Welcome Joseph.' She invites Joseph to remember what he has, without success, tried to forget. 'Look through the raindrops. Listen to the wind. Look at me. Look at you. We were in love. We will always be in love. Of all the men who have lain with me in my fields, I love you more than any other. Because *you*, with your machete in hand, cut *me* to the quick, so *I* grew to be beautiful again and again. You were the best lover.' Sugar seduces Joseph. 'My magnificent Joseph. The time has come. Remember the drama you witnessed, the drama you experienced in my fine-looking fields.' Sugar whispers. 'Remember.'

Joseph recalls the remarkable night, the night during the hurricane, the night when he ran in the hammering rain, when he ran to Lily, when he told her that her husband Carter was dead. He remembers how he touched Lily's shoulders with his filthy hands. He remembers how she kissed his hands. She kissed him. Lily kissed Joseph. They made love in the rain. In between the stalks, in the mud, naked in Sugar's soaked fields, they made love until dawn.

Sugar moans. 'There, there. Feel your body tremble. Feel me as I break under the weight of your body. Listen to me. Sugar *still* loves you, Joseph. Lily loves you, but Maria is waiting. Maria will forever be the one who is waiting.'

Joseph cries, 'Maria! Forgive me! I am foolish. I am a foolish man!' With all his might Joseph throws his machete into the bloated fields. The machete vanishes. In vain he tries to find it. He yells. 'Goddamn it!' Suddenly, he turns around. Someone is watching him. 'Who's there? Who's watching?!'

'It's you, Joseph. You're watching. You're walking on the edge of my field. It's such a beautiful, hot, sunny, June day. Remember the day, Joseph? Do you remember that day? Theodore's running in the field. You hear his feet crushing my cane. You hear his ecstatic voice. His voice fills you with joy. He throws his shirt high up in the air. You watch it as it falls. Finally, you see Theodore. He runs and runs until he disappears into my hot, sultry field.'

Joseph remembers the hot June day. He remembers hearing a man's voice, a familiar voice. He remembers two figures running in the field, two figures rolling in the field. He remembers the boy's laughter.

Theodore laughs so loud. Sugar laughs with him. 'Uncle Steven, listen to the sugar. It's laughing. It's laughing.'

'Sugar loves it when you run in between her stalks. She loves it when we roll in her fields. Sugar loves us when we play, together.'

'I love you Uncle Steven.' Theodore jumps on top of Steven. Steven wraps his arm around Theodore. They roll and roll in Sugar's fields. They stop rolling. Joseph hears Theodore moan. Joseph stands perfectly still on the edge of the field. When Steven touches Theodore, Joseph turns away. He turns away for a moment, then he turns back. He watches. He does not stop Steven. He watches. He sees everything. He will never tell anyone, never tell anyone that the man who married his daughter has touched Charlotte's boy. He will never tell anyone that this man, who is his son-in-law, who is the son of the woman Joseph loves more than any other woman

in the world, has touched Theodore. Joseph will go to his grave with the shame of these two secrets embedded in his soul.

Joseph begins to cry. 'I have sinned. I have ruined lives. I wanted what wasn't mine.' Sugar wraps herself around Joseph's body. 'I am not a man. I am a coward.'

'Hush. Hush. Your secrets are safe with me.'

Maria appears. She kisses Joseph's hand. She begins winding the filament around his body. 'Come. It is time,' she says.

'Oh Maria. I have missed you. I love you.' Maria finishes her weaving. As Hurricane Katrina wreaks havoc in Joseph's fields of memory, Joseph begins his long journey home.

When Joseph and Maria arrive at the portal, Lily and Doreen are waiting. Charlotte is busy with other chores.

At nine a.m. on August 29th, when Katrina touches down near Napoleonville, Louisiana, Winston walks out of his house onto the porch. He wears Steven Jr's football jersey. He sits in a rocking chair; getting wetter and wetter by the minute. He rocks harder and faster. He is nonplussed by the hurricane. He enjoys the wind, the rain, the pounding on the roof, the flooding in the fields. Until this hurricane, Winston barely noticed the beauty of weather's destruction. 'There is something to respect and admire in a low pressure system,' thinks Winston. 'Low pressure made Charlotte crazy. Not me. Never me.'

Winston's favourite hunting hat blows off the porch. 'Why risk my neck for that stupid hat. Right, Charlotte?' Ever since the party, Winston imagines himself in intimate conversation with Charlotte. 'Aren't I right, Charlotte?'

'Hello, Winston.' Charlotte leans against the railing. She gazes at the soaking-wet field.

Winston rocks back and forth in Lily's antique rocker. He rocks so hard the rocker nearly tumbles down the porch steps. 'I missed you at the party.' He rocks harder still. 'Mama told me you spent some time with Theodore.'

'I did.'

'Theodore never told me anything about it.' Winston clears his throat.

'How could he? You hardly speak to the boy.'

'He's not a boy any more, Charlotte. He is a thirty-five-year-old man.' Winston takes off his rain boots. He throws them over the railing. 'What's the point? How's Mama?'

'Fine.'

'How's Doreen? Are you all having a good time in ... wherever?'

'I wouldn't call it a good time.' A gust of wind rips some shingles loose from the roof.

Winston rocks harder still. He is soaked. 'I bet the Atchafalaya's going to flood like mad today. Those marshes are going to be one hell of a mess. You still love the Atchafalaya, don't you?'

'I do.'

'Those were good times.' Winston begins to daydream about the good ol' days in the Atchafalaya. He conjures up a peregrine falcon or two. 'I loved those birds. We had good times, didn't we?' Winston waits for a response. 'Didn't we?' He wipes the rain from his eyes. 'I can still see you looking through your binoculars, looking at those peregrine falcons, lying on that ugly green and black blanket your mother gave you.'

'She *made* that blanket with her own two hands!' Charlotte sighs. 'She never *made* anything else.'

'She made plenty of trouble.' Winston laughs. 'She sure didn't like me much.' He mutters, 'Real pain in my ass.'

'What did you say?'

'Real pain in my ass! Your mother.' Winston takes off his new waterproof rain slicker and heaves it over the side of the porch. 'When it rains this hard, all the newfangled rain gear doesn't keep you dry. I was going to return it. There's one less thing I have to do.' Winston gets up from the rocker. He walks toward the railing. He smells Charlotte, but cannot quite figure out her exact location. He strokes the railing. He talks to the railing as if it were Charlotte. 'Did you ever love me, Charlotte?'

'Oh, Winston. Let's not have that conversation again.'

'Did you?'

'I wouldn't have married you if I didn't love you.'

'I don't understand. Why were you so unhappy?'

'Winston! This is the last time you are going to have *this* absurd, absolutely bizarre conversation with yourself. Is that clear?' Winston shrugs his shoulders. 'I never wanted to have children. I didn't want to be a mother. *You* made me a mother, Winston. It was your fault. I hated taking care of you and Alice. I loved you both, but I didn't want to be a doctor's wife, stuck in the sticks, hanging out laundry on a hot humid day, where nothing would ever dry. It seemed stupid. I wanted my mother's life. I wanted freedom, freedom to explore the whole wide world. You shrunk my world, Winston! I longed for private time in the swamp, by myself! You insisted on coming with me! I wasn't interested in sharing those beautiful birds with you or anyone else. They were my birds! You acted like they were your birds! I hated it. That's what killed me, Winston. Hate. I'm sorry I hated you, but I did. I am sorry. I loved you, too. I loved Alice. Where is Alice?'

Winston is crying. 'She's in New York with the kids. They're staying at Theodore's apartment.' He sits down on the porch step, picks up a piece of roofing and flings it into the air. He wipes his eyes with his wet sleeve. 'Damn rain burns my eyes. The kids wanted to see some stupid show about a lion.'

'Where's Steven?'

'I don't know. He's probably travelling; another one of his funny business trips. I can't keep up with his shenanigans.'

'In the middle of a hurricane?'

'I guess so.'

'Honestly, Winston, he's your brother. Where's Theodore?'

'Don't you already know where everybody is?'

'Not really.'

'Port Fourchon. Your son is with Cleveland Alexander in Port Fourchon. Can you beat that? Rheta B.'s long-lost son shows up, out of the blue, next thing you know he and your son become bosom buddies. Isn't that something special?'

'Very.'

'That boy of yours is so much like you, it scares me to death.' Winston laughs so hard he nearly falls off the step.

'Be careful.'

'He's a good boy. Your son. The kids like him a lot. He might move back home one day and take care of his old man.'

'You never know what *might* happen.' Charlotte disappears. Winston sits on the bottom porch step. He catches raindrops with his tongue.

Another piece of roofing falls to the ground. Winston picks it up, he plays with it, he talks to it. 'Crazy. It is getting crazy around here.'

✻

At ten a.m. on August 29th, long after Katrina has hit New Orleans, Steven Duvalier looks at himself in the cracked bathroom mirror of the Hyatt Regency Hotel. He asks himself, 'What have I done with my life?'

At the same time, in the same hotel room, while Steven asks one unbearable question, Jason Stickley, crouched crying in the corner of the room with bad art strewn around him, scared out of his pants, asks a similar excruciating question. 'What am I doing with my life?'

While these two men are trapped inside the Hyatt Regency Hotel, during the unrelenting storm, the question that torments them both is how will either one of them escape when there is absolutely nowhere to go.

Steven Duvalier and Jason Stickley made plans. This was to be a celebration, a six-month celebration of their ongoing, clandestine relationship; a relationship that an entire football team, one priest and members on both sides of the family were aware of and repulsed by.

On August 28th Steven and Jason check into the Hyatt Regency; the fabulous New Orleans hotel situated next to Louisiana's pride and joy, the Superdome. Even though Steven and Jason know a major hurricane is fast approaching, it is vital they follow through with their celebratory agenda.

Steven's personal agenda is to ask Jason, who is forty-eight years his junior, to move in with him. As if that weren't enough for young Jason to consider, Steven is ready to offer the lad a permanent position at Pine Grove Plantation. They will travel together. Jason will tend to Steven's sexual needs and more important than that, Jason will help Steven sell sugar. As far as Steven is concerned, Jason is the necessary ingredient for Pine Grove's future success. Within the next two years, when Steven retires, Jason will take over the business. Even if Jason is not particularly smart, he is beautiful. Jason Stickley is the most beautiful male Steven has encountered anywhere on earth. Steven dreams about the future. *'Carter Jr will welcome Jason into the family business with open arms. I'm sure of it. He won't argue against a smart decision. Anyway, I'm the boss.'* At the beginning of August, with nothing but ulterior motives, Steven makes the reservation. Jason agrees to the plan.

Jason Stickley has an entirely different personal agenda. He is going to tell Steven, once and for all, he can no longer *be* with him. Jason does not want to *be* with a man. He has mended his wicked ways. His priest has warned him, 'It is a sin to sleep with someone of the same sex.' It is a sin to sleep with someone of the opposite sex, out of wedlock, but sleeping with someone of the same sex, *ever*, is a far greater sin. *'You will be damned for life. Purgatory forever!'* That is what the priest said. *'Damned for life! There will be no salvation. No salvation!'* For almost a month the priest's words have echoed in Jason's head, keeping him up nights, making it impossible for him to focus during football practice. Jason is terrified by his sin.

When Jason's father finds out about Jason's affair with Steven

Duvalier, he beats the living daylights out of his son. The day after his father beats the living daylights out of his son, Jason arrives at football practice with a black eye and bruises on his behind. Jason tells the coach, 'I've had a fall. I fell on some gravel.' Even though the coach is concerned, even though the coach knows gravel does not bruise like that, the coach is aware those bruises are none of his business. Jason's coach has known, for a very long time that Jason is queer, but, that, too, is none of his business. What matters to the coach is that Jason is one heck of a wide receiver.

When the hurricane hits the Hyatt Regency Hotel, Jason and Steven are ... fucking so hard, they barely realize what is happening around them. When the windows blow out on the north side of the hotel, Jason and Steven become aware of the seriousness of the situation, personal and otherwise. Neither has a clue that the roof has been shaved off the Superdome, that New Orleans is under water or that they are in harm's way. What they *do* understand is that they are stuck on the top floor, stuck in a room without electricity or water, stuck on the south side of the Hyatt Hotel, stuck in the middle of a natural disaster without anywhere to go. If that is not Purgatory, then what is?

Steven picks up the phone. 'Hello. Hello,' he screams, 'Hello!' The phone is dead.

As if he were possessed, Jason screams. 'It's wrong! What we're doing is wrong!' He begins to cry.

Steven tries, without success, to calm Jason. 'Shh. Shh. Don't be silly, sweet boy. Come back here. Nothing's wrong. I promise.' Steven tries to stroke Jason's curly head of hair. Jason pulls away. 'You are such a beautiful boy.' Jason cries. Steven pleads. 'Please don't cry. I love you.'

Jason pulls away. 'I can't do it any more! After the hurricane, I don't want to see you again. Ever!'

Jason hears the priest's voice. *'Damned for life.'*

'*Damned for life.*' Those were the words Steven's priest said those many years ago. '*Damned for life.*' Those are the words that one priest, after another priest, after another priest say to boys and men the world over; men who walk into the confessional looking for comfort and advice. '*Damned for life.*' Those words are their comfort.

Jason Stickley does not want to be damned for life. 'I can't. I can't.' Hundreds of windows shatter on the north side of the hotel.

Steven tries desperately to console Jason. 'It's not a sin. I promise. To love is never a sin.'

Jason pulls away. 'Get away from me! You dirty old man! Get away! You smell! You smell sick. You are sick!' Because he is so much stronger than Steven, Jason gets free in an instant. In the dark of the hurricane's light, Jason looks around the room, finds his pants, grabs his shirt, grabs his jockey shorts, throws his clothes on, runs for the door, opens it, looks out into the waterlogged corridor, where he sees people running every which way. He wonders where the hell is he going to go, slams the door behind him, stands frozen in front of the door and glares at Steven. 'Where the hell am I going to go? Tell me? Where do I go now!? You've ruined me!' Jason bursts out crying. Again. Because he does not know where to run, he runs to Steven; the only devil he knows.

Steven insists that Jason crouch in the corner, the corner of their honeymoon suite. Jason will be safe. No more art can fall off the walls. All of the fine art has already fallen onto the floor.

Steven runs into the bathroom. He picks up the house phone. The phone is dead. Steven looks in the mirror. He looks dead.

He feels dead. He asks himself, '*What have I done with my life? Oh Doreen, what have I done?*'

Jason curls up in a blanket on the floor of the Honeymoon Suite of the Hyatt Hotel. He asks himself, 'What have I done? What have I done?'

As the personal drama unfolds at the Hyatt Regency Hotel,

the personal lives of thousands of people, running in the streets of New Orleans will forever be changed. Many unsuspecting citizens of the ravaged city ask themselves, *'What have we done to deserve this hell?'*

For years to come, the Hyatt Regency Hotel will remain closed. For weeks on end the Superdome will house those with nowhere to go, nowhere to go unless they head for Houston, find a new home, make a new life and start all over again. How do you do that? When you have no choice, you do what you need to do.

Steven and Jason will wait out the hurricane. This tragic day will mark the end of their unfortunate affair. For their friends, for their families, for an entire football team and for many religious counsellors, the end will be a great relief.

Sixteen to eighteen per cent of all oil pumped, poured or pipelined through the United States of America comes through Port Fourchon, the southernmost port in Louisiana, which is located in the Gulf of Mexico, in Lafourche Parish. In these parts of the Gulf there are at least six hundred oil platforms with men working overtime day and night. If Port Fourchon gets hit by a hurricane, everyday life turns upside down, because everyday life requires a great deal of oil and its by-products. If weather causes serious damage in the Gulf, which is an all too common occurrence, Minerals Management Service will swoop down and evacuate every single person in and around the area. Gas prices can triple over night, the salt marshes and barrier islands can be destroyed and many hundreds of people can die in an instant, like Carter Sr died, those many years ago, in New Orleans. When a hurricane is about to hit the Louisiana coastline, all eyes are on Port Fourchon.

In 2002 Hurricane Lily caused 882 million dollars worth of damage: 121 oil platforms and forty-two rigs were evacuated, salt marshes and barrier reefs were, in fact, destroyed and crops, especially the sugar-cane crop, were damaged. Sugar-cane damage totalled over 175 million dollars. Lily was a nasty hurricane. She was the worst hurricane of that year.

On August 28th, 2005, because of the memory left from Hurricane Lily, the good folk of Port Fourchon pray for the Good Lord's mercy. They anxiously await the arrival of yet another devastating hurricane, Hurricane Katrina.

※

At eleven a.m. on August 29th, in a small white wooden house in Port Fourchon, Cleveland Alexander Hicks, his mother, Mrs Norma Hicks, a vibrant seventy-year-old woman, and Theodore Faulkner Duvalier are seated at the kitchen table. As the lights flicker and the weather threatens to destroy their convivial game of Scrabble, a competitive feeling fills the air. Challenged by mother and son, Theodore looks up the word 'denary' in a beaten-up 1966 edition of the *Random House Dictionary*. The dictionary takes up an enormous space on the already cluttered kitchen table.

Cleveland Alexander is dumbfounded. 'Where'd you dig up that word?'

Theodore laughs. 'LSU was good for somethin'. When I wasn't daydreamin' in class, which I did most of the time, I memorized words in the dictionary. Assumed it would stimulate my under-stimulated brain from atrophy. In my four years of college I almost made it through the Ds.'

Norma scratches her head. 'What's that word mean? "Denary." Looks wrong, whatever it means.'

Theodore leafs through the dictionary. He finds the word.

'Here it is.' He reads. 'Relating to a number system that has ten as its base, as in the decimal system.' Theodore closes the dictionary. He gloats. Norma Hicks and her son Cleveland Alexander push back their chairs.

'Theodore, I don't think I want to play with you any more,'

says Norma. 'You are way too smart for me.'

'Don't be silly. I'm only good through D. I'm a misery with the rest of the alphabet.' Theodore is embarrassed by his good memory. 'Hard to believe I remembered that word.'

'Don't get shy on me. My boy's told me all about you. He didn't say anything about you bein' shy. Did you, honey?' Norma winks at her son.

Cleveland Alexander looks at the board. 'He's killin' us, Mama. It's a bloodbath.'

Norma Hicks listens to the pounding rain on the tin roof. 'I remember Lily. She was much worse than this hurricane. That hurricane scared me to death.'

'Theodore's grandmother's name was Lily. Wasn't it, babe?'

Theodore blushes. He closes the dictionary. 'Uh huh.'

Cleveland Alexander gets up, walks over to the kitchen counter, picks up a pitcher of lemonade and pours some liquid into his empty glass. On his way back to the table he squeezes Theodore's shoulder, then sits down.

'My father called her "Spider Lily". She drove him crazy.' Theodore pushes back his chair. The chair tilts precariously on its hind legs. 'Drove him absolutely crazy.' He straightens out the chair. 'When I was a child, it was Lily and Rheta B. who raised me. Rheta B. was kind and gentle. Lily, Lily was another story altogether. She scared me to death. Mmm mmm mm. She was tough. You couldn't pull the slightest thing over on her. I tried many times.' Theodore gets up, walks over to the pitcher and pours the lemonade into his glass. He stares at the rain outside the kitchen window. '"Tough as nails." That's what my father said about her. "Tough as nails." But, when I was an infant, if I cried, she picked me up, kissed my tears and then, apparently, she melted like butter. That's what my sister tells me anyway.' Theodore sits down. He wipes the bottom of the glass with his shirt sleeve, then sets the glass on the table. 'I do miss her. She bossed me around, made me pick up after myself, taught me to be respectful to whoever or whatever I came in contact with in the world.' Theodore picks four tiles from the Scrabble box. 'And, oh my goodness, did she love sugar! Loved those fields! Loved 'em! She taught me to love sugar.' He sighs. 'That's for sure.'

Norma is touched. 'She sounds like a wonderful woman. You were lucky to have such a powerful lady lookin' after you when you were growing up. It's not easy for a boy without his mother.' Theodore place the tiles neatly on his Scrabble stand. Norma scrutinizes his every move. Finally, she asks her next question. 'How old were you when your mama died?'

Cleveland gives Norma a dirty look. 'Mama!'

'I'm curious, son. That's all.' Norma takes Theodore's hand. 'You don't mind me askin', do you?'

'She died when I was born.'

Norma is taken aback. 'Oh my goodness! I am so sorry.' Theodore takes a swig from his glass. 'That is terrible.' Norma gets up from the table. 'You know what they say, don't you?' She walks over to the counter, tries pouring herself some lemonade. The pitcher is empty. 'What a shame. No more lemons and nobody is goin' out shoppin' in this weather. I'll drink water.' She opens the refrigerator door, she grabs a pitcher, she pours, then closes the refrigerator door. She sits at the table. She sets the glass on top of the dictionary. Finally, she drinks until the glass is empty. She looks at Theodore. 'When a mother dies while giving birth, it is considered a miracle, a blessing. The child who comes in on the wings of an angel is blessed. Those who have the privilege of knowing the child are also blessed. Even though there is enormous grief, it is an *even* exchange. One soul is taken so another can be born.' Norma gets up from the table, walks over to the sink and washes her glass. The lights flicker. 'Didn't they teach you that in Seminary, son?'

Cleveland Alexander shakes his head. 'Where'd you learn that, Mama?'

'Here and there. Nowhere special. Here and there.' She looks at Theodore. She waits for him to acknowledge what she has told him.

Theodore plays with his tiles, continuously moving them from one end of the Scrabble stand to the other end. He does not look at either Cleveland Alexander or Norma Hicks. 'A lot of wonderful women had a hand in raisin' me; Rheta B. protected me from my big sister. My big sister could be mean.' Theodore whispers, 'Meaner than a coiled snake in a bad mood.' He remembers where he heard that phrase. 'Actually, that's what my father said about my Grandma Lily. Truth is my father hated everyone. Rheta B. told me I *had* to forgive him, said he was missin' my mama so much, he couldn't help his behaviour.'

'Theodore. You were a lucky boy. You were blessed by the love of many women. Men don't know how to nurture like women do. When Cleveland Alexander lost his father, it was horrible, but he had me to help him, teach him, dress him, love him and now, look at my boy. My boy is goin' to serve in the House of the Lord. Amen.'

Cleveland Alexander gives Norma a big hug. 'Amen.'

'And to think one of the women who raised you is my boy's blood mother and here you two are thick as thieves. Now, if that's not a miracle, I don't know what is.' Norma stands up. 'Let's go to church.' She puts on her hat. 'Let's give thanks for the many riches we have been given.' Even if it is raining cats and dogs and the wind is howling at the back door, both men realize they had better walk Norma to the House of the Lord.

Theodore pulls on his cap. Before he leaves the house, he picks up the receiver on the wall phone. The phone is dead. Norma holds the kitchen door ajar. 'Who are you callin', son?'

'Melanie.'

'Whoever she is, you won't be callin' her tonight.'

Theodore hangs up the phone. 'My mother's mother. My other grandmother. She lives in Baton Rouge.'

'You have *another* woman in your life? Tell me *all* about her on the way to church. There's a whole lot to learn about you, Theodore. You have got layers and layers of secrets inside that heart of yours. Don't you?'

After Theodore and Cleveland Alexander have left the house, Norma Hicks closes the kitchen door. 'Good-lookin' boy,' she says to herself. 'Nice boy. Not playin' Scrabble with him again.' Norma steps in a puddle. 'Damn.' She reopens the door, grabs an umbrella, then closes the door. Theodore and her son are halfway down the street. 'Hey, you two! Wait up!'

Cleveland Alexander, Theodore Faulkner Duvalier and Norma Hicks walk down the middle of the street in the middle of a hurricane. They hurry to the church where Minister Leroy Jones (the minister who, many years ago, found Cleveland Alexander a good home) will lead his congregation in prayers of hope and survival for the good people of Louisiana and the good people of the world. Tonight will be Leroy's last sermon. In the early morning, on August 30th, Minister Leroy Jones dies peacefully in his sleep after a long and illustrious career serving the good people of Port Fourchon.

At noon on August 29th in Baton Rouge, Louisiana, as usual during a hurricane, there is no electricity. Bud and Melanie Brickman's condominium is dark. Bud is taking advantage of the storm. He is fast asleep on his recliner. Melanie and Rheta B. are seated together on the couch. Except for the beam of light emanating from the two-pound, yellow and green, all-purpose Maglite Melanie holds in one hand, as she turns the pages of her favourite photo album with the other hand, it is dark and gloomy in the living room.

Even if Rheta B. has seen each picture at least one thousand times over the last thirty-five years, she acts as if it were her first viewing. It is, in fact, her first viewing with a Maglite. 'Melanie's Movie House,' Rheta says, 'When you look at these pictures with a spotlight, it's like you were sittin' in a movie house at a world premiere watchin' *Gone with the Wind*. Hold on a second! You turn those pages so fast, I can't keep up with you.'

'Sorry. I look at these pictures all the time. They remind me how to remember. Theodore loves my photo album. I wonder where those boys are?'

'I believe they're with Cleveland Alexander's mother.'

'Rheta! You're Cleveland Alexander's mother. What you mean is the boys are with Cleveland Alexander's *adopted* mother.'

'You're right, Miss Melanie. His *adopted* mother.' Rheta grabs Melanie's hand. She kisses it. 'I love you and your family so much. I love the Duvaliers.' She looks straight into Melanie's eyes. 'So many sad things happen in life. Lord tests those who walk through the fire in spite of the flame,' Rheta cries. 'So sad about Steven Jr. He had his whole life in front of him.' Melanie hands Rheta a tissue. 'The next thing you know he's up there in Heaven with Charlotte and the rest of 'em; Miss Lily, Miss Doreen. All of 'em.' Rheta blows her nose.

Melanie shakes her head in disgust. 'Poor Carter Jr. His father is such a mess, his son is dead, the Army Corps of Engineers is up his ass all the time with this rule and that rule and then there's that crazy wife of his. Someone ought to tell her you can't knit your pain away. You can't. Can you, Rheta?'

'No, you can't. But, you can clean your pain away. That's what I did. Now, I don't have the pain.' Rheta stops Melanie mid-turn 'Look at that picture. You look so happy, Miss Melanie, pushin' your little girl on the swing. Look at you. I have never seen you smile so wide.'

Melanie turns the page. She turns back, peers at the picture for a long, long time. 'Look at my little girl. She was a beautiful girl, wasn't she, Rheta? My beautiful baby.'

Rheta says, 'Beautiful mother. Beautiful child.' Melanie turns off the Maglite. As the wind howls, as the streets of Baton Rouge flood, Rheta B. and Melanie sit quietly in the dark living room. 'What was she like, Miss Melanie? When she was growin' up, what was your baby like?'

Melanie listens to the rain on the roof, listens to Bud snoring, listens to the dark. 'That girl of mine, that little girl, she was the most changeable child in the world; this way one minute, that way the next. You had to go to bed early at night, wake up early the next morning to keep up with my Charlotte's moods. I never knew what she was going to do next, what crazy ideas were going to pop out of her mouth. She was smart, Rheta. She lit up a room. Wherever she went, whoever she met, they wanted to know her. Everyone wanted to be Charlotte's friend. Everyone wanted a piece of my girl. But, you couldn't have her, not all of her. She had so many parts that were invisible to the eye, you couldn't see or know her completely. Nobody knew my girl.' Melanie sighs. 'I knew her. I knew her inside out.' Melanie touches the picture of Charlotte on the swing. 'I think I knew her. She thought she had me wrapped around her little finger. She was wrong. She had her father wrapped around her little finger, but not her mother. I could tell when she was hiding behind one of her many selves. Those many selves made her the most intriguing, unpredictable child in the world.' She turns on the Maglite. 'Whenever there's a hurricane, I can't stand the change in the atmosphere. It makes me feel restless, crazy inside. Come to think of it, Charlotte didn't like it when the barometric pressure changed either.'

Rheta B. says, 'She was her own storm.'

'She was indeed.' Melanie centres the light directly on the faces in the photo. 'Rheta. Have you ever been in love?'

Rheta shakes her head no. 'I love Theodore.'

'I don't mean that kind of love. I mean your heart-breaks-apart-like-broken-limbs-during-a-hurricane kind of love, no-sense-to-the-world kind of love, no-sleep-at-night kind of love.' She takes out a picture from the photo album. 'Morning love. Early-morning love.' She tucks the picture inside her blouse pocket. 'I think I'll keep this photo in here for a little while.'

'You must love Mister Bud an awful lot.'

Melanie chuckles. She closes the photo album, opens her arms, gives Rheta a big hug. 'Yes, I do. I really do.' She doubles over in gales of laughter. 'Oh Rheta. What would we have done without you? Precious, precious Rheta.' Melanie turns off the Maglite. 'You know what I want to do, maybe in late September or early October, if it's nice, not too hot, I want to go on a swamp tour.'

'But, Miss Melanie, you hate the swamp. Why would you want to go on one of those terrible tours? I can't imagine.'

'I don't know. It's just ... something ... I think I should do at least once. It might even be fun. It's about time I looked at some cypress trees, spent an afternoon floating down Lake Martin, had a stare down with an alligator, hung out with the blue heron like Charlotte did. My baby loved the swamp, she loved the cypress and oh, how she loved those peregrine falcons. Do you want to come with me?'

'You crazy! Why would I want to do that?'

'We'll have a great time. Have you ever been on a swamp tour before?'

'Well ...'

'Well what?'

'No, as a matter of fact, I haven't.'

'End of conversation. We are going on a swamp tour.' Melanie claps her hands. 'Fun, fun, fun. I might even invite Winston.' Rheta B. gives Melanie a look, a look like Melanie has lost her mind. 'That is the best idea I've had in the longest time. Maybe Bud will come, too, if he's not sleeping, which he seems to be doing more and more of these days.' Melanie has another idea. 'We'll make a picnic. You'll make your famous fried chicken, I'll make my famous pulled-pork sandwiches. Hell, if we do that, even Theodore will come along. Cleveland Alexander can take a day off from church. Maybe the whole family would like to join us!' Melanie pulls out the picture from her pocket, kisses it, then puts it back in her pocket. She opens the photo album. She leafs through its many pages. When she gets to a certain picture near the end of the album, she stops, she stares at a picture for a very long time. 'Look at my boy. If he doesn't look like his mother, I don't know who does?'

Charlotte parks herself at the entry portal. As the portal opens and closes, like a blinking eye, she watches hundreds of souls pour through the opening. Their luminous threads unwind and spin like multicoloured spinning toys. Charlotte daydreams about Alice as a child. I would prefer Charlotte participate in comforting the confused spirits as they enter Afterworld, but Charlotte is busy. What can I do?

I address the new arrivals with my most soothing, sonorous tone, always making sure that each spirit finds its way to the appropriate healing area. 'Next. To the left. Next. To the right. Next. Straight ahead. No, not that way, turn around, move over here. No … not you, you go over there. Next. Make way for the next one, slowly, no rush, no need to hurry. You, back there, feel the pulse of our world. I am sure you will enjoy its unique rhythm. You, up there, no need to bother with that. Why bother looking for what was familiar? Nothing is as you know it, not in here, not yet, anyway. Next. Look at your thread. Watch how your thread releases and disappears. Your thread has completed its journey. That is a beautiful sight. I have seen the sight of spinning threads infinite times. It remains the most beautiful sight in any world. Excuse me. You, yes you. Move over this way. You! Over there! Do not be afraid. Move over that way. If you move that way, you will have a much better view. Isn't your shimmer breathtaking? Do you know your shimmer has been with you forever? It has. Time to let it go now.'

Charlotte does not assist, she does not help with the new arrivals. She admires the parade of spirits. 'Look at that shape! I've never seen an oblique shape like that before. Spectacular!' Every time the portal opens Charlotte peeks through it. She watches the world where hurricanes roar. She watches Maria weave the thread through Joseph's body. They are on their way.

Lit by stars. When they arrive, Charlotte will, most probably, be of no help. She will be absolutely hypnotized by one shape or another.

Human beings cannot possibly imagine what they will become after they are finished being flesh and blood. How *could* they imagine such a superb thing?

A new soul enters. Charlotte takes the opportunity to peek through the blinking eye. She sees Winston lying on the porch, laughing at the rain.

'I know you're here, Charlotte. Isn't the rain beautiful?' He rolls onto his belly, kicks his legs in the air. 'I love you, Charlotte. Let's go to the swamp. It's been too long since I've seen a peregrine falcon; much too long.' Winston pounds his hands on the porch. 'I'm going to tell your mother I forgive her, even if she is the biggest pain in the ass I have ever known.' He roars with laughter. 'And since you are somewhere, somewhere with my mother, you can tell her I forgive her, too. I have come to understand that she had to deal with the biggest asshole in the world. I forgive him. I forgive her for being a bitch. But, I still don't understand why she was so mean, so mean to Steven and me when we were young. I would appreciate it if you would find out the answer to my question. She didn't need to act like a "Spider Lily". She could have been a hell of a lot nicer to her children.'

There goes Winston; talking a blue streak, thinking Charlotte has nothing better to do than listen to his ranting. If only Winston could see the beautiful souls passing through Afterworld, he would not fear life or death. As far as Winston's mother or Charlotte's mother are concerned, there is nothing Charlotte can do about either one. Winston needs to clean up his own mess. We, in here, are unable to tidy up anyone's untidy problems.

Another soul passes through. The eye opens. Before it blinks again, Charlotte sees Steven. He sits on the edge of the bathtub in the bathroom of the Hyatt Regency Hotel. He cries uncontrollably. 'What have I done with my life? Oh, Charlotte, what have I done? Please forgive me. I broke my promise.' Steven examines the razor perched on the sink. 'Doreen, I loved you so much. I am so sorry. I know you died because of me.' Steven realizes what a mess it would be if he killed himself; what a mess it would be for poor Jason Stickley, who is curled up on the floor on the other side of the bathroom door.

Fortunately, Steven cannot hear Charlotte yell, 'Steven Duvalier, you had better stop your nonsense or I'll tell your mother what's going on with you! I'll tell Doreen as well. She doesn't want to hear about your self-disgust! She knows what happened. We all know what happened. Leave us out of it! We're busy! We are dealing with a disaster! Dealing with a disaster requires total concentration. What we are dealing with in here is way more important than you and your self-indulgences! You are nearly seventy years old! Go get yourself some help from someone who's alive! Talk to somebody in the living part of the family! I'm sure somebody can help you out of the mess you're in, just ask for Christ's sake!'

'Charlotte! We don't say that in here.'

'Oh. It's you again.'

'I am pleased you are trying to help Steven. You understand he does not hear you.'

'I know. I know. It's so frustrating.'

'We need your services ... here. There are souls passing through who need our assistance.'

'I know. I know. I'll be right with you. But, I've never seen anything like it before.'

'No. I guess you have not.' What am I to do with her? Wait. Wait for Charlotte.

Charlotte smells gardenias. Lily arrives at the portal. They watch the eye open and close. They are delighted that circumstance has brought them together again. They look through, they look beyond, this beyond, that beyond. Tucked away in Port Fourchon, at 17077 Main Street in Galliano, Louisiana, is the

South Lafourche Baptist Church. The congregation sings, the choir sings and Minister Leroy Jones praises the Lord for his almighty miracles.

Oh happy day oh happy day oh happy happy day;
Oh happy day when Jesus washed oh when he washed
When Jesus washed he washed my sins away!
Oh happy day.

Norma, Cleveland Alexander and Theodore sing like angels. Charlotte notices Theodore is wearing a cross around his neck. 'When did Theodore start wearing a cross?' Charlotte asks Lily.

'That's my cross. I gave it to him at the end. He asked if he could have it.' Lily is nonchalant about the cross.

As a choir from The Ninth Ward passes through the portal's eye singing 'Oh Happy Day', Lily and Charlotte watch in awe.

Oh happy day oh happy day oh happy happy day;
Oh happy day when Jesus washed oh when he washed
When Jesus washed he washed my sins away!
Oh happy day.

Lily says, 'The whole world is singing "Oh Happy Day".' Enormous sins are being washed away with the hurricane. We are witnessing a great blessing.' Lily hums with the choir. 'I love that song. I love "Amazing Grace" almost as much.' She hums what she can remember of "Amazing Grace". 'Do you mind that Theodore is going out with a black man?'

You could bowl Charlotte over with that question, that question in this of all places. Charlotte catches one more glimpse of Theodore. The cross glistens on his beautiful chest. 'I don't care about the colour of the man he takes to bed. I don't care what he does, as long as it gives him some peace. If it makes my boy happy, I'm happy.' Charlotte hums 'Amazing Grace'. She stops singing. She never could carry a tune.

※

As Lily and Charlotte pierce the veil between worlds, between times with their remarkable sight, Charlotte glances at Gran' Isle, where she focuses on the rickety house on stilts. She remembers a time, a time when Winston, Alice and Charlotte drove down flooded roads to make sure their home was still standing. When they arrive, they discover the roof blown off the dwelling.

Winston climbs on top of a pile of rubble. He tries to pry open the basement door, which is swollen shut. Charlotte shouts, 'Be careful, honey! Don't break your arm! If the door wants to open, it will open. If it wants to stay shut, it will stay shut, no matter what you do.'

Winston tries yanking open the door. 'Damn!' He wrestles with the knob. The knob falls off. It disappears into the rubble. 'Son of a ...'

Alice bursts out crying. She becomes so upset, she hiccups herself into hysterics. 'What're we gonna do? How're we gonna fix it?' She tries to figure out how *she* can climb up the side of the house with a tack hammer and a bucket of nails, so *she* can re-roof the Gran' Isle home. Herself. Oh, what a family.

While Winston huffs and puffs and tries to shove the doorknob back into its hole, while Alice has a hissy fit over the roofless house, Charlotte comes up with her personal truth. 'Listen! Listen to me! Ours is a happy house, a free house! She is free from whatever held her back from being an independent structure without a roof to hold her down. For as long as she wants, our lovely house has an unobstructed view of the sky and all its many mythical creatures!'

※

Now Charlotte is in the sky. She realizes *she* is a mythical creature. She sings 'Oh Happy Day'.

Lily sings with Charlotte. Doreen joins in with her unique sound and her lovely scent. As the eye opens and closes and opens and closes, the three Duvaliers watch in amazement. I have not asked them to do much; not yet. What they *are* doing is fully appreciating the mystery around them.

❋

As they watch the Broadway musical, *The Lion King*, Daphne, Alice, Lily and Billy are spellbound. Winston is correct. It is a show about a lion.

Look at Doreen and Charlotte's children. Look at Lily's grandchildren. Look at Daphne's grief. Daphne relives that horrible day. She watches herself running through the sugar fields, running faster than she ever thought possible. She runs and runs until Sugar shouts, 'Stop!' That is when Daphne turns around. Steven Jr is on his knees, breathless, beyond life. The image is embedded in Daphne's mind. Let go of the image, Daphne. Stop blaming yourself. It was his time to be here with another part of the family. There are other things that need tending. What are you waiting for, Daphne? It has been two months since you received the letter. What about the other letters? Now is as good a time as any to tell your father. If he does not come clean, his lies will destroy the family, as well as the family business.

When the time is right, the three Duvaliers will find their football hero. First, he must find himself.

How fortunate that some of the family got away before the hurricane. It is doubtful they will return any time soon. Alice's husband Rob, is somewhat inebriated at some local bar on Forty-Second Street. He could care less about a musical, no less a musical about lions.

❋

Charlotte pleads for one more peek. 'Please! I promise I won't ask again.'

I agree to her request. 'Go ahead.'

'It looks like the future. Can I stop the future?'

'No you cannot.'

'No matter how hard I try to change the inevitable destruction of time, time can't be controlled, can it?'

'Correct.'

'Will you look at that! Another fuckin' hurricane!'

'Language, Charlotte. Language ... *Her* name is *Rita*. She is, excuse my language, a bitch on wheels. Because of Rita's raging rain, Atchafalaya is swollen, waters are degraded into a black slime, the aching rivers around the swamp are swollen with silt, banks overflow, huge ruts run through the earth's crazed surface, crazy wild seas eat up more of the shoreline and powerful winds blow off entire roofs in Gran' Isle. Sugar is blown down, branches of beautiful golden rain trees ready to bloom are strewn every which way.'

'She is a wicked woman! Look! Look at what she's done! Damn her!'

'Calm down, Charlotte. What you see is nature's business. It is not our business.'

'She won't be satisfied until she tears through whatever's in her path, will she? Cunt!'

'Language.'

Swamp screams. 'I can't take much more of this! I need healing time!' Rita could care less. Her heart is cold as stone. She rearranges the landscape according to her desire. She is a woman without reason.

Charlotte cannot turn away.

I, of course, am powerless to change what has been decided by that which is greater than me. I see through the lens, but I am merely a witness to whatever is on the other side of my puny sight. I am helpless to rearrange the rising water as it pours through breaches in the patched Industrial Canal levees devastating the Ninth Ward. Again. I am helpless to save the people who are waist-deep in water. Again. I am unable to rescue the weary individuals who cling to rooftops and scream for help. Again. Nature's devastation is more than anyone can endure in any world.

Sugar cries out, 'Yes!' She screams! 'Bring the boy home or all hell's gonna break loose! I am sick of waiting!'

'It has broken loose, you crazy-ass fool!' Charlotte screams at Sugar. 'Leave my boy alone! Do you hear me?! You have ruined enough lives!' Charlotte screams so loud, Lily and Doreen make themselves visible.

'Isn't it like watching the best Easter parade ever? Isn't it, Charlotte?' Lily says, with a delirious excitement. Obviously, Lily and Doreen are watching a different movie from Charlotte. 'Isn't it?' Lily asks.

The portal remains open for viewing the known and unknown worlds of time past and time to come. I am torn apart by the world of suffering, elated by the world of joy. Whether past, present or future, Sugar and Swamp are forever part of the landscape.

'This is the best theatre I've seen in any world,' says Doreen, as she drifts through somebody's twirling thread. 'Excuse me.' She untangles herself. She turns around. She asks, 'Who was that? It felt so familiar.'

'It's your father, Joseph,' Charlotte says. 'Enjoy the dance.' Charlotte watches Doreen spin away with her father. Doreen's mother follows close behind them. Charlotte wishes she could dance with her father.

'Good for them,' Lily says, as she spins off into a direction of her own.

A hush comes over *our* world. All of a sudden, through the portal, from the Ninth Ward, during one hurricane or another, enters a gospel choir, singing 'Oh Happy Day'.

Oh happy day oh happy day oh happy happy day;
Oh happy day when Jesus washed oh when he washed
When Jesus washed he washed my sins away!
Oh happy day.

Charlotte applauds. She is not alone. There are many satisfied onlookers in the audience. Until the next wave of celestial beings arrive, the portal's eyelid remains closed. How Charlotte wishes she could be like the eye, how she wishes she could wait patiently for the next blink.

If the Army Corps of Engineers had done its due diligence with regard to levee systems and soil erosion, most of the devastation caused by Hurricane Katrina could have been averted. Faulty design and substandard construction have been cited in the failure of the levee system. These inexcusable oversights caused levees to breach again, during Hurricane Rita.

The Army Corps of Engineers answers to no one, absolutely no one. Who dares question the organization that built the Panama Canal, the organization that protects 38,700 acres of wetlands, the organization that dredges 255 million cubic yards of whatever materials are needed for construction or maintenance of its many projects both here and abroad? How dare anyone question the integrity of an organization authorized and funded directly, with absolutely no oversight, by Congress!

＊

For many years the Army Corps of Engineers has had numerous dealings with the Duvalier family; dirty dealings. In the 1920s, when William Duvalier owned and operated Pine Grove's sugar business, he had good friends, other sugar-plantation owners, who had land near South Lafourche, Louisiana. The Army Corps of Engineers convinced William Duvalier to buy up the land from his so-called 'friends'. William made deals, paid a fair price for what was, at the time, useless land. There was one minor detail William forgot to tell his 'friends'. In the not-too-distant future the land would be worth a fortune. There were numerous gas and oil fields underground. The area would soon become of immense importance to Louisiana's energy business.

The fields would make a rich man out of whoever owned them.

When the deal was struck between the Corps and William, the Corps promised to overlook the fact that Pine Grove had illegally planted sugar on valuable wetlands – strictly against the law. For overlooking the monstrous misdemeanour, Pine Grove (owned and operated by William Duvalier) would split all future gas and oil profits with the Corps. Although William Duvalier knew 'damn well' there were no such wetlands on his property, the deal was struck.

Like most deals in Louisiana, it was an under-the-table deal. Lily's father, Daddy, William Duvalier's attorney, took meticulous care to protect the family from any potential lawsuits. So the Corps could not claim ownership of the land at some later date, Daddy expedited the wetlands issue with two words: 'in perpetuity'. He created a personal accounting system that fully explained how the gas and oil rights would be paid out for generations to come. After Lily's father dotted his i's and crossed his t's, he locked the papers inside an old filing cabinet in Pine Grove's back office under the file name 'Miscellaneous Records'. He was the only person who knew where the documents were hidden. As far as the Corps was concerned, there were no documents.

William Duvalier was the Corps' front man. Because he played the role with such finesse, he acquired thousands of valuable acres for very little money. He became a very rich man.

William Duvalier became much richer than most men in the sugar business. His greed brought an unspoken, unknown shame to his family; unknown until Daphne's discovery.

After Chris's death, Steven hires Daphne to take care of the books. Daphne decides to do more than just bookkeeping. She spends oodles of hours ogling the 'Miscellaneous Records' file; a file shoved underneath a stack of papers in a rusty drawer, in the rear of the filing cabinet, in the dank corner of Pine Grove Plantation's storage room.

On the day of Winston's birthday party, the day of Steven Jr's graduation party, the day Steven Jr dies, the day when the first threatening letter arrives in the mail, Daphne decides it is the right time, the right day to tell her father the family business is in jeopardy. But, as it turns out, it is not the right time or the right day.

Now, two months later, it is still not the right time. *The right time.* How do you tell your father that the entire world knows he has had young boys, wherever he travelled, wherever he sold his goods and his bads, in each and every sugar-buying state? How do you tell your father Pine Grove's business is built on a pack of lies, just like his life? How do you tell your father that his father not only ruined his sons, but he ruined whatever he touched and he touched many innocent women? And finally, how do you tell your father that his grandfather was an absolute, unadulterated thief? How do you do such a thing to a man you adore? You wait until *the right time.* Maybe after the hurricane, it will be the *right time* to break your father's heart like he broke your mother's heart. But that hurt happened a long, long time ago. That hurt lives in those old curtains hanging in a dark room. Those old curtains are hanging inside Daphne's heart.

While Daphne pretends to be watching *The Lion King*, she remembers a time in the sugar fields with Theodore; her skirt pulled above her head, her arms waving in the air. '*Look at me, Theodore. Look at me. I'm the sugar swaying in the wind. Don't you love me. Look at me. I'm the sweetest thing you'll ever know.*' Daphne remembers how she slid out of her dress, arms outstretched like a scarecrow on the make. She remembers how she ran after Theodore. Theodore ran so fast – in the opposite direction – Daphne didn't know which way to turn. Steven Jr ran just as fast, even faster. He ran toward Daphne. Two months since he dropped dead and Daphne still hasn't a clue which way to turn.

Daphne remembers the drink in her mother's hand, she remembers the ice cubes. She remembers the Bibles in every room of the Mansion. *'Those Bibles didn't do anyone much good, did they? Faith is wasted on the guilt of its sinners,'* thinks Daphne.

Maybe she should tell Carter Jr about the letters. Carter Jr can handle his father for a change. Daphne is not interested in handling any of them right now. What Daphne wants is to relive those sweet childhood days in the sugar fields.

＊

Daphne hears Sugar's voice inside her head. 'I have seen you Duvaliers playing, lying in my fields, running in the sun, running after one another, taking each other for granted, taking me for granted. I take nothing in my world or any world for granted. I survive what you people can't tolerate. I will survive this hurricane, the next hurricane, the next blight, the inevitable death that comes with life. I will survive your silly notions about me, about you, about life, about death.'

When the curtain comes down on *The Lion King*, the audience jumps to its feet. Daphne is unable to stand. She is distracted by Sugar's merciless chattering.

Sugar begs, 'Bring him back home, Daphne. Talk to Theodore. He will listen to you. He loves you almost as much as he loves me. Please. For everybody's sake. You know what to do. Now, do it!'

＊

Charlotte languishes in a dormant state of wait. Doreen is off tripping the light fantastic with her mother and father. Lily has disappeared. The eye has been shut for what seems like an eternity. Charlotte needs stimulation. She needs company; quite a notion in here, isn't it? She wants to dance with *her* mother and *her* father. She wishes she could disappear from herself, but herself is no more self than other. She deliberates. *'If I am infinite, why do I feel finite?'* These are questions she feels

I should have answered a long time ago. 'Afterworld. You're nothing but a trickster.'

'Charlotte. Would you like another verse of "Oh Happy Day"? Would that cheer you up?'

'Maybe. When Alice was a child, when she came home after church, she would sing spirituals to me. In those days, "Amazing Grace" was my favourite spiritual. What was the verse? Maybe, if I listen, I'll hear Alice.' Charlotte listens.

Yes, when this flesh and heart shall fail
And mortal life shall cease;
I shall possess, within the veil,
A life of joy and peace.

Charlotte cries, 'If only it were true.' Without my help, Charlotte realizes how foolish she is being. *'At least I can hear Alice's voice. I have developed the capacity to hear my little girl singing my favourite hymn.'*

Having recently returned from New York City, in a van, with her relatives, twelve days after Hurricane Katrina, an exhausted Daphne walks up Winston's back porch steps. Steven is by her side. He carries a stack of files under his arm. He looks exhausted.

Daphne says, 'Come on, Daddy.' Coaxing him as if *he* were *her* child, she says, 'Come on!'

'What am I going to say? How am I going to ... You've got to help me, honey.'

'There's absolutely nothing you have to do, Daddy. Uncle Winston will understand whatever you tell him, whatever you say.'

'Winston? I doubt it.'

'He's changed, Daddy. Ever since Steven Jr died, something's happened to Winston. He's different. He's a very different man than he used to be. He'll understand and, Daddy, you don't have to tell him anything you're not ready to tell him.'

Steven kisses Daphne. He shuffles over to the porch swing, sits down, rubs his sweaty palms together, looks at a lone rectangular piece of shingle leaning against the banister. 'What's that doing there?' He walks over to the banister, bends down, grabs the piece of shingle, throws it over the railing toward the sugar field. 'Oh. I hope Winston's not saving it for something.' He walks down the steps.

'Daddy! Get up here! Stop hemming and hawing. You're acting like a child. It isn't becoming to a man of your age.'

Steven waves the folders in the air. 'I don't know what I'm ...'

'Whatever *you* are ready to tell him.' Daphne kisses her father. 'Go on.'

Steven knocks on the screen door. Winston yells from upstairs. 'Come on in. I'll be right down. Be with you in a minute. I brewed some coffee. Mama's old mugs are in the breakfront in the living room. Make yourselves comfortable.'

Daphne and Steven walk into the kitchen. Plants and vegetables are placed in every corner of the kitchen; positioned on small tables, hanging from the ceiling, spilling over the sides of beautiful ceramic pots on small wooden stools. The kitchen looks like a jungle. Steven and Daphne are amazed at the living things growing in Winston's house.

Daphne remembers Steven Jr walking into the kitchen, out the back door, down the porch steps. She shivers at the memory. She strolls into the living room. She remembers the moment when Theodore confronted her, the moment he realized Daphne and Steven Jr had fortified the family's sexual dysfunction. 'Shame on me. Shame on me.' She slams her hand on the breakfront. She grabs the Tulane mugs from the bottom shelf. She remembers how, no matter how much she drank that evening, she could not numb herself, could not forgive herself, would not let Steven Jr forgive himself. Now she asks herself, 'What would Chris think?'

When Daphne walks back into the kitchen, she finds her

father leaning against the kitchen sink, gazing out the window, looking at the sugar fields. The files are under his arm. 'Put the files down, Daddy.' Steven doesn't move. 'Daddy. Put the files on the table.'

'Have you ever seen anything more beautiful? The harvest will be coming up soon. How many harvests? I never get tired of the harvest. I love the sound of the trucks driving down the road, driving our sugar to the sugar mill. Our sugar.'

'Our sugar.'

'I miss Joseph. Joseph and his harvest. Your mother and me. Joseph and his harvest.'

'Daddy! The files. On the table. Sit down. I'm going to pour you a hot cup of coffee.' She pours the coffee into a red mug. 'Do you want sugar?'

Steven turns around, looks at his shoes, stares at the floor, kicks an invisible piece of dirt. He looks adoringly at his daughter. He smiles a winsome, unfamiliar smile. 'I never touch the stuff. It's bad for you.' He drops the files on the kitchen table. He sits on the metal chair with the red vinyl seat, the chair that once belonged to his mother. He drinks his coffee without sugar.

Winston strolls into the kitchen. 'I didn't know you were coming over. What a nice surprise. I thought you were stranded up there in the big mean city. I can't believe they didn't quarantine you before they let you back in our ruined, but wonderful, state of Louisiana. You missed one hell of a hurricane.' He hugs Daphne. 'Ouch. When hugging hurts, you know you're getting old.' Winston laughs at his bad joke. 'Thank God I'm not as old as him.' He walks over to Steven. He hugs him. 'Oh, that hurts.'

Steven is taken aback by Winston's affection. Winston sits next to Steven. He rests his arm on his brother's shoulder. 'Where the hell have you been? I've been worried sick about you. We were worried about you, Steven. Once we got our phones working, had our lines of communication back in order, we called and called, but nobody answered at your house.'

'I wasn't home.'

'Well, where the hell were you!? You could have been dead.'

'I'm sorry. I should have called, but ...'

'I don't like it when you disappear. Our father did that. Remember?' Winston gets up from the table, he pours himself a cup of coffee, then he sits down. 'Where were you?'

'New Orleans.'

'New Orleans? In the middle of that insane hurricane!?'

'Right in the middle.' Steven sips his coffee, slowly. 'Daphne, honey. Do you mind waiting on the porch?'

'What's the problem, Steven?' Winston asks. 'Have we got some kind of a drama going on here for a change?'

Daphne replies. 'When don't we have a drama going on in our family, Uncle Winston?' Mug in hand, Daphne walks over to her father. She kisses the top of his head. 'I just love that bald spot.' She walks out the back door, down the steps, looks for and finds the piece of shingle, walks up the steps, drinks her coffee, then plays with the shingle like it were the most fabulous toy in the world. While she plays with her new toy, her father and his younger brother have their first heart-to-heart.

The brothers talk and listen and talk and listen. They reminisce about their mother and father, Lily and Carter, two people who never should have married, two people who never should have had children. Their parents were ill-equipped to nurture anyone. They were selfish people, people who wanted what they wanted, when they wanted it, no matter what the emotional price. That is who they were.

The conversation curls back in time to childhood. Winston remembers how Steven, the elder son, took care of his mother, took care of his younger brother, tried taking care of ironing out the deep creases in a ruined family. Entering into a conversation about childhood is painful but necessary. Those childhood years were the years that damaged these two men beyond emotional repair. Anyone who tried loving either one of the Duvalier brothers would find it an impossible task. They were ruined goods. It was during those childhood years when their mother had them sleep in her bed with her, because their father was somewhere, somewhere else, sleeping in someone else's bed. At a very early age the boys were told about their father's infidelity. Their mother took it upon herself to share her pain with her children.

There was no doubt in their minds that their mother and father hated each other. It was an arranged marriage of sorts. That's what she said. Her father, Daddy, believed their father, Carter, would settle down. One day he would become a fine upstanding man. As it turned out, there was nothing upstanding about Carter. His moods blew hot and cold like the changing winds. Whenever he returned home, returned to Pine Grove, he made his presence known by screaming so loud, even the sugar whimpered.

Carter hated the sugar. He hated the business. He hated it. He tried to unearth a deeper meaning inside his unfulfilled life. The only time he found a deeper meaning was inside a bottle or inside some other woman; any woman but his wife. Living with Lily reminded him how his miserable father, William, ruled Carter's life. Lily was William's choice. Carter found Lily beautiful, but he never wanted a God-fearing woman to become his lawful wedded wife. He wanted *his* woman to be a hater of all gods, a rule-breaker not a ball-breaker.

If only he could leave the business behind, but he had responsibilities; children, wife, business obligations. The albatross that hung around his neck made him the most unhappy of wanderers. There was no place for family in Carter's psyche. His world could not survive within a family structure. The man could not survive within any structure defined by society.

※

Finally, hours later, the brothers talk about their wives, their lives without their wives. Winston confides to Steven that he has recently seen their mother in some other worldly form, that he hears his departed wife in some other worldly voice, that things are not what he believed them to be, that life and death are hovering within each other at all times. Winston has fallen in love with life. For the first time in his many living years, he sees possibility in the morning sun and the evening rain. He accepts the dancing shadows in his heart. He accepts his brother for who he is, even if he doesn't understand his brother's choices.

The playing field is wide open. Steven confesses his sexual cravings for young men. He confesses to having been at the Hyatt Regency Hotel with Jason Stickley during Hurricane Katrina. He confesses to being a sex addict, a lover of beautiful bodies, a chronic liar, a lousy father and a man in need of help.

Steven describes his aimless wanderings after he was evacuated from the hotel; how he roamed flooded streets, walked through unrecognizable neighbourhoods of New Orleans, how he watched people of all ages weeping, holding each other, helping each other through the worst disaster they would ever experience. How Steven wanted to help, to hold, to touch each person in need, but Steven was afraid that if he touched, he would want something more than just a touch.

As far back as he can remember, Steven has wanted more than just a touch. He has wanted to get inside the touch, underneath the touch, underneath the guilt and shame of wanting to be in the arms of young men who might help heal his ruined psyche; young men in every sugar-buying state. That is why Steven likes to travel. Just like his father, he gets it out there, in bars, in cars, in public toilets, in motel rooms on the road, where nobody knows his name, where nobody knows about his sexual crimes. Unfortunately, he has ruined his cover with Jason Stickley. He was in love with Jason. Now, a hurricane has come between them. Steven wants help. He wants to break the habit that has ruined his life, the habit that could ruin the family as well as the family business.

The family business. There is, of course, that gigantic albatross; always that burden. Steven shows Winston the files. Winston peruses the fine print. 'Oh dear.' Winston mutters. Finally, he understands his family legacy, understands his father, his mother, his brother and himself just a little better. Now, he fully comprehends the insidious lies, the tortured lives, the self-inflicted misery of a family with untold enemies from one end of the state to the other, from one generation to the next.

Winston's epiphany leaves him with a heartache the likes of which he has not felt since Charlotte's death. 'No wonder Charlotte had to die,' thinks Winston. 'She was too good to be one of us. Poor Charlotte. Forgive me,' he says. There is no response. Charlotte is busy with more pressing matters.

Steven sits in a corner. He wonders how he will, if he will, ever be able to pick up the pieces of his degenerate life. Winston continues to read one damning document after another. Since he was a child, thanks to his father's frequent ranting and raving, Winston has forever hated the Army Corps of Engineers. Now that he sees the documents confirming the Duvalier's collusion with the Corps, he is furious, furious like he was before he talked with his mother in his bedroom, before he saw his father in the sugar fields, before he witnessed Steven Jr being wrapped and readied for his journey. Winston feels an all-consuming rage; a rage that has ruined his life. That rage kept him from loving Charlotte the way she needed to be loved. He did love her. If only he had known *how* to love her.

Steven hands Winston one last file. The Corps has offered Steven (Pine Grove Plantation) a paltry sum for an enormous piece of land; land planted with sugar, land planted with soyabeans. Since the Duvaliers owe their wealth to the Corps, payback time is overdue. Since the Corps needs the parcel of valuable land, because the land contains clay required to repair the roads, bridges and levees destroyed by Katrina's storm, the Duvaliers have to sell the land to the Corps at a discounted price. They owe it to the Corps. They owe it to the good people of Louisiana who have been duped again and again by both the Corps and the Duvaliers.

Finally, Steven pulls out the letters. For all Steven knows, they could have been written by anybody in any sugar-buying state. Steven has come to the end of his lies.

Winston swears on his life. 'I promise we will work this out together, even if it means giving up the family business.'

Winston and Steven promise to change the family tradition; a family tradition built upon generations of lies and deception. If such a thing is possible, they will find a way.

With so much revealed in one afternoon, there is no need to confess the biggest secret of all. Steven is unable to tell his brother that he seduced his brother's son in the sugar fields those many years ago, on a hot summer day, when his brother's son was just a boy without a mother's love or a father's kindness. There is no need to bring up such a complicated piece of ancient history. Enough history has been exposed for one mid-September afternoon.

The brothers embrace. They kiss without shame or regret.

There is nothing like a swamp tour on the bayou, especially when the swamp tour takes place on the back end of two terrorizing hurricanes. Why else would Duvalier friends and family be crazy enough to embark on a swamp tour, during the hottest, most unpleasant, stifling, overcast October afternoon?

Melanie and Rheta B. are responsible for the swamp tour mania. During Hurricane Katrina, Melanie had the idea, after Hurricane Rita, Rheta B. ran with the idea. They have been frying up finger-lickin' food for days. These two ladies are, without question, two of the best cooks in any state north or south of the Mason-Dixon Line. Nobody will miss a picnic packed with pulled pork and fried chicken. Nobody, especially Cleveland Alexander and Theodore Duvalier, who have driven from Port Fourchon to Baton Rouge, picked up Melanie and Rheta B., packed up the food and are driving to Thibodaux for the experience of a lifetime: Slam's Swamp Tour.

At the last minute Bud decides he would rather stay home and sleep in the recliner than set out on a swamp tour. He went looking for alligators in the swamp with his daughter a long time ago. Once was enough.

Steven and Winston have driven together, for the first time in a long time, in the same car, to the same place. Before today, neither one of the brothers has experienced a swamp tour. Maybe once. Maybe once, when they were children, their father took them to some bayou, somewhere near Napoleonville, held them under his arms, threw them in the water, screamed, 'Gator! Gator! Swim for your lives!' If that happened and it probably did happen, the brothers have erased the horrific memory from their consciousness, forever.

While devouring two bags of barbecue chips, Daphne and Alice gossip about whether Theodore and Cleveland Alexander have any sort of a future together. Since both girls have been privy to Theodore's sexual wanderings for as long as they can remember, the consensus is negative. Although the girls are fond of Cleveland Alexander, they think it unlikely that Theodore is cut out to be a minister's wife or a minister's husband.

Lily and Billy bicker in the back seat of the car. After two major hurricanes and no power or water for weeks, the bickering is getting on Alice's nerves. The twins have entered into a heated debate over faith-based issues, the legalities of abortion and whether or not the end of the world is close at hand. Alice is thankful their father, Rob, was called to the hospital for an emergency operation on some famous football player's torn tendon. Rob, being a liberal, would have rather died than listen to his children rattle on about faith-based issues, particularly the issue of abortion.

＊

Carter Jr and Faith drive the back roads. That is what they do these days; spend endless hours driving here and there, so they can be together. Since Steven Jr's death, Faith's knitting has been rolled up inside the wooden knitting box on the back seat of the car. Faith hardly knits anymore.

Carter Jr energetically exhales. 'The sugar is as strong as I have ever seen her, honey. Those ferocious hurricanes didn't come close to destroying the crop. Sugar! She is something else. We are going to have a fantastic harvest!' In the middle of a winding country road Carter Jr stops the car. 'I love you, Faith. I adore you. I can't, I could never, ever live without you. I am such a lucky man.' He takes her hands in his. He kisses them. He looks into her eyes. He cries. He quietly cries.

She wipes the tears from Carter Jr's eyes, kisses him on the mouth. 'Honey.'

'What, baby?'

'Do you want to ... would you like to ... do it?'

'What? Here? Are you out of your mind?'

'I want another child, Carter.'

'But, honey. Isn't it a little late for kids ... at our age?'

'I still have viable eggs in me. And, if I don't have viable eggs, there are ways. They have newfangled ways to get a woman pregnant.'

Carter is stunned. He sits straight up, bangs the steering wheel with his left hand, grabs Faith with his right hand. 'If you say so, let's see if we can fry those eggs and have another child. A boy. A girl. It doesn't matter to me. Does it matter to you, honey?'

'It doesn't matter.' Faith and Carter Jr climb into the back seat of the automobile. They throw the knitting box out the window. They make love. They giggle. For the first time since Steven Jr's death, they dare to dream of a future.

After making love, they hear a familiar, faraway voice. '*But the man, though he die early, shall be at rest.*' They will hear that familiar, faraway voice for years to come. One day, not this day, but one day, they will talk about the voice that guided them through the dark days of *that* unbearable summer.

❋

Carter Jr looks askance at the surroundings; rusted cans, upside-down picnic tables, old boat parts and broken glass are scattered on both sides of the road. 'Where the hell are we? Would you look at this shithole, honey.'

'Carter Jr! I haven't heard you swear in the longest time.' Faith claps her hands in delight. 'It's lovely.'

They pull into Slam's parking lot. The lot is packed with half-built Harley-Davidson motorcycles, empty beer cans and a couple of baby goats nibbling on garbage scraps. Adjacent to the parking lot, in the middle of an algae-ridden pond, on a rock, a six-foot alligator is sunbathing.

❋

Swamp hollers. 'It's time! The rest of the family has arrived! I realize you're busy with the death of so many individuals from one hurricane or another. I, myself, am full up with tears from the Ninth Ward. My banks are wet with grief. I'm tired and overworked, but I'm ready for today's events. Have you made your selection?'

I reply. 'I am exhausted. Exhausted. Yes. There is a plan in place. When the moss hanging from your bald cypress trees dances and sways in three-quarter time and the moss hanging from the live oak trees dances and sways in three-quarter time, when the wind blows the moss so hard the moss looks like a sea of sugar-cane blowing in the afternoon sky, shimmering like sugar-cane right before harvest time, that is when the sky, when the dark sky will turn violet and the thunder will roar. When the thunder roars, I will send you the necessary elements to complete the cycle. Remember, there are other forces at work here. Sugar prefers to work alone. Who knows what she has got up her sleeve. Sugar is not on my watch.'

'Or mine.'

'She could bring in other players. You never know with her.' Swamp sighs. 'Have you seen Charlotte?'

'I have. She is busy watching the comings and goings of the last month. She just sits in front of the eye, waiting for the blink, waiting for something extraordinary to happen. Can you imagine?'

'I miss her. After all these years, I still miss her love for my trees, for my birds, for my sky. I'm glad she's with you. Take good care of her.'

'I have no idea how much longer she will be with me. As you well know, it is not up to me. Is it?'

'Not up to any of us.'

✳

Slam, the swamp man, is a godlike creature. His hair is waist length, straight and blonde. He has blue eyes, bulging muscles, a smile that could and has seduced many swamp visitors straight into his makeshift bed that is located behind the rock where the sunning, six-foot alligator spends the better part of his day. Slam does not bring strange bedfellows into his cosy swamp house, because Slam is the proud father of a violent, teenaged son; a teenaged son who has been known to aim a .22-calibre rifle at unwanted visitors.

When Slam's son, Sam, entered puberty, he vowed he would punish his father for divorcing his mother. His mother recently moved to Ashville, North Carolina with her boyfriend, Wichita.

Today's tour will be operated by Slam's sadistic son, Sam. Unfortunately, Slam is driving to New Orleans, where some fortunate lady will win a night on the town with him. Ultimately, Slam will raise a tidy sum for his favourite Baptist church in the Ninth Ward.

The Duvaliers are not overjoyed at the prospect of Slam's son, Sam, being in charge of their two-hour swamp tour, but Slam has promised them a good time, whoever is guiding the vessel. 'Alligators aren't sleepin' today. Birds are circlin' high, gettin' ready to put on their finest aerial show. You people are in for a rare October treat.'

Sam nudges his father. 'Dad, I gotta get somethin' back at the house.' Sam runs home to get his gun. The wary guests board the boat. There is no shelter on Sam's swamp boat. If it rains, you will get wet. If the bugs are biting, you will get bitten. If it is hot, which it is, you will sweat. If you tried, you could not ask for a worse day to tour the swamp. To top things off, here comes Sam toting his .22.

As she grabs the tow line, pulls herself on board, Faith asks Carter Jr, 'Honey, are you sure it's safe out here? That boy doesn't look like he's old enough to drive a car, a boat or a bicycle. Look at him. He's barely fourteen years old. Barely.' She takes a good look at Sam, rolls her eyes, then whispers. 'He looks crazy to me. Did you see the grenade tattoo on his forearm?'

Carter Jr jumps on board. 'Every little thing is fine, honey.' He winks at Faith. They sit in the front of the boat, holding hands. Carter Jr yells. 'Hey, Captain! Have you got any cushions?'

Melanie snaps. 'We've got pulled-pork sandwiches and fried chicken. Who needs cushions? Sit on your bony ass and enjoy the ride!'

Winston, who is seated next to Steven, on the starboard side, sighs. 'I never knew anyone her age with such a big mouth.'

Steven whispers in Winston's ear. 'Our mother had a pretty big mouth. When she wasn't preaching the gospel, she was busy damning anyone who disagreed with the gospel. The Bible got none of us anywhere, did it?'

'I'm not sure.' Winston notices the moss dancing in the air. 'Beautiful, absolutely beautiful. How we *interpreted* the Bible to serve our personal needs, that didn't get us anywhere.'

'I don't believe in God.'

'It doesn't matter whether you do or you don't.' Winston watches a peregrine falcon dive and circle overhead. 'Miracles.

Wherever you look. Miracles.'

The wind blows, the moss dances, the boat slams in and out of inlets, the birds fly high and low, the bugs nibble at the sweetest person on board; that person being Faith, who would rather be home in her air-conditioned house, sitting in front of the flat-screen television, watching the Home Shopping Network. Daphne and Alice continue gossiping about Theodore's sex life. Theodore and Cleveland Alexander sit next to Rheta B. and Melanie. Where else would they be? That is where the pulled pork and fried chicken is situated. Those are two smart men. Steven and Winston plot and plan solutions to fiscal and family problems. Lily and Billy hang, upside down, over the railing, hoping to see a hundred-foot alligator ... at least.

Alice screams. 'Hey! You two! If you fall into the swamp, nobody, I mean *nobody* is coming in after you! You hear me?'

'We're lookin' for 'gators, Mom! Ooh, ooh. There's a baby 'gator!' A baby alligator peeks out from underneath the water.

Sam slams the boat into a tiny inlet. The boat comes to a screeching halt. He shoots his gun off in mid-air. He roars with laughter. 'Bet you're all wonderin' how the hell we're gonna get out of here? Aren't you?'

A pall comes over the passengers. Theodore is furious. 'How the hell are we gettin' outta here?' Theodore walks toward Sam, stands next to him, waits for an answer. 'Huh?'

Sam stares him down. 'I'm gonna put this here throttle in reverse.' He does just that. The boat rears like a horse being broken. The frightened guests, including Lily and Billy, hold onto their seats. No one is amused. 'Where's your sense o' humour, folks? We're on a swamp tour! What's a swamp tour without a little bit of excitement?' Sam backs out of the inlet. As soon as he is far enough away from the cattails and brush, he steers the boat forward, full speed, full throttle, scaring his passengers absolutely out of their minds.

'Slow this buggy down! Damn it!' Theodore grabs hold of Sam's arm. 'You got some elderly people on this boat, boy. You don't want to give someone a heart attack and have a lawsuit on your hands? Do you, boy? You don't want to get sent away to some military academy, where they'll beat the shit out of you for bein' such a punk-ass pussy? Do you?'

'Fuck you,' Sam mutters. He slows down the boat. 'Just playin' with you guys. My dad made me promise to give you an excitin' tour. Didn't mean to scare you.' He glowers at Theodore.

Theodore pushes Sam aside. He takes over the steering. 'Let me drive for a little while, boy.' A petulant Sam sits next to Rheta B., who is nearly having a full-blown heart attack.

Sam smirks. 'Aren't you havin' a fine time, miss?'

Beads of sweat pour down Rheta's forehead. She nods furiously. 'Havin' a fine time, young man. Fine time. Aren't we, Miss Melanie?'

Melanie's head tilts slowly to the left, tilts slowly to the right. She stares at the moss dancing in the trees, dancing on the branches. She mutters. 'Look at that. I have never seen that. I have never been on a swamp tour ... have I, Rheta?'

'No you haven't, Miss Melanie.'

Melanie rocks from side to side. As if it were her long-lost friend, she talks to the moss swaying in the trees. 'You know Bud has been on a swamp tour. Years ago. My daughter, Charlotte, took Bud on a swamp tour ... long, long time ago. Long time ago. My baby loves the swamp.' Melanie talks incessantly. Rheta B. thinks Melanie is talking to her. 'My daughter, my baby loves nature ... loves the spirits ... loves ... the swamp. Dancing spirits.' The moss begins moving in a rhythm unfamiliar to nature's design; moving in three-quarter time, like a waltz in a dream, a perfectly syncopated waltz. Soon, the sky changes colour; the dark grey sky turns violet. The moss looks like sugar-cane growing high, like sugar-cane grows right before harvest time. But, the sugar-cane is growing in the sky; glorious, dancing, sugar-cane in the violet sky. 'Look. Look. Look at that. Look at my baby. Isn't my baby beautiful? ... Dancing ... Dancing in the sky.' The peregrine falcon circles directly above Melanie's head. 'I love you, baby.' Melanie waves at the peregrine falcon. 'Love you ... for ... ever.'

Rheta B. realizes something is terribly wrong. She wraps her arm around Melanie's shoulder. 'There, there, Miss Melanie. Your baby's beautiful. She'll always be beautiful.'

Melanie shakes her head, grabs her hair, opens her jaw wide, pulls away from Rheta B. 'Don't like it! ... Barometric pressure changing! Ow! Ow! Swollen brain! Feeling crazy, baby feel crazy. When my ... baby lives ... spirit ... creatures in swamp. Ow! Ow! Crazy ... Swamp. Baby. Baby. *My baby ... Where's my baby!?* Where the hell's my baby!?' Melanie becomes hysterical. Her eyes bulge. Her mouth quivers. '*Owww ...*'

Winston notices the sudden change in the sky, he notices the moss dancing on the branches of the trees in three-quarter time. 'What the hell is going on here?' He notices Melanie acting crazy; crazy like Charlotte acted before she used the knitting needles. Theodore notices Melanie's insane behaviour. Rheta B. notices the sky rapidly changing colour, like an out-of-kilter kaleidoscope. She notices the wind is blowing in all four directions at the same time.

'That's not possible. Oh no, no, no,' Rheta B. says to herself. 'Not possible.' Her heart beats hard and fast like a tribal drum in some faraway jungle.

The boat rocks from side to side, backwards and forwards. As he makes his way to the rear of the boat, Winston holds onto the rails. He approaches Theodore. 'Let me take over, son. Melanie's in trouble. Terrible trouble. Go see what you can do to calm her down, son. I'm steering this piece of garbage back to the landing!'

Theodore sits on the other side of Melanie. Melanie shakes, cries like a frantic infant in a pitch-black room. 'Shh. Shh. Goin' ... goin' to be fine.' Theodore remembers the hot June day, when Melanie picked him up at the Greyhound bus terminal. She said it was going to be fine. It was not fine then, it is not fine now.

Rheta B. holds Melanie in her arms. She strokes her hair, the same way Melanie stroked Charlotte's hair when Charlotte was getting ready to leave the world of day and night, getting ready to ride the ribbon in the sky to my world without corners.

Sam laughs at the crazy people on his father's boat. 'You shut the fuck up, boy!' Winston screams at the top of his lungs. 'Show some respect or you won't know what happened to you and your father won't know how it happened! Do you understand me?' The boy winks, spins his .22 rifle in the air, then stores it underneath his seat. He spits on the floor, folds his arms and glowers at Winston.

Charlotte screams. 'She is my mother! You fucking trickster, you bastard, you manipulator of all the dead beings in this lousy dead world! Let me out! I'm tired of waiting! Tired of watching! All the dead ones! Where's the cord? Whose cord am I going on? How am I getting the hell out of here? Where the hell are you? You bastard, you motherless, fatherless, non-human life-sucking liar! Liar! Let me go back!'

'Shut up, Charlotte.' I shout so loud all the choirs from the Ninth Ward stop singing. 'I am sending someone else, someone other than yourself, someone who will carefully wrap your mother, so your mother can have an effortless journey home, someone who *has* learned forgiveness, someone who does not need to be the centre of attention all the time, someone who *is* compassionate, someone who has suffered and grieved because they were one of the human beings *you* left behind without ever questioning what your death would do to them. Charlotte Duvalier! You have not learned anything. You have not changed!'

'That's not fair. That was a long, long time ago. I have changed. Damn you! I'm not the same. After these last few months, how could I be the same? Steven Jr; the miracle of winding his golden thread; the miraculous journey back; the witnessing of hundreds, thousands of souls coming through the eye. How dare you say I haven't changed!'

In a quiet tone I try to explain the inexplicable. 'Listen to you. Listen to you. You harbour such resentment, such rage. You are selfish, silly, caught up in your deluded views of life and death, just like so many in the other world. Why else would you spend hours sitting in front of that eternally blinking eye, waiting for something to happen? Waiting! As if you had nothing better to do with time.'

'I like it.'

'That is not the point, Charlotte. There is always work that needs to get done in here, out there. Someone needs *your* help every moment. You cannot keep waiting or watching what has already happened. I am sorry, but you are forbidden to leave. I have orders. When your mother arrives, she will find you. You will help her to acclimate to our astonishing world of in-betweens. That is *your* role in *her* crossing. Do not take it lightly.'

'You liar of all liars!'

'You selfish, angry angel!' I bellow my most glorious tone. 'Lily Duvalier! Get ready for another important journey! *I*, excuse me, *we* have created a thread of light, especially for your travels. I have received orders. You will be returning to Louisiana. You will bring back Melanie Brickman's splendid spirit; quite a blessing for both of you.'

Lily is perplexed. 'Why isn't *she* going? Melanie is *her* mother?'

'Obviously, that is not the point.' I hand Lily a shimmering golden filament, filled with dazzling threads of light. The eye opens. This time, for some unknown reason, Lily does not resist the ride. She disappears in the blink of an eye. She travels back to the family she loves; the family she loves as much as the light that has guided her since the beginning of her many lifetimes.

✳

Melanie lies comatose on the floor of the boat.

Cleveland Alexander kneels beside her. 'The Lord is my shepherd: I shall not want: He maketh me to lie down in green pastures. He leadeth me beside the still waters. He restoreth my soul.' Cleveland Alexander continues to pray. 'He leadeth me in the paths of righteousness for his name's sake ...'

Theodore and Rheta B. kneel at Melanie's side. Rheta B. whispers in Melanie's ear, 'Charlotte's waitin' for you. Your girl's waitin' to welcome you home. Hallelujah.'

'You're goin' to have 'em dancin' in Heaven. Wish I could be there, wish I could watch the celebration.' Theodore kisses Melanie on the forehead. 'They won't know what hit 'em.' Out of the corner of his eye, Theodore is certain he sees Sugar dancing in the sky. Absolutely certain. 'Lord. Will you look at that.'

Lily and Billy are hysterical; screaming, crying, hiding behind Alice. Alice cannot stop gazing at the dancing sky.

Steven sits next to Carter Jr and Faith. As they witness Melanie's final moments on earth, Carter Jr, Faith and Steven hear a soothing voice from some heavenly realm.

'*After these things I looked and saw a door opened in Heaven and the first voice that I heard, like a trumpet speaking with me, was one saying, "Come up here and I will show you the things which must happen after this."*'

Daphne stands next to Alice. Daphne, Alice and Cleveland Alexander recite The Lord's Prayer.

Alice is crying so hard, she can hardly breathe. At one particularly hysterical moment she is certain she hears a voice, her mother's voice, Charlotte's voice whimpering in some corner of the dancing sky. 'Oh my God! Mythical creatures in the sky. They will be mythical creatures, together ... in the sky.'

Winston cannot, for the life of him, get the boat to move in any direction. The boat is stuck in reeds and thickets. 'What the hell is going on here? This hunk of junk won't move an inch!' He yells. 'Hold on, Melanie! We'll get you back ashore! I promise. I promise!'

What occurs next is impossible to describe in a logical way. There is no logic to Mystery. That is why it is called 'Mystery'. Human minds are but small wonders compared to the fantastic apparitions that inhabit the unseen, veiled world of a profound elemental order.

A formless, glowing Lily descends from the moving sky; a streak of light, a tender voice with the sweet scent of gardenias, a spirit come to do her work. As Lily descends, Winston, who is trying his damnedest to get the boat out of muddy waters, knows, without question, his mother has returned.

Lily shouts, 'Focus! Winston, I need you to focus! Help your mama get your mother-in-law ready for the journey. Can you do that for your mama?'

'I can do anything, Mama. Tell me what you need.'

'Stop playing with that damned motor! Come over here.'

'Where, Mama? Where?'

'Right here, son. Right behind Melanie's head. Give me your unconditional love and support while I wrap the filament around her soul. I need your help. I have never wrapped the golden thread by myself.'

Winston rushes toward Melanie. Lily and Billy stand frozen in place, mouths agape, sniffing gardenias, staring and staring, as Lily's light dances around Melanie's head.

Lily asks Billy, 'Do you smell Great-Grandma?'

'Yeah.'

'Me too.'

Alice yells at her children. 'Children! This is no time to be playing games. Stop your nonsense, now. Do you hear me?'

'We're not playing games. We smell Great-Grandma. Just like at the party. Can't you smell her?' As fast as they can, they run from their mother, run toward Great-Grandma Lily's scent and light.

Alice grabs them. 'Hush up now. Behave yourselves!'

Winston winks at Lily and Billy. 'Great-Grandma is helping her good friend Melanie.'

Before Alice or Daphne contradict Winston about Melanie being Lily's good friend, the sugar-cane sky opens up, pouring down rain, sweet as sugar; buckets and buckets of sugar rain pouring down from the violet sky. Inside one violent downpour appears a spirit, filled with the violet light of the sky. Suddenly, Carter Sr's sugar-coated spirit plunks down next to his son, Winston. Winston stands directly behind Melanie's head. Carter Sr has a roll of golden twine wrapped around his iridescent body.

'Hello son. Let me give you a hand with this here spirit.'

Sugar laughs so hard. 'Surprise! Surprise! Don't ever underestimate Sugar. I rule this world. You best not leave me out of the game.'

Swamp calls out to me. 'I told you we were in for a surprise!'

Disgusted, I reply. 'I don't care any more. When have they ever given us the correct information? I am sick of it. I am sick of these last-minute changes.'

Lily chastises Carter. 'Carter Duvalier, what the hell are you doing here, again?' She continues to wrap Melanie's spirit.

'You asked me the same question the last time I came to your rescue. My dear, sweet Lily, I have come to help you.'

'I don't need your help.'

'Obviously, you do or else I wouldn't be here. Now, if you don't mind, let's wrap Melanie's spirit with our mutual threads. You keep forgettin' we have an awful lot in common. Many souls will need our help on their final journey: children, grandchildren, cousins, friends. We have an entire world of family. Why shouldn't we work together?'

'Carter, you are so full of shit it astounds me. I do not understand *why* you are here, but I will accept *that* you are and that we are meant to do the Lord's holy work together, for reasons that will forever escape me.' The two spirits wrap Melanie's body with their complimentary threads of light. Lily mutters. 'I simply don't understand. Why him? Why now?'

Though Lily has no interest in Carter's story, Carter explains the reason for his return. 'When I was a young boy, one night at the dinner table, I was caught chewin' gum. My lousy, stinkin' father, William Duvalier, yelled, "*Spit that crap out of your mouth, boy, or else I will give you a thrashing, the likes of which you will never, I mean never forget!*" Right in front of his eyes I took the gum from my mouth and stuck it underneath our very expensive antique dining table. The bastard beat the shit out of me. When my mother tried to defend me, he smacked her hard, on the mouth, shut her up good. Then, the bastard locked me in a storage room for three days; all on account of a lousy piece of chewin' gum. There was an old file cabinet in the storage room. I found some wire lyin' on the floor. Bein' handy at breakin' and enterin', I opened the file cabinet, read some fascinatin' papers. Those papers explained how my almighty father had become such a rich bastard. There was only one signature on the bottom of those papers; *your* father's. When *your* father and *my* father decided we should get married, I didn't want anythin' to do with you. But, when I met you, I fell in love with you. Problem was my hate for your father and my hate for my father were stronger than my love for you. Hate poisoned me for my entire life. Poisoned our marriage.' Carter stops his winding. 'I'm awful sorry, Lily. I don't know why I couldn't tell you that story before now, but I couldn't.'

'Thank you, Carter. I appreciate your honesty ... You're a good man after all.'

As they weave, Lily and Carter Sr create a beautiful, well-built design to carry Melanie home.

Lily inspects their intricate work. Satisfied, she boards Melanie's spirit. The spirit begins to ascend. Carter grabs hold of the tail end of the filament. Instead of travelling back to Sugar's world, Carter tries, with all his power, to hitch a ride to my world.

I think, 'Oh no.' I do not say a word.

'Are you absolutely certain that you want to do this, Carter? Are you sure you want to leave Sugar behind? Do you think you are ready for Afterworld?'

'I'm ready. Ready for a change. If Afterworld'll have me, I'm ready for another chapter in another life, in another world.' Carter Sr takes a good look at his progeny. Proud to have been an unforgettable character in their human development, he climbs aboard Melanie's spirit. Hundreds of peregrine falcons circle on concentric currents in the dancing, sugar-coated sky.

✳

It is a beautiful, cool, sunny day in Baton Rouge, Louisiana. After the ceremony at Beth Shalom Synagogue, Carter Jr, Steven, Winston, Faith, Rob and Daphne congregate on the front steps of the temple. Bud and Rheta B. have gone home. Rheta will prepare the food and drink. Bud will nap. The Duvaliers are amazed at how eloquently the rabbi captured Melanie's unconventional spirit in his sermon. No one in the family had any idea Melanie was such a vital member of the temple's congregation. She rarely talked about her faith. The family assumed Bud was the only family member active in temple life.

The Duvaliers are worried about Bud. If ever there was a time Pine Grove Plantation needed his accounting expertise, this is it. Though the Duvaliers know it is inappropriate to talk business on such a day, when have the Duvaliers been appropriate? So, they talk business. Steven is worried that without Melanie's constant nudging, Bud will not get up from his recliner. Carter Jr is concerned, because the Corps is trying to steal their land. Bud is the only man alive who can figure out how to keep the valuable parcel in question from being sold for a pittance. If the land is sold, Pine Grove could be out millions of dollars on the deal and might possibly have to shut its doors. This is serious business.

At some point during the conversation Carter Jr realizes they are talking business. 'Let's not talk business, not today of all days. Let's show some respect. We have lost a loved one.'

Now is a time to celebrate a life, to celebrate a woman who

refused to compromise her needs or desires. And look at what she did for Theodore. She slayed dragons for Theodore, wrestled with the devil himself for that boy. She loved him, gave him a unique and passionate view of life. She gave him a mother's love without being his mother. If Melanie had not been there to raise Theodore, what in the world would Winston have done? Melanie, with the help of Rheta B., raised Theodore Faulkner Duvalier and Lily lent her strong hand.

Steven reminds his family of one curious fact. 'Don't forget she commuted between Baton Rouge and Atlanta just to take care of Theodore. Why she didn't live in Napoleonville, that's a question none of us can answer. The answer isn't important. What's important, what truly matters, is Theodore needed someone to confide in, someone to take care of him and Melanie was that person. Melanie knew Theodore's darkest secrets.'

Many years ago, on a hot June day, Melanie had a talk with Steven about Theodore's darkest secret, about Steven's awful secret; one talk. Steven never forgot the look in Melanie's eyes. If she could have, she would have killed him. 'I better get home. I've got some work to do. I'm out on the road next week for the last time.' Steven hugs his children, kisses his daughter-in-law, walks down the temple steps and waves goodbye to his brood. 'Good sermon. That was a first-rate sermon.'

Carter Jr excuses himself. He runs after Steven. 'Wait up, Dad.'

'Hey son. What a time. What a time. We've got real problems, don't we? ... I am so proud of you and Faith. How you two survived this summer is a mystery to me.'

'We had to, Dad. There was no other way. We love each other. That's how we got through it. That's how we will continue to get through it.'

'You have turned out to be a fine, upstanding man, son.' Steven starts to walk away.

Carter Jr grabs his arm. 'Dad. Daphne told me everything.'

Steven blushes. 'Has she now? I don't think she knows ... everything.' Steven laughs. 'At least I hope she doesn't know everything.'

'Please don't quit the business, Dad. No one knows the sugar business like you do. If you want to get off the road, fine. But, please don't quit. We need you. I need you.'

'I'm the wrong man for the job, son.' He shakes his head in disgust. 'I made a mess of things; a real mess.' Steven shifts from side to side. He can hardly look at Carter Jr. His eyes dart here and there, finally, they focus on his son. 'I made a mess with your mother, with you kids, with the business. I made a mess.' Steven sits on the temple steps. He thinks out loud. 'Get Theodore to come home. He's your man. He can charm anybody in any sugar-buying state. That boy has always loved the sugar. Convince him to come back. It's the right time for him to be with his family. I'll help in any way I can.' Steven gets up, clasps his hands behind his back, cracks his knuckles, then walks away. As he walks away, he stretches his arms up in the air. 'That feels good.'

'I wrote the letters, Dad.' Carter Jr hurries after his father.

Steven stops. 'Oh. I see.'

'I couldn't help myself. I blamed you for Mama's death. For years I thought it was all your fault; her drinking, her insecurities, her sitting in that dark room chewing ice cubes. I blamed you. I blamed you when Rheta B. left us for Winston's family. I blamed you for everything bad that happened in my life, even Steven Jr's death. I blamed you. I figured my boy made bad choices like his grandfather, that's why he died.' Steven tries to hold back his tears. 'I was wrong. I was terribly wrong.'

'No, you weren't, son.'

'Do you understand why I ...'

'... You did what you had to do. Now what matters is that you forgive me for all the terrible things I did to our family.' Steven breaks down crying.

Carter Jr hugs his father. 'You're too good a man to humiliate yourself because of a stupid football-playing, dumb-ass, mama's boy. You are so much better than that, Dad! You are, you know?' Carter Jr takes a good look at this father. 'You are a wonderful man with a heart full of pain. Let it go, Daddy. Let it go.'

Steven cries harder than he has cried in his entire, shameful life. 'I am so embarrassed. I'm not angry at you for what you've said. I love you for it.'

'You're my father. It doesn't matter to me that you like men. What matters to me is that you don't like yourself.'

The rest of the family joins Carter Jr and Steven. Before today, none of the family has seen Steven Duvalier cry. But, it was an emotional day. Melanie is gone. Melanie was an important part of the Duvalier family.

BOOK IV

AMEN

harlotte mulls over my accusations. Hoping to be helpful during her mother's transition, she anxiously awaits her mother's imminent arrival. I am delighted with Charlotte's progress.

While Charlotte waits, she questions: 'Why did I abandon a husband, two children, a mother, a father, a family, friends, a world filled with untold adventures? How could I have taken life for granted?' Charlotte realizes she did not give any thought to the impact her actions would have on those she left behind; the *human* beings who, without her presence, muddled through her death without realizing, that as far as Charlotte was concerned, her death had nothing to do with them. Charlotte was a selfish, impudent child; full of fear, self-loathing, rage and terror. She covered her monstrous nature with an incandescent kindness that made her appearance seem saintly to others. She was able to understand a stranger's pain, but in order to understand her own pain, she had to acknowledge her aggrandized version of herself.

Charlotte had secrets tucked inside her mind, inside her blood, inside her guts, inside her bones. She was not meant to live an ordinary life. An ordinary life! What a foolish notion. Nothing is ordinary in life. Charlotte abandoned the world. She believed the world had hidden its mystery from her. She coveted the mystery. That is why she spent so much time in nature. Nature had written the mystery. Nature *was* the mystery. Nature *is* the mystery. As far as Charlotte was concerned, nature needed her. She was nature's greatest creature.

Nature said, '*Charlotte. Come with me. Come to me. I will wash away the pain. You don't have to live in pain. You will be free. Your family, your friends, they will join you. They will follow. There are worlds far greater than the world of time and space and birth and death; other worlds. Come.*'

Many years ago, not long after her death, I overheard Charlotte railing against nature. *'Without the living to appreciate you and your exquisiteness, you are no more than me. If you are unseen and unappreciated, you are nothing! You seduced me into this world of nothingness.'*

When Charlotte was pregnant with Theodore, soon before she died, she knew having another child would kill her. She longed to be free. How could she be free? She was shackled with two children, shackled with a husband who craved her unconditional love; a husband who demanded her undying attention, a husband who followed her whenever she tried to escape. How could she be free?

Charlotte did not want to hurt the world. She wanted to be free from it. How else could she liberate herself from that gnawing unrest? How ironic she *still* suffers from that insistent unrest. Even if Charlotte has transcended time and space, as far as I can tell, she has not transcended her unrest.

＊

Melanie arrives. Her light is bright. Her scent is sweet. She looks like an ecstatic flame flickering in the wind. Two travellers arrive with her. As she enters through the eye, the travellers break away from Melanie's body. Lily and Carter have transported Charlotte's mother back to Afterworld. Carter plays cat's cradle with Melanie's thread.

As Carter's spirit bangs and shimmies against the atmosphere, his unfamiliar, erratic force demands attention. 'Now that I'm here, where do I go?'

'Carter! Calm down. Easy does it in this domain. After having spent so many years with Sugar, are you prepared to transition into my realm?' How am I going to manage another restless soul? Why me?

Lily shrieks. 'That man is not fit for Afterworld! I know him well. He will run away tomorrow or the day after or the day after that, but he is sure to change his mind! I know that man better than he knows himself!' Lily smells like gasoline; it smells as if the whole of my world is on fire.

Carter is furious. 'What's the matter with you, Lily? Who helped you wrap the thread? Who helped you transport Melanie? Who entertained you for the duration of the trip? Tell me. Who was it?'

'Carter. You are such a blowhard!' Lily spins and spins. Her frenzy makes me dizzy.

Charlotte says, 'Hello, Carter.'

'Hello, Charlotte. You're lookin' beautiful, as always.' Carter's force field settles down a bit.

Before Lily says something ghastly or Charlotte has the opportunity to gush over Carter's flattering remark, I say, 'Charlotte. Your mother will awaken soon. When she awakens, embrace her, lift her from her sleep, dance with her until you hear a choir. Follow the voices into the Healing Hall. There will be other souls in the Healing Hall. Like your mother, each soul will be watching its personal movie. Sit with your mother's spirit. Listen to what her spirit has to say. As your mother journeys back in time, as she witnesses all that has gone before, give her the support she needs. Do what she asks. She has memories to share with you. You have an opportunity to share what you have learned in your many years away from her.'

'I, I don't know if I've learned anything.'

'Charlotte! Please do not waste any more of my time. Come here, child. Take your mother. Now, *she* is *your* responsibility.'

Charlotte hovers over Melanie's spirit. 'Hello in there! Can you hear me!'

'Not like that, Charlotte. Be gentle. Invite her to our world. Invite her to follow you. Like this.' I whisper, 'Come with me, Mama. Come dance with me ...'

Charlotte whispers. 'Come. Come with me, Mama. I have waited such a long time. How's that?'

'Much better.'

'Is it time for us to dance between the stars?'

'It is.'

Charlotte hovers directly above her mother's spirit.

I send them on their way. 'Stop dawdling, Charlotte. Move!'

Charlotte embraces her mother's glistening body. They glide through space like angels on ice skates. 'Look at me. Look at me. I'm dancing with *my* mother.'

'Enjoy yourself, Charlotte. As for you Lily, Doreen is waiting. She needs your help. Her parents have been directed to another frequency. There is absolutely nothing I can do about their placement. Go. Find her. Take her to a quiet corner in the sky. Comfort her. I will send for Steven Jr. He has some free time to experiment with unresolved issues. If Doreen is kept busy with his problems, maybe she will forget her own problems. That is the plan.'

'Poor Doreen. She was ecstatic dancing with her parents.' Lily begins to recite a prayer of gratitude. 'The eye of the Lord ...'

'Lily!' I interrupt. 'Doreen is waiting.'

Lily shouts so loud she pierces the sound barrier. 'Goodbye Charlotte. Take good care of your mother. Goodbye Melanie. It was an honour and a privilege taking you on your journey.' Lily spins away like a gigantic tornado ripping through the expansive sky. She spins her way toward Doreen without ever saying goodbye to Carter.

'Carter.'

'Yes, sir.'

'I am not a sir, Carter. You have one lunar cycle to decide if our realm suits your needs. If it does not, Swamp or Sugar will be more than happy to take you back. Since you broke free from the world of time and space, the three of us, Swamp, Sugar and I have been in constant communication. We have been trying to figure out how to handle your placement problem. It is a bit of a mess.'

'Sorry.'

'No need for apologies.'

'Where do I go in the meantime?'

'I haven't the faintest idea. I am too tired making life and death decisions to think about a location assessment. Go wherever you feel called. I leave it up to you, Carter.'

Charlotte hears my voice. As she dances with her mother, she hears the quiet in my world. She is stunned into a stillness; a stillness she has been searching for, for as long as she can remember.

Melanie awakens. Mother and child dance wildly, passionately; turning this way, turning that way. They listen for the choir that will lead them to their mutual healing; a blessing few mothers and daughters experience. But, Melanie and Charlotte have been anointed by some great goodness.

Bud has not risen from his recliner in three weeks. Rheta B. feeds him, clothes him, warms his milk at night, puts him to bed and wakes him from his stupor in the morning. She answers the telephone, takes down the messages from those concerned about Bud; concerned that without Melanie Bud might never get up from his recliner.

It is harvest time. The Duvaliers are busy. No matter how busy they are, one member or another visits Bud Brickman every day. Without Melanie, the house feels lifeless. The photo album sits on the coffee table. When Theodore flies south to visit Cleveland Alexander, he makes it a point to spend some time with Bud. Since Theodore and Bud are both men of few words, the visits do not last long.

After the men have talked about Melanie, they sit around and play cards. After they play cards, Theodore opens the photo album. He almost always turns to the picture of Melanie pushing Charlotte on the swing. Charlotte looks like the perfect child. After Rheta B. has finished washing the dishes, she looks at the photo album with Theodore.

Every now and then Bud leafs through the photo album. 'Theodore, look at this picture of your mother. She was a wild child. Look at her eyes. She is swinging all right, but her mind is in some faraway place up in the sky, just like her mother.'

'What'd you like most 'bout my mother?'

'The same thing I liked about your grandmother. Unpredictable. When Charlotte woke up in the morning, when Melanie woke up in the morning, neither one of them was the person who went to bed the night before. I had to be on my toes with those girls. Unpredictable and outspoken. If your grandmother knew I had spent the last three weeks in this recliner, she would give me holy hell, tell me to get off my ass, play bridge, play golf, solve Pine Grove's problem once and for all, and get the books in order.'

'Mr Brickman? I ...'

'Rheta! After all these years, don't you think it's about time you called me Bud?'

'Why yes, Mister Bud.'

'Not Mister Bud. Bud.'

'I will try to call you Bud, Mister Bud.'

Four weeks after Melanie's death, Bud rises from the recliner, walks to the kitchen wall phone and dials Carter Jr's number. 'I have been sitting around on my ass for nearly four weeks, mulling over the situation with the Corps, Carter. Why don't you come over here.'

When Carter Jr arrives, Bud greets him at the door with a smile on his face, a smile Melanie had seen maybe once, maybe twice in their many years together. Bud has figured out a solution. He once met a man, a man who once worked for the Army Corps of Engineers. That man, a married man with a wife and children, now holds a high position in the Louisiana State Legislature. If Bud's memory serves him correctly, which it still does, he remembers an evening quite some time ago, a Christmas evening, when Steven and this fine upstanding man of politics, this man whose name will remain anonymous, disappeared into the bushes.

On Christmas night the two men struck a deal; not necessarily while they were in the bushes. Probably after the bushes is when they struck the deal. The deal protected Pine Grove Plantation from having to sell any of its land to the Corps. Ever. Both men acknowledged Pine Grove's previous South Lafourche oil and gas agreement. The South Lafourche financial agreement would remain intact, but Pine Grove's valuable land would forever be protected from any future claims made by the Army Corps of Engineers.

The day after the Christmas party Steven sent a handwritten memo to the honourable mister so-and-so who, soon after, signed his name to the handwritten document, forever protecting Pine Grove's sugar fields from any and all future excavation. The young man had the document hand-delivered back to Pine Grove Plantation, care of Mr Steven Duvalier.

After sitting in his recliner for four weeks, mourning the death of his wife, Bud remembered where he had hidden the memo; in a file cabinet in Pine Grove's storage room, along with all sorts of other incriminating documents.

When the Corps receives Bud's letter, hand-delivered of course, the upstanding man in question places a phone call to a very important man in the Louisiana Legislature. After that timely phone call, the Corps buys the much-needed clay, for a pittance, from some other sugar plantation.

Bud swears on his life, if it weren't for Melanie's divine guidance, he would not have come up with such a scheme. Who else but Melanie would be clever enough to blackmail the Army Corps of Engineers?

Daphne tries to convince Theodore that Louisiana is where he belongs. 'Come on, Theodore. The family needs you. You can run the business with Carter Jr.'

'I don't see myself runnin' anythin' with Carter Jr.'

'Fine. Do whatever you want.' Daphne pouts. 'Please. I miss you. I love your ass.'

'So does Cleveland Alexander.'

'I bet he does. Cleveland Alexander's good for you. He's a fine man. Please. Come back for him.' Theodore does not respond to Daphne's plea. 'Even the sugar misses you. She told me so.'

But, Theodore is not ready to make the Louisiana commitment. He likes the big city. He loves the noise, the lights, the restaurants, the crazy people who come in and out of his life leaving some indelible imprint on his psyche. He enjoys the random sex he finds around the corner, up and down the streets, in the restaurants and bars around town. Most of all, he likes how the city makes him feel inside his heart. The din of the city is the single most significant mechanism to help him block out his vast grief; the grief of losing Melanie to the violet sky, the grief of losing Steven Jr to drugs and a malfunctioning heart, the grief of losing his mother before he was old enough to speak her name, the grief of losing Lily to cancer. The grief. The grief. If you need to get away from the grief and the pain, New York City is a great place to live.

Simply put, Theodore is not ready for Sugar's fields. He is no longer the young boy playing hide-and-seek with Daphne in Sugar's fields. He is no longer the innocent child sitting next to Joseph, riding in the combine in Sugar's fields. Joseph. He is gone. Doreen is gone. She hated Sugar's world. Uncle Steven has finally let go of Sugar's strangling grip. He has stepped down from his position, walked away from selling sugar, walked away from buying sweet young boys who don't know any better than selling themselves as cheap trade. Theodore is pleased with Uncle Steven's choice.

Theodore is not ready to make a lifetime commitment to Cleveland Alexander. He loves the sex, but Theodore does not want to live with him or hang out with his devoted parishioners on Sunday morning. Theodore is not ready to babysit for Lily and Billy. Though his father is a changed man, Theodore is not ready to listen to his father or take his father's advice. Theodore Faulkner Duvalier needs, at least, a few thousand days and nights before he returns to the fields that changed his life, the fields that changed everybody's life in his family; all the many generations, all those beings living in the seen and unseen world.

Sugar yells. 'Bring that boy home or else!' In a quiet tone, Swamp says, 'Or else what?'

I am too exhausted to fight, so I say, 'Leave the boy alone. He will come back home when he is good and ready, not one moment before.'

'What do I do now?' asks Sugar.

'Concentrate on your harvest! If your harvest does not go well, you will be completely ruined and *we* will be forced to clean up *your* mess.' I return to the work at hand; finding the appropriate placement for Carter Sr which, by the way, is not an easy task.

As the Louisiana sun sets, Swamp calls out to the jack-o'lanterns. 'If it's possible, could you light up the Atchafalaya with your magical powers. We have a serious problem! There are many men working throughout the night. They need your light to shine like diamonds, so they can assess the damage caused by these two terrible hurricanes. Once the men ascertain the damage, they'll figure out how to control the flooding along the Mississippi. When they figure that out, then and only then, can you jack-o'-lanterns rest.'

For the next many weeks and months the jack-o'-lanterns shine brighter than ever recorded before or since October 2005.

Charlotte discovers that the Healing Hall is not a hall. It is an atmospheric, perpetually circling, tunnel filled with sound and light, like no place in any galaxy. Charlotte is next to her mother. Her mother watches a movie. They are surrounded by numerous souls. Each soul watches a movie; weeping, laughing, moaning, gasping, screaming, pleading, shaking and ultimately settling into the entirety of a unique understanding of the world left behind.

Thousands of choirs sing.

Hallelujah! Hallelujah! Hallelujah!

Thousands upon thousands more sing.

For the Lord God omnipotent reigneth.

Voices from all worlds sing.

Hallelujah! Hallelujah! Hallelujah!

And sing. And sing. And sing.

Hallelujah! Hallelujah! Hallelujah!

'So beautiful.' Melanie says at least a hundred times. 'Look at my baby.' She says at least a hundred more times. 'Where's my baby?' she asks again and again.

'I'm right here, right next to you.' Charlotte's voice is quiet and comforting.

'Come closer.'

'I can't get any closer.' Charlotte tries to get closer, but fails.

'Oh yes, you can. Come in here with me. Come inside the tunnel filled with memory. Come here, baby.'

'I don't know how.'

'Don't be silly. Of course you know how. We're no longer separate.'

'We aren't?'

'Haven't you learned anything, baby?'

'Maybe not.' Charlotte laughs a precious, childlike laugh.

'That's impossible. Absolutely impossible. We'll discuss it later. Right now, let's watch the movie together. Come here. Experience my life like it was your life. It was your life. You were my life. You are my life. Not for one moment have we been separated. My silly girl. You don't understand, do you? Look at the photographs. You'll figure it out. Look at this one in particular. What do you see? Come in here, honey.'

Charlotte glides inside Melanie's light. She views Melanie's movie. 'There I am.' She says. 'That's me swinging on a swing, swinging forward and backward and backward and forward. Look at you pushing me higher and higher.' Charlotte is elated. 'There it is! The photo you always look at. The wind is blowing my hair, my mouth is wide open, you're laughing, I'm laughing … I love that photo.'

Melanie asks. 'Do you remember the day when that picture was taken?'

'Uh uh.'

'Do you remember how happy we were?'

'It was such a long time ago. I don't remember.'

'Do you remember the man?'

'Maybe … Yes. I remember a man was holding the camera.'

'Do you remember what I said to him?'

'Uh uh.'

'I said, "Take the picture already, you crazy man! Take the picture of your girls!" That's what I said. Can you see him?'

'No. I only see you and me.'

'Look beyond the photo, look behind the camera. Don't you see a good-looking man behind the camera?'

Charlotte shouts! 'Oh yes! I see him now! What a beautiful smile. Why is he wearing sunglasses on a cloudy day?'

'The poor fool's afraid he'll be blinded by my love.'

'Who is he?'

'*He* is your father, Charlotte. *He* is your father.'

'I don't understand.'

'You do understand. You are so like him.'

'I am?'

'No more questions. Let's watch the movie, listen to the healing voices, lose ourselves in the past and celebrate how we've come together without form. When I said goodbye to you, I knew I would see you again, feel you again. Otherwise, I wouldn't have been able to let you go. And I did let you go.'

'What about the man?'

'I couldn't let him go. Even when he was torn from me, I never let *him* go.'

'Torn how?'

'No more questions. Let's watch the movie. Soon enough you'll find out what you need to know about yourself.' Melanie laughs so hard that I roar with delight. She plays her movie many times. Sometimes she laughs, sometimes she whimpers; no matter what she does, she holds Charlotte close inside her.

❋

I am awakened by thunder, lightning, howling winds; awakened from my momentary rest. I receive an audible directive. 'Transport Charlotte to the eye. Immediately! Frequency upgrade.'

'No. No! Not now. Please! I cannot. I will not!'

'Excuse me? Orders are orders!'

'Please. Please.'

'Oh, I see. You've become attached to Charlotte. When did *you* become so sentimental? Haven't you learned anything about selfless control?'

'Where Charlotte is concerned, I have learned many things, but certainly not that.'

'Your work is complete. Call her. She's ready.'

Unbeknownst to me, Doreen, Lily, Steven Jr (looking like a spectacular lightning bolt), Carter and many Duvaliers from past and future lives form a radiant circle. The eye blinks furiously.

For the last time, I call Charlotte's name. 'Charlotte. Charlotte. Come here!'

She arrives in an instant. 'Yes.'

'Yes. You have been called. The time has come for you to leave Afterworld. You will travel to a more subtle frequency.'

'I have been? ... Why me?'

'I ... I do not know why. I only know that you have been called.'

'What about my mother?'

'She has not been invited. She has more healing to do in my

world.'

'I can't leave her. Not now. I don't want to go anywhere else. Why would you do this to me now of all times?'

'This is not my doing. Nothing would make me happier than to have you stay here, but you have been called by a greater force than me. It is an honour.'

'Honour my ass!' Melanie fires up. 'More bullshit! You get out of that world, come here thinking things are bound to be different and what do you get? The same old bullshit! My baby's not going anywhere!'

Lily twirls red rings of fire around Melanie and Charlotte. 'Charlotte. It *is* an honour. When you are called by the divine, you must follow! If I was asked, I would certainly go.' Lily rants. 'Melanie! You are still, after all these years, a horse's ass! Let your *baby go*! If the truth be told, Charlotte is no longer *your* baby.'

'Shut up, Lily! I had enough of you down there. Don't tell me I have to put up with your horseshit in here, too! You and your pious, old-time religious crap!'

'You and your lies and secrets!'

'I have no secrets!'

'Stop it!' I yell so loud that millions of stars randomly shoot into each other creating a frightening display of fireworks. 'Both of you. Stop it! I need some peace and quiet. I have important decisions to make.' I turn my attention to Carter Sr. 'Carter, I am having difficulty placing you in my, excuse me, in our world. Would you like to go with Charlotte? Maybe she can drop you off on some suitable wavelength along the way?'

Melanie faints. She spills like black ink pouring out into the unholiest blob imaginable. 'Over my dead body!' she hollers. 'Over my dead body!' She shakes with such an uncontrollable rage, the lining of my realm begins to pull apart. Black jagged particles fly every which way.

Lily hovers over Melanie's spirit. 'This *is* your dead body, you crazy fool!'

'Carter is staying right here with me. So is Charlotte. Right here. Nobody's going anywhere. Do you hear me? Nobody!'

I am at my wits' end. 'Melanie. Melanie. Control yourself! Get up from your slime!' I snarl. 'No one behaves like that in my world. No one!'

'I don't give a damn about you or your world!' Melanie picks herself up, glides over to Carter and transforms herself into a blazing golden ray of light. The ray connects Melanie's spirit to Carter's spirit to Charlotte's spirit. 'Charlotte! Honey! *He* is your father! *He* is the man on the other side of the lens. Look at him in his purest light. There is no mistaking the genetic link between you and him.' Lily is stunned into some useless prayer of forgiveness. Doreen is flabbergasted into the same futile prayer. Hoping to console his great-grandmother, Steven Jr glides toward Lily. He prays, for the first time in any world, he prays for someone other than himself. Melanie approaches Charlotte. Charlotte is unable to move or speak. All Charlotte *can* do is absorb the information with the absolute understanding of its enormity.

Carter is furious with Melanie. 'Damn you, Melanie! You promised. You promised you would never say a word to anyone. You promised. Especially to Charlotte!'

'Carter. These are unusual circumstances. I had no choice!'

'Damn you, woman! Look at what you've done. Made a mess of things again!'

'I told the truth, Carter. That's what I've done. I did what I've wanted to do for so many years. What a relief. No more secrets. If you want to run from our love? Fine. Go on. Keep running. Go with Charlotte, take a ride, take a trip, take yourself to some other galaxy, but be aware you are, once again, running away from the love of your life, from the light of your life.' Melanie turns to Lily. 'Lily. Could you stop praying for just one second. Please.'

Lily says, 'Amen.' Her heartache is infinite. Hopefully, her capacity for forgiveness is equally as infinite.

'When Carter came to Atlanta to hire Bud, Bud invited

Carter to our house for drinks. He wanted Carter to meet me. I remember serving Carter a double bourbon on the rocks. I thought to myself, "*This man is nothing but trouble.*" But, when I looked into his eyes and he looked into mine, we fell in love, trouble and all ... in a glance. There was nothing we could do about how we felt. Love captured us and swept us up. Bud saw it with his own eyes. He knew we were meant to be together. He knew *when* we *were* together. He knew I needed to spend time in Louisiana with Carter. Bud was and is a very generous man.'

'The man is a fool.' Lily mutters one final prayer of forgiveness.

'No, Lily. Bud is a very wise man. Lily, I am so sorry. Carter didn't mean to hurt you. Loving me was as hard on him as it was on you. He tried, but he couldn't let me go.'

'I understand so much now; so much more than I would like to understand.' Lily turns away. Her pride is pummelled to pieces.

'On the night of the hurricane that killed Carter, Carter was in a drunken stupor. He was trying to get home to tell you about us. That's how drunk he was. He had to leave me in the middle of a hurricane, in the middle of a goddamn hurricane. When he left the hotel room, he was half naked, dazed and crazed. Before he left, I tried to stop him. I begged him to sleep it off, to please wait until morning. I begged him.' Melanie mumbles. 'You left anyway.' Melanie relives that terrible night. She hears the wind beating against the hotel window, she hears the rain pounding on the siding of the building, she feels her heart pounding with fear. 'You all know what happened after that! The damn manhole cover blew and killed him in an instant. Joseph was waiting downstairs in the hotel lobby. Whenever Carter went out drinking, whenever he got drunk, Joseph was the man who made sure Carter got home safely. Joseph knew about us. He was Carter's confidant. Somehow, he understood Carter's pain.' Melanie cannot go on, but, of course, she does go on and on. 'When Carter died, I died one more time; first time I died was when Charlotte died. The second time I died was when Carter died. I had to let go of my baby, then I had to let go of my man. I can't let go of either one of them now. Don't ask me to do that. Honestly, I can't.'

'Carter.' Hoping against hope not to get the answer she is going to get, Charlotte asks the question. 'Are you really my father?'

'Could be, Charlotte. Very well could be.' He laughs that rowdy laugh of his. 'Lord knows we have some similar traits.'

'We do, don't we?' Charlotte understands the complexity of her relationship to Winston and the children. 'Oh my God! Carter. Mother. You mean Winston is my ...'

In unison Carter and Melanie say, 'Yes. He is, Charlotte.'

'Why didn't you stop us? Why did you let us get, oh God! Married?'

Carter says, 'We couldn't say anythin' to either one of you. And honestly, Charlotte, Winston would have married you, no matter what we said. Even if you were his whole sister, it wouldn't have mattered to Winston. You were the love of his life. You were his goodness.'

'I tried to warn you, honey. I told you they were a no-good, rotten family. I have always believed Swamp talked you into it. I'm quite sure it was Swamp's fault.' Swamp does not deny Melanie's charges.

I am flabbergasted by the current Duvalier drama. I collect my muddled thoughts. 'Charlotte. In light of the situation, I will put in a request for you to remain in Afterworld, with your mother and father. Would you like that?'

Charlotte mulls it over, much like I have been mulling over so many things during the recent past. 'I don't think so. It *is* tempting, but if I have completed my work in your world, I probably should go. Travel. Travel on and on to wherever I belong. Lily's right. It *is* a great honour. *I* have been called. *I have* been called.' There is a peculiar friction in the atmosphere. Soon, the friction subsides.

The blinking eye opens so wide, it looks like the mouth of a giant whale, like the whale in the biblical story of 'Jonah and the Whale'. Though I will miss her, I have the distinct feeling that the giant whale will heave Charlotte's soul into some new and remarkable dimension.

Charlotte absorbs one final moment in my world; the world she is about to leave behind. 'I'm not leaving any of you. If I haven't learned that lesson by now, what have I learned?' Charlotte transmits her ineffable scent toward her mother, father, Doreen, Steven Jr and the rest of the family. 'I am so pleased to see you; all of you together. At last.' She turns to me. 'Thank you, Afterworld. I will miss you.'

'And I you, Charlotte. And I you.'

As she slides deep inside the inner circle of the blinking eye, Charlotte is released into space. She flies on the wings of many peregrine falcons that have been awaiting her return.

Charlotte hears a choir.

> *Behold, I tell you a mystery; we shall not all sleep, but we shall be chang'd*
> *Behold, I tell you a mystery; we shall not all sleep, but we shall be chang'd.*

Voices surround her. She hears Winston's voice.

In a moment, in the twinkling of an eye, at the last trumpet.
She hears Steven's voice.

In a moment, in the twinkling of an eye, at the last trumpet.
She hears Alice's voice singing in perfect harmony.

In a moment, in the twinkling of an eye, at the last trumpet.
She hears my voice, Sugar's voice, Swamp's voice. We sing, and sing and sing some more.

> *The trumpet shall sound and the dead shall be rais'd incorruptible and we shall be chang'd.*

Charlotte's ecstatic spirit sings with the rest of us.

The trumpet shall sound and the dead shall be rais'd incorruptible and we shall be chang'd.

She asks one more question. 'How? How? How shall we be changed? When will it happen? Who will take care of the earth?'

Choirs sing out from the past, present and future. Choirs sing out from invisible and visible realms. Choirs chant for eternal grace.

Worthy is the Lamb that was slain and hath redeemed us to God by His blood, to receive power and riches and wisdom and strength and honour and glory and blessing.

Charlotte asks her final questions. 'Theodore. Can you hear me? Do you hear the voices? Can you hear my voice among the many?'

'I hear you.' Theodore says, 'I hear your voice. Your voice is the silence between the noise, between the pain.'

'Can you forgive me, son? Do you forgive me?'

'Yes. Yes, Mama. I forgive you. I've heard so many speak your name, so many times, but I've never, not once, said your name. Listen to me. Charlotte. Charlotte. *I* am your son. *You* are my mother ... Now let go. Let go of me. Now is our time to let go.'

'Listen, Theodore. Listen to the masterpiece. Behold the magnificence of the mystery. Now, we *can* let go.'

Blessing and honour, glory and pow'r be unto Him that sitteth upon the throne and unto the Lamb, for ever and ever.

Let go.

※

AMEN

ACKNOWLEDGEMENTS

I would like to thank Charlotte Sheedy for recommending Ann Patty who gave me the courage to cut and carry on without regret. Thank you Ann. You are an astounding editor and a wonderful friend. Thank you Pat, for showing me how sugar and its many by-products are made and manufactured. Thank you Gibbs, for the facts, the fun, the thrill of learning about the world and history of sugar. I will never forget the look on your face when I walked barefoot in the mud-soaked fields. Thank you to my friends. You know who you are, especially Phillippa who fed me right up until the deadline. Thank you to the great, unstoppable people of Louisiana. Thank you Mary, for letting me read out loud. Thank you Mackenzie, for your honesty. Thank you Gary Pulsifer. You are a writer's dream and to think you are my publisher. Thank you Piers, Karen, Angeline, Colin and everybody at Arcadia Books. Thank you Margot Harley, for your patience, love and support. I am the lucky one. Thank you to the seen and unseen spirits who guided me on this journey.